# The Huntress
*War Torn Trilogy Part One*

## KIMBERLY HUMPHREYS

Copyright © 2020 Kimberly Humphreys
All rights reserved.
ISBN: 9798657500912

Scripture quotations are taken from the Holy Bible, New Living Translation, copyright ©1996, 2004, 2015 by Tyndale House Foundation. Used by permission of Tyndale House Publishers, Carol Stream, Illinois 60188. All rights reserved.

# CONTENTS

| | Acknowledgments | *i* | | | |
|---|---|---|---|---|---|
| 1 | Hidden | *1* | 13 | Wisdom | *125* |
| 2 | Communal Threat | *5* | 14 | Silence | *136* |
| 3 | Firefight | *19* | 15 | Take Heart | *142* |
| 4 | The Blood of a Stranger | *27* | 16 | Duty Station | *151* |
| 5 | Translation of a Psalm | *35* | 17 | The Common Rule | *156* |
| 6 | Tightrope between Hope and Despair | *48* | 18 | Mission Essential | *171* |
| 7 | Buttons and Scattered Memories | *58* | 19 | The Window | *179* |
| 8 | The Great Cleansing | *68* | 20 | A New Dawn | *185* |
| 9 | Strangers | *76* | 21 | Formation | *196* |
| 10 | Cultural Conflict | *87* | 22 | The Prophecy | *203* |
| 11 | Symbol of Commitment | *102* | 23 | A Golden Glow | *208* |
| 12 | Memory Lane | *114* | | Epilogue: A General Warned | *212* |

# ACKNOWLEDGMENTS

Praise to my Heavenly Father, who redeemed me, and protected me even when I lived in a place the inspired Auctairea.

There is no greater love, than the love of God.

I want to thank my husband, who has been an invaluable help, support, and partner in my life. God truly joined us together, "let no one split apart what God has joined together." Mark 10:9

For my children, thank you for every single evening and weekend that you've spent with your dad to give me time to write this story. From the first story I write as a child, my mom has always inspired me to keep writing. Thank you.

Thanks to God that I love in America. I pray it never falls into socialism. And thank YOU, dear reader, for investing your time into Kira's life. I hope her faith inspires you, the way it has inspired me.

# CHAPTER 1
## *HIDDEN*

The drone is coming...

Kira Westin's brow creases in fear. "It's almost dark."

Nadia continues writing her arithmetic lesson on the small chalkboard above her lap. Her little hands are thinner than Kira would like, but at least she's alive.

"I know, mommy," Nadia whispers. Her light brown hair reflects the fire's glow.

Their living room is their classroom, but today they started late. Auctairea always has a layer of fog covering the landscape, but as the sun begins to set, the gray light above the curtains fades. It's almost time for Nadia to hide.

"There!" Nadia hands her mom the chalkboard. Her Seventeen Addition Family is perfect.

"Fantastic job!" Kira's lips curve into a smile, and for a moment, she forgets the time. The mechanical voice outside reminds. Kira's smile fades. She knows the drone is on her street.

"I'll go hide." Nadia rushes upstairs to the only room in the house without a window.

With a quick pat on her chest to make sure her cross necklace is hidden, Kira embarks on her nightly routine. First, she checks her rifle, making sure it's not visible. Rushing through her house, she yanks open every curtain. Kira must expose her home to the patrol, or risk appearing suspicious.

The voice of the drone is close enough to be understood. Out of breath, Kira fixes her hair and relaxes her shoulders to seem nonchalant. She strolls downstairs and takes a seat on her faded blue couch. Crossing her legs, she casually picks up an old magazine.

The mechanical undertone of a man's voice makes her hair stand on end. Kira can't risk showing her discomfort and buries her mind in pictures from the past. Real estate listings advertised to private buyers, from before the government owned everything.

"Neighbors…" The voice is right outside of her house. "Watch out for your neighbors, by reporting violations now." A continuous static hums with each recorded word. "An enemy to Auctairea is an enemy to us all." Camouflaged by thousands of transparent sensors that reflect the scenery, the drone could be an oval mirror. Solid, with each sensor layered like small waves. It slowly flies up to her first living room window. Kira tries not to look at her own image because the eyes of Auctairea record everything they reflect. It glides to her second living room window and slowly records the view. "The war effort needs your sacrifice…"

Kira's muscles tighten, but she catches her breath before it can release. This is the announcement she feared.

Like an oversized, reflective bullet, the drone makes its way to her backdoor. It hovers up to the top window. "There will be no drop-off this week."

No drop-off. No rations. It's been two weeks, and the Commons are sure to venture their looting out here. Kira feels sweat beading down her neck, but she can't let her anxiety show.

The drone might not be the only one watching. In Auctairea, to show need is suicide.

Focus. The magazine's largest advertisement is a listing for the Tanner's house next door. At fifteen hundred square feet, with three bedrooms and two baths, it was listed for three million dollars. Kira glances up at the ruins that are nothing more than the frame and a stone chimney, rotting in the mist, two acres from her window.

The drone rises to scan the windows upstairs. Kira silently prays Nadia will stay quiet.

It checks each window, repeating itself four times before leaving her property.

Kira can't move until it's out of earshot.

Once silence replaces the static, Kira sets her magazine down. She casually stretches, before closing each window covering, tightly.

Saving her bedroom for last, by the time Kira reaches these four windows, her hands are shaking.

A mixture of hunger and fear threatens to make her collapse. Kira closes the last drapes, before dropping to her knees. Her body lets out a silent scream, and she squeezes her eyes shut in agony. She deserves this fate, far worse, but Nadia doesn't.

Kira pulls her eyes open and lips a prayer. "Please don't let Nadia starve. Let her live God, let her live. Don't punish her for my sins, please." Kira's eyes close, but it's no use. Her tears still flow.

Abruptly she stands. Nadia can't see her like this. Kira looks at her dresser mirror and is ashamed to find her brown eyes bloodshot from crying. She violently wipes the tears off her cheeks. In the low lantern's light, her skin resembles porcelain, making her feel breakable.

"It's gone now." Kira hates that her voice cracks. "You can come out."

Silence.

Always this foreboding, always this fear. Kira's face hardens before she marches down the hallway to her daughter's bathroom.

The door is cracked open, revealing nothing but darkness. Kira pushes it open all the way and flips the light switch.

Giggling sounds from the darkness. "That's never worked." Nadia jokes, stepping out into the light.

Kira sighs in relief, before embracing her. "You know it used to," Kira kisses the top of Nadia's head, "Back when you were a baby."

"How could I remember that?" Nadia asks, making Kira laugh.

"Alright, the drone's gone. How does dinner sound?"

"Mmm!" Nadia's brown eyes sparkle.

Kira doesn't want to frown, but this is only their second meal for the day. Breakfast was hardly enough to be considered a snack. Through it all, her daughter is grateful. Somehow, that gratitude makes it worse. Starving would be so much easier to deal with if Nadia constantly complained. Then Kira would have to tell her to count her blessings. Instead, Nadia is content with their pitiful existence, and it breaks Kira's heart. There's so much more she wants to give her daughter, but the only thing she can offer her now is life...

***

# CHAPTER 2
## COMMUNAL THREAT

Light beams break past the drapes, like silver bars above each enclosed window. Kira's eyes open to find Nadia curled up beside her. Kira vaguely remembered her crawling into her bed last night. It's been getting harder and harder for Nadia to stay in her own room. Kira sits up. It's the same black furniture, the same canopy bed, the same burgundy couch at the foot of her bed. While the memories of safety in this room remain, now, safe is nonexistent.

Kira can't wallow in self-pity. She has to milk Feisty before the Commons wake up.

Walking to Nadia's room, a toddler mattress rests on the floor, layered with unused blankets. Nadia's bleached oak changing table stands under a layer of dust across the room. It's been almost four years since it's been used, but now, nothing can be wasted. A concrete block by Nadia's bed holds what Kira needs. A little white spray bottle, filled with kepweed infused water.

Kira takes it to her nightstand, before caressing Nadia's hair. "Good morning to you," she whispers in song, "good morning, sweet Nadia. Good morning to you."

Nadia's brown eyes open. "Morning…"

"Do you see where I put the bottle?" Kira points at her nightstand.

Sitting up, Nadia's five-year-old eyes focus on it. "Yeah."

"Good. I'm going to milk Feisty."

"Okay." Nadia's head plops back on the pillow.

Kira stands and admires her daughter lovingly, before covering her with a burgundy comforter.

Strapping her rifle over her shoulder, Kira marches downstairs. Morning is the only time it's safe to go outside. Tapping a hand over her black shirt, she makes sure her cross necklace isn't exposed. Kira steps up to her back door and takes in a deep breath. Letting it out slowly, she knows when she steps outside, she risks death. Silently asking God for help, Kira readies her rifle, unlocks the deadbolt, and swings open the backdoor. Pointing the barrel to the right, then to the left, Kira walks down the two concrete steps to the dirt. It appears as though she's alone.

Not even the dawn's light can kill the layer of fog presiding over everything. The birds are singing, a good sign. Kira's shoulders relax before she uses the key on her charm bracelet and locks the backdoor of her house.

Her well-worn, black boots crunch the hard soil before the ground softens underfoot. She's almost to her shed.

The splintered gray boards make their appearance through the fog. Kira gets her key ready. Before she can unlock the bolt, something to the left catches her eye. It's a tall mound of dirt. At first, she thinks it's from a groundhog. Walking closer, her visibility improves through the fog. What she sees makes her stop. Knees weak, her eyes assess the damage. Rows and rows of trial and error have been destroyed.

Her garden is gone.

Kira slowly kneels. The Commons were here last night and she didn't even hear them. Hot tears roll down her cheeks. How will she and Nadia eat now? Devastation churns into anger before she salvages what they didn't steal.

Eight potatoes, a single carrot, and two onions are all she can recover. Dirt compacts deep under her fingernails. Kira holds the little gain in her hands. Her body shakes. "Okay, God, I trust you." Tears blur the pitiful harvest she holds. "Make this enough, somehow." Kira grits her teeth and shoves the vegetables in her jacket pockets.

Her eyes focus on the shed. Surely if they got Feisty, she would have made some sort of noise. Kira's heart races, and she presses her lips together in a moment of cowardice. She doesn't want to go in there. She can't handle seeing that shed empty, not now.

The longer she waits, the more likely whoever was here will come back.

Her face trembles. She manages to stop her tears, before reaching for the shed's door. She lifts up the black padlock, to find the paint has been scraped off in several long scratches. She momentarily closes her eyes before gathering the bravery needed to open the door.

Except it won't budge.

Kira gasps and fumbles for the key on her bracelet and shoves it in the lock. It turns, making her smile. They didn't get in.

Joy fills her, and once she swings the door open, Feisty looks at her, chewing hay. The three chickens behind Feisty are huddled securely in their coop. A sigh of relief escapes her before Kira gets to work.

Once the milk and eggs are gathered, Kira locks up her shed.

Locking her back door, Kira sets the pail of milk on the counter and empties her pockets. Two eggs and a few pitiful vegetables are all they have. Kira can't focus on preparing food, not while there's so little. She looks around the stale kitchen. Espresso cabinets, creamy tile floor, and brown speckled granite countertops are all dingy without the proper solutions to clean them. Heart heavy, she knows she doesn't deserve God's grace but needs to hear from him. Her strength is depleted, and God's word is the only thing that can refill it.

Finding that Nadia is still asleep in her bed, Kira's eyes soften. The more Nadia sleeps, the less time she'll spend being hungry.

Lifting the beige carpet from a corner under her black nightstand, Kira pulls her Bible out from beneath the baseboard. She's managed to hide her great-grandmother's Bible all these years and will protect it, even if it costs her, her life. Tiptoeing out of the room, Kira allows herself to read it in the loft. Sitting on a black couch under the gray light from behind the curtains, Kira closes her eyes to pray. "Dear God, thank you that Nadia and I have survived this long, but God, our garden..." Kira grits her teeth in agony. "You know who did it, and I ask that you forgive them, but please, fix this. Don't let us starve. Give me favor and wisdom on how to survive this." Kira sobs. "Speak to me, my Lord, my God, speak to me. Give me strength, in the name of Jesus, amen." She opens her Bible to Isaiah 62:2-5.

The nations will see your righteousness. World leaders will be blinded by your glory. And you will be given a new name by the LORD's own mouth. The LORD will hold you in his hand for all to see—a splendid crown in the hand of God. Never again will you be called "The Forsaken City" or "The Desolate Land." Your new name will be "The City of God's Delight" and "The Bride of God," for the LORD delights in you and will claim you as his bride.

Kira's brow furrows. Splendid crown? Bride? Understanding floods her, and she breathes in deep. She hasn't felt peace in bartering it all this time, but the closest thing she has to a crown is her wedding ring. The mayor always coveted it, and Cheryl is sure to have rations. She may even have seeds. Using the last symbol of her marriage to George is what will save them.

"Thank you, God." Kira whispers. She reads her favorite verse, the one which God has spoken to her through, so many times before.

So be strong and courageous, all you who put your hope in the LORD! Psalm 31:24

"Yes, Lord, give me the courage I need. Strengthen mine and Nadia's hearts, for we hope in you. Deliver us, in the name of Jesus, amen." Kira gently puts her Bible away before pouring herself and Nadia some milk.

Nadia smiles with a milk mustache, before taking a bite of eggs that were scrambled over the fireplace.

Kira returns her smile while sipping on her milk.

The shed lock being tampered with plagues Kira's mind. She will need to add another one before nightfall. Even so, what's to stop the Commons from finding a bolt cutter?

"I'm done." Nadia slides her half-full plate across the table.

Kira caught on to Nadia's honorable tactic to save her from starvation months ago and has since doubled her portions. "Thank you, sweetheart."

She takes a bite from half of the two eggs she scrambled. It physically hurts Kira to eat. Each bite she takes is a reminder that everything is running out. Nadia watches intently to make sure she finishes it.

"We are blessed to have Feisty." Kira forces a smile. "But the rations aren't coming and..." She knows the reaction that's coming, but there isn't any other choice. They can't survive off nothing but milk and eggs for long. Kira's smile fades. She has no choice but to tell Nadia. "Our garden is gone."

Nadia's brow rises. "Gone?"

Ashamed, Kira looks down. "Someone ransacked it last night." She slowly looks up. Her heart stings with the anticipation for how much this will scare her daughter. "I must go into town."

Nadia doesn't move for so long, Kira fears that she may not have heard her. Finally, Nadia whispers, "No."

"I have to."

Nadia's lips tremble. "Please don't leave. I don't want to be alone!"

Kira fights tears. Kneeling in front of Nadia, she takes both of her tiny hands into her own. "All you have to do is play quietly in your room. The doors will be locked, and I'll come home as fast as I can."

Tears roll down Nadia's face. She turns towards the heavily draped window. "What if someone comes inside?"

"You spray them. The kepweed will do the rest."

Nadia looks at her mom, her eyes strengthened, though her ivory face is still red from crying. "Okay."

Kira kisses both of her daughter's hands. "That's my brave girl." She smiles past her breaking heart. "So be strong and courageous..."

Nadia whispers the rest of Psalm 31:24 with her, "all you who put your hope in the LORD!" Bravery drains from Nadia's face before she wraps her arms around her mother's neck.

"I know." Her daughter shouldn't have to be so afraid. She's only five, and should never be left alone, but what choice do they have? "God is bigger than us, he will deliver us." A tear escapes Kira. "You'll see. God will protect you."

"I'll be strong, mommy." Nadia pulls away and wipes away her tears. "I will."

"Of course you will." Kira stands. "And I'll be quick."

Nadia runs upstairs to hide in her room.

Kira's lips tremble, but she can't let herself cry anymore, or else someone might notice. No one can know she is in need. Wiping the dishes clean, Kira puts them away before checking her hair in a mirror by her dining room table. Kira's brown eyes are bright. Her face is far too youthful for these circumstances, and her dark lips have retained their fullness, under sharp cheekbones that flatter her heart-shaped face. Tightening her ponytail, her brown hair hangs just past her shoulder blades. She hates being pretty. It only attracts the wrong kind of attention, the attention of *him*. Nauseated by the thought of bringing herself under his radar, Kira slings her rifle over her back.

Walking out into the mist of the fog, Kira locks the backdoor and steps onto the street. Besides her own home, the Langton's house, though vacant, is the only one still standing on her cul-de-sac. Directly across the street, the stables of the Langton's have long since been burnt to ash. Every window of their house is broken, and the front door hangs by a hinge.

She can't focus on that now. Kira holds her head up high. This is not the time to grieve what's been lost.

Her street opens to a desolate road. Daylight has burnt off some of the fog, but the sun is still obscured by the clouds, the way it usually is in Auctairea. A few pines stand tall in the yellow grass, and an occasional rooftop comes into view. Beyond the field to her left is a forest of which overflows with pine trees. Off the open road, there are homes spread out across the land. Some of them even show signs of life. A trail of smoke from a chimney, or the upkeep of a yard, gives them away. Otherwise, most of these pillars of luxury are vacant, rotting with the rest of society.

The peace of the country is overcome by violent laughter and the obnoxious sounds of the less refined.

Kira looks up at the bare branches of a nearby tree. Through the fading mist, the beady eyes of a dozen blackbirds hunt her. She has to look away.

Kira knows all too well how they feed, and it gives her the shivers. Fear is not an option, not now.

She's reached the Commons.

Two apartment complexes seem out of place in the picturesque setting. Their inhabitants are those whom the city deemed unworthy of its perks, sent into exile out to the country. This is Hanover's biggest leech and main threat. Back when she still had a choice, if Kira had known this project was in the works, she never would've moved here.

Keeping her face stern, Kira tries to ignore the approach of a scrawny woman wearing nothing but a dirty white tube top, over fraying black shorts. Her bones protrude past her pale skin, and not even the makeup plastered over her face can masquerade her homeliness.

"Look, it's the Modest Snob!" Meredith Cove has never kept her jealousy of Kira hidden.

Kira ignores her.

"Still think you're too good to talk to me?" Meredith's shoulders slouch as she struts towards Kira.

Behind her, several figures make their way from the Commons. Even through the fog, Kira can tell by their silhouettes that they're male. Her muscles loosen once she sees that *he's* not with them.

She needs to say something to ward off their attention. "My business is none of yours." Kira continues looking straight ahead.

"She speaks." Meredith laughs abruptly.

Two of the five men behind Meredith, stroll up. Kira recognizes Jeb and Marten, but the other three are strangers. Their eyes are just as lustful, and their clothes just as dirty. Past them, she sees his frazzled hair.

Nausea overwhelms Kira. *He's* watching her.

Perched on the rooftop of the first complex, a shirtless man observes her every move. Shivers run up Kira's spine. The Principal is the designated warden of the Commons. His primary job is to control its inhabitants by deceit. He does this well, so well that each set of eyes that watch her are brainwashed enough to believe he is their friend. In a world where there is no religion, it would be sacrilegious to harm a Principal.

Yet she's almost killed this one…

He holds his post well. Like trained animals, the Commons stop at the corner of Main Street. They're too frightened to venture from the grounds of their government-funded cells, stacked into two huge eyesores in the country. Their seeming obedience to their societal status won't fool Kira. She knows they venture out at night. She has a pretty good hunch it was one of the ones watching her now, who stole from her garden.

"Come on, Kira, we'd love to have you join us for a grouping," Marten shouts from behind her.

Just the thought of their debauchery makes Kira cringe. Without acknowledging him, she keeps walking.

Soon, the Commons are out of earshot, and the white picket fence of the Mayor's estate reflects the pale daylight. A charcoal drone flies back and forth over the gate, to guard the Prime Minister's spy of Hanover.

Beyond the acre of well-trimmed, yellow grass, is a three-story farmhouse, complete with a wrap-around porch. Unlike the Commons brown paint, the white of this house doesn't have a single chip in sight.

The drone stops pacing and turns its pointed front towards Kira. Much like the patrol drones, these sensors, though darker in color, record everything they reflect. She ignores her reflection and holds her chin up. "My name is Kira Westin, and I would like to speak with the Mayor."

The drone does not move. Regardless, the information is being transmitted.

A buzz fills the air, and the drone pulls back to the fence post. "You may enter." The voice is the same as the patrol drone. Kira doesn't acknowledge it while walking past the gate.

Before she reaches the porch, an older woman steps through the double mahogany doors. She holds a crystal glass filled with whiskey. The breeze can't move her thick, blond hair that rests at her shoulders. Cheryl's gained weight since the last time Kira last saw her. Her blue eyes are glazed, but her thin lips are curved in a welcoming smile. "Kira Westin, my favorite citizen, how are you?"

Kira playfully cringes. "Don't say that too loud, or the Prime Minister might hear you."

Cheryl laughs. "He owes you more than I do." She takes a drink before holding an arm out to the house. "Come in, come in."

Kira steps into the shadows and frowns. Only candles and lanterns give the dark walls any light. "When was your electricity cut off?"

Cheryl momentarily frowns before giving her best politician smile. "A few months ago, the Commons threatened to riot over my crime against the planet. The Prime Minister had to keep the peace." She points at the chandelier overhead, where glass bulbs do nothing but collect dust. "My crime stopped." Cheryl flings her hair back indignantly. "Everyone's okay with the Prime Minister and his army having electricity. They're essential. People like you and me, well…" She shrugs before marching down the hall to an oversized dining room, where a dark oak table with twenty matching chairs rests. On top of the table are several plates of fine china with various processed snacks and bowls of fresh fruit.

Kira's stomach growls.

"Of course, Joplin hasn't stripped me of *all* my dignities." Cheryl takes a seat in front of a crystal bottle that's half-filled with whiskey. "Would you like some?" Cheryl offers, her hands shaking as she refills her glass.

"No, thank you."

Cheryl eyes her playfully. "So, what brings the Modest Beauty to my neck of the woods?"

Kira winces at being called that, making Cheryl laugh before Kira reaches into her pocket. "I woke up to find my garden ransacked."

"Oh?" Cheryl's eyes drop. "I don't investigate crimes anymore, but you can still report it to the patrol drone."

"I'm not seeking justice." Kira takes out the black velvet box, laced with purple, before opening it. Even in the low lighting of kerosene lanterns, the sparkle of her cushion cut, yellow diamond solitaire reflects rainbows across the room.

"The Roberta," Cheryl gasps in reverence since only the most coveted diamonds are named. Nine flawless carats in a coveted shade of yellow that sparkles like the dawn. "I remember when it was on the cover of Auctairea Weekly." She laughs once. "Only you would be able to keep something this special hidden all these years. What do you want for it? Ammo?"

Kira's heart races. Ammo is what she needs more than anything, but she can't let it show. "A girl can never have enough ammo."

"Not these days." Cheryl crosses her arms. "Are you out?"

Kira's shoulders stiffen.

Cheryl's eyes may be cloudy, but they noticed.

"No." Kira doesn't lie since technically, one round doesn't mean she's out. "I would like more than what I have, but when it comes to lead, I'm greedy."

This time, Cheryl's eyes smile with her lips. "I have twenty rounds of .22 that I can spare. What else do you need?"

"A rifle to match them." Kira points at hers. "This shoots .308."

Cheryl frowns. "I don't have that. Gilligan uses .22, and I can't break the law."

One rifle per household, but with the high cost of firearms, very few Auctaireans can afford self-defense.

"Of course." Kira forces a casual grin to hide her disappointment. "I need four months' worth of rations, seeds, and a bottle of kerosene."

"That's a lot of rations just for you." Cheryl looks down at the yellow rock that's held with double platinum prongs, gripping each corner like eight sharp claws.

"It's going to take time to replenish my garden."

"Hmm, let's not be coy. You're in the company of a friend."

Kira's discernment screams otherwise.

Cheryl's eyes dance at her. "I know about your kid."

Kira's heart drops, making her smile fade.

Cheryl leans forward to whisper. "Who do you think erased her record?" Her eyes look down at the gaudy ring before she smirks. "The scale has always tipped in your favor, but now it seems you owe me. My, my, how times have changed..."

Kira never expected this and glances towards the hall while her fight or flight mechanism kicks in. Running away would be stupid. "Why would you do that?" Kira raises her chin, faking confidence, before looking back at Cheryl.

Cheryl glances around the dining room that's so dark they might as well be in a cave. "I raised my boy. Of course, back then, it was legal." She shrugs, and Kira sees sincerity in her eyes for the first time.

"Does anyone else know?"

"No."

Kira slouches in her chair. "Thank you."

Cheryl doesn't smile before taking another drink. "I can't give you any rations. My drone didn't come last week."

Kira's eyes bulge since the Mayor should always receive a drop-off. "No."

Cheryl smirks. "I'm on my last case of whiskey." She holds up her glass. "And I barely have enough to keep the Commons inline. What I can give you are seeds and kerosene. You may also pick what your pockets can carry from my orchard. There's not much left. Gilligan's a growing boy." She finishes her drink and coughs a little, before setting the glass down.

"Is it the Kaddains?" Kira whispers.

"I don't know. Joplin hasn't said a word about who attacked us." Cheryl pours herself another drink. "Sometimes, I think it's just propaganda." She smiles, but her eyes remain hard. "That was a joke."

"Of course."

"I can call him on your behalf. I'll bet he would love to put you back to work." Cheryl's brows rise.

"No," Kira was more firm than she meant to be and is afraid she overstepped her bounds.

"The kid," Cheryl whispers.

Kira is surprised by the understanding that seeps from Cheryl's eyes. "Yes."

"You must consider that if you can't feed her, you shouldn't keep her. Education Centers aren't THAT bad. She'll be taken care of. You can move to Quandii, and get your life back."

"I'll feed her." Kira's lips press together in anger. Nadia is her life. But she must keep her thoughts to herself. She's already treading dangerous waters by showing her face. Staying out of sight helps keep her and Nadia safe. Without food, their lives are at risk either way. Besides that, if the government isn't giving rations to the mayors, they probably aren't supplying the Education Centers, either.

Cheryl eyes her cynically. "It's your life. Makes no difference to me."

Kira's tight lips manage to smile. She knows she's not in the company of a friend, no matter how hard Cheryl pretends to be one.

Thirty minutes later, Kira has seeds for carrots, potatoes, onions, and green beans in her pockets. A jar of kerosene tucked under her arm, and three pockets full of green apples. It's not enough to last until these seeds amount to anything, but better than nothing.

Kira walks past the wrap around porch, where Cheryl sits at her rocker, still drinking.

With a friendly wave, Kira is dismissed from the property. Behind her, the drone continues its zig-zag patrol.

The mist has cleared, but a haze of thick clouds block the sun, making the landscape fitting for her mood.

Passing the Commons, everyone is out of sight. Not even the Principal is at his post. Kira's hair stands on end. It's always better when they're out in the open.

"Your pockets are awfully thick." Meredith's voice is sharp. "Got anything for me?"

Kira turns to see a thin figure marching towards her. Meredith's shoulders move up and down dramatically, trying to appear intimidating...

"Only lead." Kira briefly glares over her shoulder and keeps walking.

Meredith stops. With her chin down, she snarls at Kira.

Kira walks towards her home, leaving the threat behind.

Stepping into the quiet of the country, Kira lets out a low sigh. Disappointment gnaws on her heart. She traded a $600,000 wedding ring for some seeds, oil, and a few pockets of fruit. It's enough to burn Kira's cheeks red. Gritting her teeth, Kira keeps telling herself it could be worse. Like every other Auctairean child, Nadia could be raised in an Education Center, without ever knowing God or her own mother. Still, one of her greatest earthly treasures she had was traded for something that's not even a solution. Kira's eyes harden. She's been saving her last round for defense, but she now has no choice.

She has to hunt.

How Nadia will react, is terrifying...

\*\*\*

Cheryl waits until Kira is out of sight, before using the remote around her wrist to call her drone.

The drone leaves the gate and arrives at her porch within seconds.

"Send a transmission to the Prime Minister." Cheryl sets her glass down on the white table beside her bench. She straightens her shoulders and frowns. A tinge of guilt causes her left eye to twitch before she refocuses on her reflection off the drone. "Now," She orders, smiling wide, "Stephen, hello! You forgot my drop off last week, but that's alright. I know you're a busy man. I'm forgiving, and even have good news for you. It seems Kira Westin is getting desperate..." She holds up her right hand to show off the famous ring everyone in Auctairea once adored. "Send me my supplies, and

I'll send her crawling back to you."

***

# CHAPTER 3
## *FIREFIGHT*

Moonlight causes the thin cloud cover to glow in waves of gray, white, and charcoal over the dark landscape of the meadow. A clearing breaks and brightens the scene. The cruelty of poverty can't diminish Kira's beauty, as she intently waits for her prey. Taking a moment to admire the stars, she regains her focus on the tree line.

Only the swaying pines make a sound in the night, which reminds Kira of the sea. It's a peaceful contrast to Nadia's tantrum earlier. Kira glances towards the house. She's too far away to see it, but her heartstrings are yanked in that direction anyway. Nadia may have protested this hunt, but Cheryl's right. If she can't feed her daughter, she doesn't deserve to keep her.

A cold breeze moves the October air, and bristling pines draw Kira's attention. She spots a large doe at the tree line. She's sniffing on the ground, stepping closer to where Kira placed the apple cores. A buck would be better. Still, Kira steadies the rifle against her shoulder, ready to take whatever God offers her.

The doe stalls. After several moments of hesitation, it steps out into the open.

Kira allows the doe the time to enjoy an apple, before letting out a slow breath and squeezing the trigger.

The doe falls.

Kira lowers her rifle. She's been out of practice but knew she wouldn't miss. Searching for the casing, with the full moon, it's not hard to find. When she picks it up, she feels the crack. Her heart sinks. Just like the brass in her attic, this round can't be reloaded.

The reality of hers and Nadia's vulnerability shatters Kira's heart. "God, help us," She whispers, before grabbing the handles of her makeshift wagon, which is nothing more than splintered wood hammered onto two wooden wheels. Kira braces the handles over her shoulders and drags the cart from behind. The wheels squeak, echoing throughout the meadow.

Reaching the deer, Kira sets the wagon beside her. It's massive for a doe, large enough to last her and Nadia throughout the winter. "Thank you, God," Kira whispers. She has to drag it by its hind legs to put it on the wagon. With her shoulders already stressed, Kira sets the handles on them and braces herself for the weight.

The wheels squeal in protest at the weight. Straining to drag the boisterous cart along the meadow, each one of Kira's breaths glows like fog under the moon's light.

A roar of thunder fills the sky and rattles the ground, along with Kira's heart. Instinctively, she drops the handles to her cart and looks up. It's been five years since Kira's heard a jet. All she can see is a shadow, with a red light beneath. It's a sight that should be familiar. Saffarion Air Base isn't far, but nothing, not so much as a crop duster, has flown over Hanover in years.

Another jet streaks across the sky. This one has a white light on its tail.

The first shadow maneuvers towards the second, in a wild flip, to make a 180.

Popping assaults Kira's ears, and several flashes brighten the meadow. She squats to the ground and covers her ears, while the second jet fires back. The flashing of white against the trees makes the pine needles look like curtains, and the meadow becomes an amphitheater to the light show. A show that proves the rumors of war are real. All Kira can think of now is how scared Nadia must be.

She has to get home.

Kira grits her teeth and regains hold of the wagon. Her feet nearly fumble, but she catches herself. If she hadn't used her last bullet, she would ditch the deer and run. She drags her cart and the heavy load, with desperation and fear tugging on her hamstrings.

To her left, a flash of yellow draws her eyes. Kira can't help but stop to watch a parachute glide down from the first jet.

The mechanical bird crashes beyond the tree line, and the explosion is close enough to rock the ground.

Mesmerized by the parachute as the pilot maneuvers it down, Kira feels such grace is unfitting in battle.

Crack!

The gunshot seems to have come from the forest.

Kira's heart skips a beat. Someone nearby has ammo, when she doesn't.

The pilot continues his descent. He's getting close to her, too close.

Kira must move, but her knees won't budge. Fear has never paralyzed her before.

The second jet creates a mighty gust that nearly blows her over, as it veers across the meadow. Three bursts and the parachute enfolds on itself, sending the pilot crashing on the ground with a thud. There's no way anyone could've survived that fall.

Overhead, dozens of jets zoom in, brightening the night with more flashes. The once peaceful scenery is now filled with ear-splitting bursts of combat.

Kira rushes towards home before an unwanted and primal thought enters her mind.

Surely the dead pilot has a sidearm…

Everyone at the Commons has to hear this commotion, and those vultures always rush to loot the first chance they get. Kira doesn't want to be like them. God expects better from her, but without ammo, she can't protect Nadia. It's only a matter of time before they seek more than just her garden.

The idea is dangerous, stupid even.

Kira rushes in.

The sounds of battle drown out the squeaking of her cart. It only takes Kira twenty paces to reach the fallen pilot. Through the gray haze, light from the moon reflects off several white pages on the ground surrounding him. Kira can't understand why anyone would fly into battle with a book.

"He's over here, I think," a man shouts from the tree line. His voice is far too close for her liking.

She must hurry.

The pilot's back is flat on the ground, and his arms are entangled with the cords of the parachute. On his hip, the reflection of metal catches Kira's eye. Her mouth opens in surprise. Part of her expected not to find a gun. Now, her heart races at the sight of it. Stepping closer, she gets a better look. His uniform is dark and hard to make out in the moonlight, but whoever he is, he's not Auctairean. His build is far too muscular, proving this man is an enemy of her state. She reaches for the sidearm, but the guilt for stealing from someone, even though he's dead, causes her hand to shake.

In a brief lull of battle, she hears his staggering breath.

Kira's heart stops. Instinctively she steps back. She didn't expect him to be alive. The flashes of war blaze above like fireworks, making it easier to see the stranger. Blood soaks his pants from his thigh to his knee. A large hole in his uniform reveals where the pages came from. Strapped onto his chest, is a large book. Finding that odd, Kira's lips morph into a frown. While she can't fathom what's so important about a book to warrant keeping it on one's person, Kira knows a reward for turning this him in, is guaranteed. Kira looks at her cart. Even with the doe, there's still room for him.

If she could take him to Mayor Fletcher's drone, she'll be rewarded and Nadia will have plenty to eat.

She's lifted bucks heavier than men before, so Kira is confident she could pull it off.

Looking back at the stranger, the whites of his eyes prove he's watching her every move. With his arms bound, he can't shoot her, but even after she acquires his gun, she can't let him free, or he may try to fight her. It's reckless, but Kira won't let fear weaken her resolve. She rolls her shoulders back, determined to turn this man in.

"Help him."

God's voice is unmistakable.

Confusion creates a battle in her mind. Raising a brow, she can't understand why God would ask such a daunting task out of her.

Who is this man?

She steps forward, and something foreign in this setting crinkles underfoot.

Looking down, the torn piece of white paper reflects the moon's light. Kira stares at the pilot while bending to pick it up. Maybe she'll learn who he is from the text…

She can't decipher this language, but the title is something she can read. It is the book of Psalms.

An unwanted gasp escapes her. Even if it costs her everything, Kira won't turn in one of her own.

She let's go of the page. Moving forward, she will obey God and save this man.

"You said he was over here," a woman shouts. She almost sounds like Cheryl, but the voice is too far away for Kira to know for sure.

She must remain silent, or they'll be discovered. Kira pulls her cross necklace out from its hiding place. The brightness of the full moon reflects off the platinum, showing this stranger she's not a threat.

His eyes widen.

She tucks the necklace under her shirt before drawing her knife. Reaching to free this man causes every protective alarm to blare in her head. Her eyes wince at the foolishness of this before she musters the faith to cut him free.

If God wants her to save this man, he will protect her too.

Pulling his arms out of the knotted cords, the pilot tries to sit up but grimaces in pain before falling to the ground.

Kira steps back, keeping her knife drawn, in case he tries to fight her.

The pilot unholsters his weapon.

All Kira can think of is her daughter, since helping this man was the dumbest mistake of her life. Who will protect Nadia, once she's gone?

Much to Kira's surprise, the pilot holds the gun out, handgrip first.

Goosebumps cover Kira's arms. She takes the weapon and holsters it in her pants. Pressing her finger along her nose and lips to make sure the pilot stays quiet, Kira bends down to help lift him up.

He's heavier than she expected, but she manages to get him to his feet.

His teeth are bare, reflecting the moonlight as he struggles to remain quiet.

The pain of carrying him pulls every fiber of her back muscles. Kira lowers this man to her cart, slowly. Once the pilot is beside the doe, Kira yanks off her jacket and drops it over his face.

Concealing his sidearm by untucking her shirt, the cold is not lost on Kira, before she straps her empty rifle over her shoulder.

Bracing her neck for the heavy haul, Kira lifts the cart handles over her shoulders and focuses on the shadows of the tree line.

"Kira?" A man asks, and he's close.

She has to get to the shadows before he sees what she's carrying.

"I say, Kira, is that you?"

She's almost to the shadows, just a few more feet…

"Hey!" Gilligan Fletcher, the Mayor's son, catches up with her.

"Yeah, there's quite a show tonight." Kira fills her voice with annoyance to hide her fear.

"Did you get anything from it?" Gilligan gains on her.

"I wish."

Gilligan steps up to her left. He's too close for comfort. "Looks like you've got quite the load?" He's more accusing than inquiring.

If Cheryl learns of Kira's aid to the enemy, she'll report it to her drone.

Kira drops the cart and sighs with heavy irritation. "She was huge, almost as big as you."

It may be nightfall, but it's plain to see that Gilligan's not amused. "Who was?" His face is round, his beady eyes are too close together above a flat nose that remains unattractive, even under the flattering light of the moon. While everyone else in Hanover starves, the Mayor's adult son lives overfed. Growing boy, indeed.

"The doe I shot. I'll cut you off some for a few rations." Kira pulls out her knife, ready to use it on Gilligan if necessary.

"Is that all you've got?" Gilligan says. "We don't need your gamey venison, not tonight. I'm after a more valuable catch. See, you're not the only one who's a good shot around here."

"No one's a better shot than I am," Kira snaps.

"Well, I shot a pilot midair, with a kepweed laced bullet to boot."

Kira's heart sinks at the thought of kepweed. No wonder the pilot could hardly move. He'll probably be dead before she can get him home. "I don't believe you."

"You can bet I did. Ma heard they're paying a whole month's worth of rations for one, and triple for the first that flew in. We just have to find where he dropped."

Wondering why the first pilot is so important, Kira fears the Bible may just be a cover for some hidden information. A code or a map, perhaps, might be logged in those pages. Maybe she's a fool for helping him after all? She reminds herself that it was God's voice who guided her, and God has never let her down. "Why?"

Gilligan laughs, but it's more like a wheeze. "All I know is that I shot him. And I'll be willing to share some of that reward for certain, favors."

"I'd rather die." Kira picks up her cart and heads toward home.

"You don't have to be so rude about it," Gilligan's voice is broken by her rejection.

"You're right, I was rude. Keep pushing me, and I'll get mean." Disgusted, she bares her teeth at him in the moon's light, before moving on.

Kira has to hurry. It won't be long until Gilligan, or someone else finds the parachute, without the pilot.

Behind her, Gilligan shouts, "Someday, you're going to have to accept that George isn't coming back!"

Kira cringes at the sound of that name, as she treks across the meadow.

# CHAPTER 4
## THE BLOOD OF A STRANGER

Kira drags her cart over the shallow creek, and onto the grounds of her once beautiful estate. The tan and gray stonework appears white in the moonlight, except for where blotches of mold spread like dark bruises on the walls. Several spots where tiles are missing from her rooftop appear silver, and two broken beams of the attic are exposed. If she didn't live here, it would be a place she'd naturally avoid.

A soft glow through the back window intensifies. Kira sets the cart against a large pine, before unlocking her door.

Nadia steps into the shadows that cover the bottom of their stairway. "Mommy, there was a terrible storm. I was so scared."

"It wasn't a storm, those were jets. I'm sorry I wasn't here."

"Jets?" She asks, gripping the white spray bottle in her hand a little tighter.

"Remember what I taught you about airplanes?"

Nadia's eyes are indifferent. "Oh."

"I'm going to bring someone inside. Whatever you do, don't scream." Kira steps outside and reaches to lift her jacket off the pilot. She hesitates, fearing that he may be dead. She pulls it up to find his eyes are alert.

Beads of sweat cover his brow. He is older than Kira, but not by much, mid-thirties, perhaps? Above his pointed chin, his broad cheekbones accentuate his eyes that are set under thick brows. Eyes that Kira can now tell are green. His dark hair is short but is a mess. His face is beige, but his color is draining by the second.

Kira silently asks God to protect her and Nadia before squatting beside this stranger. Her mind screams that helping him is crazy, while her heart remains at peace.

The doe needs to be drained, so Kira draws her knife.

The pilot's eyes show no fear.

Kira reaches beyond him to cut the deer's neck. It's the part of hunting she hates the most. Biting her lip, she holsters her blade.

He watches her with eyes far too calm for their situation.

"I need to get you inside," Kira whispers before sliding a palm behind his back to lift him. The pilot tries to sit up on his own. The movement causes him to not only wince but sweat profusely. Even so, he's far too calm to have kepweed in his system. Hoping Gilligan lied about lacing his bullets, Kira braces her shoulder under the stranger's arm and helps him rise to a stand. With the pilot on his feet, Kira kicks the cart down to drain the deer's blood.

The pilot glances at the doe and is clearly impressed. He keeps his weight off his injured leg and hobbles with her through the doorway. Kira kicks the backdoor shut behind them.

Nadia gasps and almost drops her spray bottle. "Who is that?"

"I don't know, but I need to get him upstairs. Can you lock the door for me?" Kira grunts under his weight.

Nadia only stares at the pilot in fear.

He returns Nadia's gaze, a smile playing at the corner of his lips, despite the pain he must feel.

"Why would you help a stranger?" Nadia asks.

"God told me to. Now please, move." Kira gasps under the pressure of the pilot's weight.

Nadia steps back, with her eyes distraught.

Kira supports the pilot with her shoulder. He manages to keep the majority of his weight on one foot, as she drags him through her dining room. Kira holds a firm hand against his back to help brace him. The sweat has drenched his uniform to where it feels like an extra layer of skin under her palm.

Nadia rushes to lock the door and leans against it to watch them, her eyes wide with fear.

The sound of her daughter locking the back door gives Kira comfort, while she continues on this reckless mission.

She has to get him upstairs. If she tends to his wounds down here, he could be seen. Kira can't risk that.

A worn mahogany table and four matching chairs stand in the low light of the fireplace. Kira has to kick one of the chairs out of their way before her feet reach the carpet of her living room. She continues to brace him up against her body, which is at least five inches shorter than his. Slowly she guides him towards the stairs.

The pilot's skin is hot, and being this close to him feels awkward, but Kira pushes past it.

"We need light," Kira calls over her shoulder.

Nadia carries the lantern up behind them, making the glow of yellow expand.

The first step is the hardest, like learning a new dance just to keep him standing. After that, each step causes the pilot to wince until they reach the first doorway.

Kira is surprised by his willingness to let her lead, before she guide him into her bedroom, then straight to another doorway that leads to the master bath. She helps the pilot into her tub. He doesn't make a sound. If kepweed were in his system, this movement would be like torture. Kira figures Gilligan lied.

Nadia sets the lantern on the counter, before scurrying behind her mother.

In better lighting, Kira's heart tanks at the amount of blood. She sees the patch sewn on the right shoulder of the pilot's green uniform. As she suspected, it's not Auctairean.

The Zyandite flag has a deep red background, with gold trim and a white cross in the center.

How could Prime Minister Joplin, be stupid enough to provoke the world's most distinguished and feared warrior kingdom?

"A Zyandite..." Kira whispers. Lifting her chin to fake confidence, she raises her voice enough for Nadia to hear. "I need to dispose of his uniform. Go downstairs and get some water boiling." After Nadia leaves, Kira closes the door to protect her daughter from the gory sight.

Rolling up her sleeves, Kira kneels and leans against the tub. "I hope some of this blood is from the deer."

The pilot only stares at her.

"You don't speak Auctrah, do you?" Kira asks.

His eyes fall to his wound.

She hopes he speaks Pazmirish. While digging out her meager medical supplies from her cabinet, she asks, *"What is your name?"* After so many years of not speaking the favorite tongue of the GPU, Kira's surprised by how fluent she still is.

The pilot eyes squint in confusion before he shakes his head.

"Figures," Kira whispers in her native Auctrah, before laying the bandages and disinfectant on the rim of her tub. She decides to try the lesser-known language of Dulboruu.

*"What is your name?"* This dialect has always been difficult for Kira since it's so different from Auctrah. It has been a long time since she's spoken Dulboruu, and her tongue gets twisted.

The pilot only glances at her for a moment, his green eyes perturbed.

"Of course not." Kira sighs, to relieve some of the stress like a pressure valve.

There's no other way to get to the wound on his leg, but to cut the uniform off. The blood and sweat have made it skintight, to where it might as well be part of him. Using trauma shears, she begins snipping the fabric. "We're in a predicament. I don't speak Zyandish." Kira peels the uniform back to discover that his leg, not the deer, is the source of all the blood.

White spots fill Kira's vision at the sight. The bullet obviously went through his thigh. The flesh is red in the center and terribly inflamed. A few black lines spiral out of each hole, but the stench confirms it. Gilligan wasn't lying about the kepweed.

Kira glances at the cupboard where the antidote is hidden, but it's reserved for Nadia, and she won't give it up. Kira looks at his leg, and her heart knows that she should give it to him, but she refuses. Since the bullet went through, maybe he won't need it? Looking at his calm eyes, she knows kepweed burns the blood. How this man can be so composed, is beyond her. Kira grabs the disinfectant and pours it liberally. The wound fizzes out a white foam, making the pilot cringe. For good measure, she pours more. She has to flush out the poison. "Sorry." She whispers.

He doesn't respond.

Kira accepts the silence.

Keeping her hands from shaking, she hesitates before suturing his wounds. Kira's only practiced on a raw chicken before, and that was years ago. The idea of sticking a needle into human flesh makes her nauseous. These holes are too big to be left alone, and Kira doesn't have time to question what the Langton's taught her. Each time she passes the needle through his skin, Kira expects him to flinch in pain, but he remains still. He doesn't even grunt. It takes longer than Kira expected to stitch up his wounds, but once it's done, she's relieved it's better than the last time she hemmed clothing. Kira unrolls the gauze and covers both wounds.

Something rumbles outside. It's the kind of noise Kira imagined an earthquake would sound like. It's thunderous but deeper than the jets. They both look up, as though they could see through the ceiling.

The rumbling shakes the house, before fading away. Kira wonders if it's a cargo plane before her eyes meet his, both speculating whose side it's on.

She can't take the silence any longer. "If the bullet hadn't gone through, you'd already be dead." As it is, she can't imagine how he isn't screaming in pain from the kepweed. Kira wraps medical tape around his leg several times. Wiping her brow with her forearm, Kira doesn't even notice the blood on her hands.

She waits to see if her stitching was good enough to stop the bleeding. The gauze remains white. Kira can now focus on the hole over his chest.

Without giving eye contact, she begins to cut along the gaping hole in his uniform.

He flinches to stop her.

In automatic response, Kira swiftly presses the shears against his neck. "You've already lost a lot of blood. Don't make me cause you to lose more." Her heart thunders, but the pilot remains calm. He doesn't look at her with fear, but rather his eyes dance with admiration.

A minute, perhaps two passes until Kira realizes that she overreacted. Zyandite modesty is ridiculed around the world. She pulls the blade away from his neck.

The expression in his eyes doesn't change. There's no sign of surprise or even relief. It's as though he knew she wouldn't actually kill him. Kira lets out a deep breath before cutting off his dark green uniform. This time, he stays still. No easy task, due to the sweat and blood that causes the fabric to stick to his skin. She then cuts down to the hole over his leg, to rip the uniform off without messing with the bandage. He leans forward to help her peel it off his back. The musk of his sweat combined with aftershave tickles her nostrils. She would rather not enjoy the smell and forces the distraction out of her mind. The armor strapped over his chest is dented. There's a tan Bible, taped under the armor, center on his torso. It's heavy and challenging to pull off, but once she does, the released pressure allows him to take a full breath.

He gasps and coughs while Kira lifts up the armor to see another bullet hole. This one must have come from the jet and would have taken his life, if not for his Bible.

"He protected you." Kira whispers, pointing towards heaven before setting the armor and his soapstone covered Bible on the floor.

Through the door, Nadia whispers, "I heard a scary sound."

"It was another airplane, everything's alright."

After a moment of silence, Nadia whispers, "I brought water."

"Leave it by the door, and go back downstairs," Kira says harsher than she meant to.

She doesn't have time for guilt and fumbles in her closet to find something this stranger can wear. Kira must be quick to get rid of the evidence of his identity and the proof of her treason.

All she has left of George's things are stored in a single chest. His clothes may be a little tight on the pilot, but they'll have to do. Kira hesitates to open the chest. The memories it holds are strong enough to cripple her heart.

She yanks it open. Kira could ask why God chose her for this task, but in Auctairea, she's his only option. She grabs the clothes on top, making sure to block out their textures and colors to keep the memories at bay.

She returns to the bathroom, where the pilot is trying to stand up, wearing nothing but black underwear and his own blood.

She raises a hand. "Stay still."

He glances at her hand, and his eyes seem to register her body language. Slowly he sits back down and grimaces in pain.

Kira wants to respect his privacy, but there are many defined lines she's never seen on a man before, which both intrigue and scare her.

Her eyes fall on his scars. This man has seen battle. On his chest, just below his collar bone, there's a rounded scar that isn't much bigger than the bullet hole on his leg. There are several long scars on his abdomen, and what appears to be a recently healed stab wound on his left rib cage.

Her cheeks warm, and Kira turns to grab a towel. She drops it into the bucket of warm water to bathe him.

He gently takes the towel from her hand, with his eyes pleading.

"I understand." Kira allows him the dignity to bathe himself.

She steps out of the bathroom and returns her rifle to its place behind her bed frame. Kira takes this moment to silently petition God for protection. God has to bless this. Otherwise, the outcome is death.

Kira can't think of that now.

Figuring he's had enough time to bathe, Kira steps toward the bathroom, when Nadia screams.

# CHAPTER 5
## *TRANSLATION OF A PSALM*

With her heart pounding like a drum, Kira rushes downstairs. The thought of soldiers waiting outside plagues her mind.

Nadia is at the bottom step, staring at the back door, coiled inward.

Expecting a search team, there's only one silhouette. "Don't be scared, Kira," a man's voice says through the door.

By the grace of God, he thought Nadia's screaming was her. Kira closes her eyes in relief. "Go hide," she whispers.

Nadia gasps, before running into the half bathroom down the hall, and closing the door.

Figuring whoever is out there is from the Commons, the handgun doesn't give Kira much comfort. Besides the fact they're illegal in Auctairea, she's never shot one. She makes sure it's hidden under her shirt, before opening the door.

Only Jeb stands there, his blond hair dripping sweat. His lustful blue eyes scan her body, before widening in terror.

Kira follows his gaze and nearly jumps at the sight of blood on her hands. She can't let Jeb see her fear and scrunches her face. "What do you want?"

Jeb's eyes have a hard time peeling away from her hands. "The Principal sent me."

Kira presses her lips together in annoyance. "You Commons aren't welcomed here."

He looks at her hands once more, and all his color fades. "Your…" He swallows hard enough for her to see.

"My what?" She asks.

He points. "Your hands."

Kira smirks and crosses her arms. "It's from draining my kill." She nods at the deer.

Jeb turns around and looks at her cart. "I don't know how you can stomach that."

Kira knows that the Commons have no problem raping, looting, and occasionally, murdering their fellow man. His judgment against hunting proves Jeb's hypocrisy. Kira glares at him, before walking towards the doe.

Jeb keeps his distance.

"You think it's any different where the rations are made?" Kira squats beside her cart to see if the doe is ready to be cleaned. "They just make them behind the walls of a factory, so you can't see the gore."

"Those are vegan, though."

"So, they say, but do you know what the ingredients are?"

Jeb doesn't respond. No one knows the truth about the rations, other than the government.

"It doesn't matter. No one can be picky now, can we?" She rolls her cart to the door.

Jeb is quick to move out of her way. "Guess not."

"Why are you outside of your bounds?" Kira is purposefully rude.

Jeb's mouth fumbles for a moment. "To tell you the war's reached

Hanover."

Kira looks past him, at the firefight that's far enough away to no longer thunder the meadow, but still close enough to decipher continues on. "I think everyone's figured that out, but it's a good excuse to get out of the Commons." She eyes him suspiciously.

Jeb looks down. Their social class defined in his shame. "Also, there's a Zyandite soldier on the run." He looks up slowly. "The Principal wants to know if you've seen him."

She plays her part as a curious citizen. "Gilligan said he shot him. Did the Principal tell you the reward is triple for the first one that flew in?"

The misgiving in Jeb's eyes morphs into competition. "Triple, huh?"

Kira sets the cart handles down and shrugs.

"I wouldn't believe a word that fat idiot says." Jeb's forced laughter doesn't fool her. "Even if it's true…" Jeb looks towards the meadow. "A bunch of Skull Smashers was dropped in the forest. They'll probably catch him before anyone else can."

So that's what the cargo plane was for. Kira hides her fear by grabbing the doe. After the pilot, the deer is easier to lift. She drags it to her table, while Jeb watches in horror.

She uses his fear, and wipes some of the fresh blood off her hands, allowing it to drip out her back door, before grabbing her cart and parks it in its place against the wall. "How do you know they're Skull Smashers?"

"I saw them combing the forest from a distance. No human moves like they do." Jeb's pale face follows the tree line. "I better go." He smirks and looks back at Kira. "If you get lonely, the Principal's arms are always open."

Kira's lips curl in disgust.

Jeb lifts up his hands in the motion of surrender. "Hey, he just wanted me to remind you, that's all. Don't kill the messenger."

Of all the Commons, Jeb is the most dangerous to her, because he's always been the slyest. Almost like a guy she could trust. Just like Cheryl, Kira knows a liar when she sees one.

Jeb backs away and turns towards the meadow.

Kira waits a minute before closing the back door. She locks it, releasing tension through a sigh. Cold, heartless machines are looking for the pilot. It won't take long before they get to her house. Kira wants to fall to the ground and cry out her fears to God, but the bathroom door opens. Nadia is watching.

Kira forces a smile. "It's alright. He's gone."

Nadia sulks to the faded blue couch and sits down.

A thud sounds above.

Kira runs upstairs to find the pilot, bracing himself on one knee and her dresser. Wearing a cream turtleneck and gray trousers, he slowly regains his footing. He sets the lantern on the dresser with shaky hands.

In this lighting, Kira can see the highlights in his brown hair, and his green eyes appear hazel. There are laugh lines that crease each side of his full lips before a square jaw, positioned symmetrically above well-defined neck muscles. He looks nothing like George, who had raven black hair and striking blue eyes, yet the sight of his clothing causes her heart to race. She pushes through the anguish of her past and squares her shoulders.

He glances down at the clothes that are far too tight on him, trying to piece the puzzle together. But the movement sets him off balance, and he tips.

She steps forward and takes his arm. Through the sweater, she feels the heat of his fever. "Come on." Kira drapes his arm around her shoulder and leads him to a burgundy, velvet couch at the foot of her bed. "You'll sleep in my room,"—she leans close to his face—"so I'll know if you move."

His pain-filled eyes show no sign of fear. He still doesn't speak, not that Kira can understand Zyandish, but some form of communication would be better than none.

Kira studies his face. She wants to trust the kindness she sees in his eyes.

Eyes, she wishes she didn't find handsome. There's also a poise lurking about him that scares her. She didn't recognize the insignia on his uniform, and can only guess what his rank is. Most Zyandite pilots are captains.

Gilligan said the reward would be higher for the first jet that flew in. Perhaps this man is a general? He's too young for that, and last she heard, the highest rank for Zyandite pilots was a lieutenant colonel. Maybe something in the jet makes this man more valuable.

The fever forces the pilot into a deep sleep. While his breathing changes, so does his expression. Kira can't deny she enjoys watching him sleep when only the opposite should be true. Disappointed in herself, Kira pulls her eyes away from him and shakes this attraction off.

Grabbing her lantern, the sight of her bathroom causes her to gasp.

There's blood all over the tub, the floor, the cabinets, and sink. After cleaning the mess, and finally, her hands, Kira grabs his uniform and boots. She must destroy all evidence of his nationality and her betrayal.

The memory of God's voice beckoning her to help this Zyandite fills her heart with peace. Stopping at the doorway, she looks at him one more time. "God must really love you," she whispers. Since, in all reality, this stranger should be dead.

Downstairs, Kira finds Nadia with her arms folded, rocking back and forth on the couch. "The machines are looking for him?"

"Yes, in the forest. Don't worry. Everything will be okay," Kira whispers.

"What if that man tries to kill us in our sleep?"

"He won't."

Nadia only sobs.

Setting the soldier's things down, Kira takes a moment to hug her daughter, while silently praying God will reveal his plan to Nadia. Her fear is one they share.

"That pilot is a Zyandite, and they have strict rules about harming civilians, especially women and children."

Nadia doesn't respond.

All of the drills teaching Nadia to run or hide from Auctairean men, fog Kira's mind. How can she make this clear for Nadia to understand?

"In the rare case, a Zyandite breaks those rules…" Kira pulls from their embrace to look Nadia in the eyes. "Their king must execute them."

"Their king?"

"King Sampson Tidal is a God-fearing, righteous man. I knew about him before…" Kira fights the urge to cry for all that's been lost. "Everything changed."

"But their king's not here." Nadia wipes away a tear.

"God is. We must have faith. God told me to save that man. He will protect our lives, as well. He always does."

After a long moment of silence, Nadia finally looks up. "Okay, I will trust God."

"That's my strong girl."

Kira steps up to the fire and watches the light dance along the white crown molding. Centered on each side of the mantle are two hand-carved pine trees. The glorious pine, a symbol on the Auctairean flag, one she has tried to scrape off, more than once. Since the Great Cleansing, Kira hasn't wanted anything that represents Auctairea in her home. Even with as good as she is with a knife, she couldn't remove these carvings. Now both sides of her mantle look scarred and ugly, and she hates looking at them. They remind her of her failures.

Kira takes a better look at the red shoulder patch sewn on the Zyandite's uniform, especially the perfect white cross in the middle. Here, she could be killed for wearing a cross necklace, and his nation has it on their flag. It's also nostalgic for Kira to see the Zyandite flag again. She almost doesn't want to destroy it. Not only because of the cross at the center but of the fond memories from when she was a child.

After the Zyandites left Auctairea for good, she learned in college that Zyandites worship the art of war more than God, and men dominate every institution, including the home. It hurt and made her feel a little betrayed. Even so, she never let go of the good memories from her prior involvement with the Zyandite Church. After the Great Cleansing, Kira learned to not trust everything Auctairea taught her. She used to believe all the lies. Not anymore.

Kira tosses the uniform into the fire and watches it burn. In her heart, she knows that flag belongs to the right side in this war.

Carrying the boots and armor outside, she knows her property so well, she could navigate it blind.

Reaching the waste hole, Kira tosses them in. It takes a few seconds before she hears them reach the bottom.

The battle in the sky wages on over the forest, but is so far away it's distorted. Kira understands why Nadia thought it was a storm. There could be a victory for either side tonight, although she is not naïve enough to believe any war is won or lost that quickly. If Zyandite falls to Joplin's mechanical army, will there be any place that's safe for Christianity in the world?

She shouldn't speak, but her heart stirs a prayer, one that must be said. "God, please help your people win this fight."

A breeze cuts through her and covers her skin with goosebumps. With her shirt still wet from the pilot's blood, the wind feels even colder. She returns inside, and to give Nadia comfort, she smiles.

Nadia gives a half-smile, before lying to her side to watch the fire.

Kira cleans the doe, sets the meat in her smoker, and disinfects her table. She takes a little longer to wash her hands with the water in the bowl on her kitchen countertop. Thankful to find Nadia asleep, Kira takes the opportunity to bathe. Wearing a black cashmere tunic over burgundy leggings, she gathers the meat. The cold is bearable in dry clothes.

After storing the jerky, Kira carries Nadia up to her bedroom, where she lovingly tucks her into bed.

Taking her lantern into her room, Kira finds her houseguest exactly where she left him.

His eyes are closed, and his breathing is deep. Kira needs to know if his Bible is something other than what it seems. There has to be some reason why the reward for him is higher. She picks up the heavy Bible and sets it on her bed. Turning the pages, she finds nothing but the books a Bible should hold. Feeling along the inside of the soapstone cover, nothing seems different. Just to be sure, she flips through the pages again. Even the ones that are torn feel comforting underneath her fingertips.

God's word always does.

The bullet obviously stopped on a verse. It's a Psalm, but Kira can't read Zyandish. Lifting the carpet from a corner under her nightstand, Kira pulls out her Bible from beneath the baseboard. Sitting on her bed with both Bibles, she turns the pages to find which verse the bullet stopped on. Kira uses her own Bible to translate the verse that is printed in Zyandish, since the chapter names and numbers are still the same. Seeing the bullet landed on Psalm 31:24 causes Kira to gasp before she whispers it.

"So be strong and courageous, all you who put your hope in the LORD!"

A floodgate of emotions bursts in her heart, for Kira doesn't know whether to cry or smile. This verse has been her strength for years, ever since George...

Kira can feel the pilot watching her, and looks up to find him staring.

Sweat drips down his face, and she stands to feel his brow. He doesn't flinch as she touches his skin to feel that his fever is gone. He must be quite the fighter to ward off the kepweed with such vigor.

Kira hands him his Bible, and points at the page. "That bullet landed on my favorite verse," she says, even though he can't understand her.

She tucks her Bible into its hiding spot, while the stranger watches her every move.

Kira turns to face him, screwing her face into a scowl. "I'm a very light sleeper and won't hesitate to shoot you with your own gun."

His lips curve into a smile. "I don't doubt it." His Auctrah is perfect.

Betrayal turns Kira's eyes to slits. "You should've told me you speak Auctrah!"

"I just did." His words are smug, but his face is humble. "Thank you for saving my life."

Kira crosses her arms. "Soon as you're healed, you need to leave, mister?..."

"My name?" He seems genuinely surprised.

"Yes, your name." His social awkwardness makes her suspicious that his fever has spiked again.

"It's Ruger, Ruger Anstone."

"I'm Kira Westin." She doesn't give any pleasantries. It certainly hasn't been nice to meet him.

Ruger's eyes widen. "The reporter?"

Kira's heart drops in shame, to where she can't look him in the eyes. "That was years ago."

"I didn't recognize you without makeup." Ruger looks around. "So, this is how Joplin treats his elite? You don't even have running water."

"Auctairea is Eco-socialist now, and we all must sacrifice to save the planet," she whispers before smirking at the hypocrisy. "Of course, the Prime Minister and his selected favorites, all still have their utilities on in Quandii."

Ruger's brows rise. "Typical."

Kira brings her eyes back to his. "I take it Zyandite hasn't deteriorated to the Stone Age?"

Ruger's the one smirking now, though his eyes remain suspicious. "Our people are good stewards with every gift God gives us, including basic utilities." He eyes where her Bible is hidden. "Why do you hide your faith?"

Kira gasps. She can't fathom how he doesn't know. "Christianity's illegal here."

His lips curve to a doubting smile. "The most inclusive country on earth has outlawed Christianity?" Ruger tilts his head unbelievingly.

Closing her mouth into a slit, Kira won't waste time defending herself. "Why are you here?"

"Your Prime Minister started this fight when his machines crossed our border."

"Joplin attacked Zyandite?" Kira's heart skips a beat. "Why?"

"I have no idea," Ruger's voice is curt. "Perhaps his robotic army gave him a confidence boost?" He shrugs.

"The whole reason Joplin gained support to build his army of machines, was to keep our neighboring warriors from invading Auctairea." Kira tries to piece Prime Minister Joplin's motives together, and all of the clues lead to the suicide of a nation.

"Zyandite never attacks unless provoked."

"I'm aware of Zyandite's history, Mr. Anstone. I went to school when it was still taught, but the public is easily swayed by the sound of a threat. Far as I know, Prime Minister Joplin has only used that army to murder his own people." Fearing she's given too much information, Kira abruptly blows out the lantern. "No more talking tonight."

"Are you truly going to be able to sleep, with an enemy soldier beside your bed?"

"I'm a really good shot."

"In the dark?"

"Especially in the dark. Now get some sleep. Your body is fighting off the effects of the kepweed." Kira says before adjusting her covers. "There are only a couple more hours till dawn, and we both need rest."

"What is kepweed?"

"The end result of a crazed botanist. He wanted to heal the planet by killing humans. He sowed it all over Auctairea before it killed him."

"That's what he gets," Ruger whispers. "I've been wondering why this is so different from the last time I was shot."

"If you try anything, I'll be the first to shoot you in the head."

Ruger chuckles. It sounds more like admiration than mockery. "You don't need to worry about that because I can't stay here."

"You're in no shape to go anywhere." She relights the lantern to find

Ruger standing. Her heart sinks in terror. She didn't even hear him move.

His face is tense, suspicious even. "Why would you want me to stay?"

There is nothing Kira wants more than for him to go, but if he leaves now and is caught, she doesn't want to think of what would happen to her and Nadia. "You can't even take five steps without falling. It's better if you leave at dawn."

Ruger's face drops, and it's the first time she's seen him afraid. "That would give the impression that I broke the laws of chastity." He looks back at her. "Thank you for the help, but I can't risk that."

Zyandite's laws of chastity vaguely ring a bell, but Kira is too frightened of him being seen to remember them now. The machines are out there, and the Commons are lurking around. If he's seen, she'll die. "They're all out looking for you. Just one night, please. No one will know you stayed here." She can't help but whisper, "No one can know."

All kindness fades from him, and what replaces it, scares Kira enough to curl inward. "Joplin's smarter than we gave him credit for..."

Confused, Kira's eyes widen. "What do you mean?"

"Regardless of what you are, I mean you no harm." Ruger holds a hand up, though trying to ease her fear. "I must go." He limps towards the door and has to catch himself on her bedpost.

"See, you're in no condition to go anywhere." Kira leaps out of bed to help him. "And I need you to stay, just until dawn." She gently takes his forearm to help him regain his balance. "Please."

Ruger looks at her hand resting on his arm, and his eyes soften, but only for a moment. "You're good. In fact, you almost had me..." Anger causes the many shades of green in his eyes to flicker like flames. "God-fearing, beautiful, strong, you're practically my dream woman. Add the poor single mother bit, and you've created the perfect formula to yank on any Zyandite's heartstrings..." Ruger's teeth bear for a moment. "Auctairean shame knows no bounds."

Insulted, Kira yanks her arm back. "Why would I care about your heart?"

"No one should have known I was here, but you were waiting for me. I'm supposed to believe that you'd give up the reward? No single mother in her right mind would do that. You're in for a higher payout, one from Joplin himself." Ruger glares at her one more time, before limping towards the stairs.

Kira doesn't bother defending herself. She should feel relieved that he's leaving, but instead, terror fills her core. "I don't want to seduce you if that's what you're accusing me of?"

Ruger takes the first step down the stairs. It's a struggle. All color drains from his face, but he continues down. "Joplin should have used someone else, someone unknown. You of all people should know who I am. To pretend otherwise, gave your act away." He smirks. "Give Joplin my regards."

"You're nothing but a pilot and a bad one too, considering how quickly you crashed!" Kira bites her lip. It's unwise to provoke a soldier.

Ruger's shoulders tense, but he doesn't look back at her.

Kira's chest rises with each breath. If he's seen and she's caught for helping him, what will happen to Nadia? Kira squeezes her eyes closed in a silent prayer to God before the words slip. "Just make sure no one knows you came from here." Her voice shakes. "Otherwise, you'll bring death to my child."

He turns and quickly limps up the steps.

Kira's instincts tell her to step back, but Ruger stops before invading her space. His eyes are perplexed, but his body language isn't intimidating, but rather, inquisitive.

"They'd kill a child?"

"Yes."

"Then why would you help me?"

Tears rise up and want to burst like a valve. Kira's body shakes to keep them from flowing. "God told me to."

He looks down. His eyes defeated. "I won't put a child at risk, even if her mother does." He walks past her to retake his seat.

His words stabbed her like a blade. "I rely on God, and I know his voice. When he told me to help you, I obeyed. Obedience is love, and even when…" She throws her hands up at the decaying walls that surround them. "It doesn't look good. I love him. I trust him." Kira hates that her lips quiver. "For whatever reason, God asked me to risk our lives to save yours. Otherwise…" Her voice gets stuck in her throat before a few tears escape her. "I would've turned you in for the reward."

Ruger's brows rise cynically. "So, what's the plan? Did that visitor come to coordinate for the machines to pick me up?"

Her jaw drops at his sarcasm. "No."

"How will you turn me in?"

"To the drones, but that's not why I helped you."

He eyes the floor. "They don't patrol here all the time, do they?"

Anger dissipates Kira's tears, and she places her hands on her hips. "How do you know about that, and not what happened during the Great—"

The sound of someone running outside fills the air.

# CHAPTER 6
## TIGHTROPE BETWEEN HOPE AND DESPAIR

"No," Kira whispers before rushing to the window.

Expecting the machines, she carefully draws back the curtain with her finger, just enough to not be seen by whoever's out there. She watches a man with long, unkempt hair run through the hay growing in her front yard, before turning down the curve of the street.

"Do you recognize him?" Ruger whispers directly behind her, which makes Kira jump.

"No, he looks like a Vag." She answers, wishing she could feel relief, but her heart still races. "Jeb told me the forest is crawling with machines. I thought it was one of them." She exhales deeply, relieved that wasn't the case.

"Vag...What's that an acronym for?"

"Auctairea's not that creative. It's short for a vagabond. Planet healers as they're known. They don't live in homes like us Dwellers do. Vags venture all around Auctairea, to share their sacred herb." Her lips twist in disgust at the thought of smoking it.

"Do you think he knows I'm here?" Ruger asks, and Kira suddenly feels his body heat radiating from his fever on her skin. He's far too close for comfort.

"I hope not. If anyone were to find you here, I'd be the first to die." Kira steps away from the window and sits on the edge of the bed.

Ruger watches her, his eyes calm before he practically falls on the couch. This time, she hears his every move. "Guess I'm trapped." He glances at the doorway.

"Oh, you're leaving," Kira whispers, "First thing in the morning. That's when the Commons sleep."

"The Commons?"

"That man who came by earlier was one of them. Lowlifes sent out to the country, to spare the city from their shenanigans." Kira frowns. "They get along well with the Vags."

"Where do you suppose the lawn runner came from?"

Kira shrugs. "Anywhere. He could be a member of a gang, or banished from the tent city outside of Quandii."

Not one, but *several* men outside start singing an off-tune song.

Her shoulders drop at knowing there's more than one potential threat outside. "They..." Kira whispers, hardheartedly correcting herself.

Ruger's stares at the window, his eyes calculating...

Nadia runs into the room. "I'm scared, mommy!"

Ruger watches her cling to Kira, and his eyes pity Nadia.

Kira wraps her arms around her daughter. The fire across the street creates a soft glow above the drapes. "I won't let them hurt you."

All suspicion fades from Ruger's eyes. "The gun your mother's holding is an import all the way from Tunaunda. It's renowned for being one of the most astounding weapons ever made. They..." He points at the window. "Are the ones who should be afraid." Weak in fever, he lets his arm drop to his side.

Even in this poor lighting, Ruger can see Nadia smile, before his eyes meet Kira's. She appreciates his words, even if they're lies.

The men outside only get louder. There's no reason to remain silent. Kira decides to sing her mother's favorite worship song. *"Though there is nothing to sustain my hunger, no worldly treasure to quench my heart's desire, I will rejoice in my God."* Nadia's muscles relax, and she joins in her mother's quiet song. *"Nothing could be all I have, since nothing compares to you, my God, so I will remain. I will remain in the Lord. I will remain strong in the Lord, though the earth may give way, yet I will remain. I will remain in the Lord."*

The sound of something crashing outside before more hysterical laughter causes Ruger to jump.

Kira and Nadia don't let it break their song.

*"I will remain strong in the Lord. He enables me to do the impossible. I will remain in the Lord. Though my enemies march towards me, the sound of war nearing to fill my mind with fear, I will sing praises to my God. Nothing could be all that's left since nothing compares to you, my God, so I will remain. I will remain in the Lord. I will remain joyful in the Lord, though the earth may give way, He will remain. I will remain in the Lord. I will remain strong in the Lord. Joyful in the Lord, He is my strength, and He enables me to do the impossible! He's already done the impossible! Lord, you've earned our praise. I will remain in the Lord. We will remain joyful in the Lord."*

Ruger can't help a tear that rolls down his cheek, at the act of worship in the midst of danger and fear. It's a beauty, unlike anything he's seen. Against his will, fever drags Ruger into sleep.

After Ruger's breathing changes, Kira lowers her voice in song to not wake him, and Nadia joins suit.

The men outside cuss and scream in fright, as howls enter the atmosphere.

"Thank you, God," Kira whispers, since nothing scares off people better than the wolves.

"Are we really safe with him here?" Nadia whispers, her eyes fixed on Ruger.

His face is ghostly white, while he lightly snores in a deep sleep.

"The kepweed is in his bloodstream, so he shouldn't be able to do much. But we'll sleep in your room, just in case." Keeping a firm grip on Ruger's gun, Kira carries her burgundy comforter down the hall.

# THE HUNTRESS

Nadia's mattress was made for toddlers, so Kira takes the floor.

Tucking Nadia in her blankets up to her chin, Kira kisses her nose. "I love you."

"I love you too, mommy."

Sleep. Kira dreads it. Most nights, her dreams are filled with terror...

\*\*\*

The Langton's house used to be beautiful. Beige siding with espresso trim and wrought iron pine trees framed the lead glass. The family inside wasn't blood-related, but regardless, they were a family Kira considered her own.

The night the convoy came down their pretty little cul-de-sac replays, with the thud of a mechanical hand knocking on the Langton's door...

Kira abruptly sits up.

Nadia remains asleep in her bed, but the sun peeks above her curtains, proving that it's late in the morning. They overslept.

Rubbing her head to nurse its ache, Kira gets up to check on Ruger. Finding him on the floor, she gasps.

Sweat covers every pale patch of skin that's exposed. His body violently shivers. His eyes are open in slits, but he's not conscious. His breathing is nothing more than a wheeze before he has a seizure. The knocking of his knee against her dresser is the exact sound that woke her.

The seizing stops, before Ruger's entire body stiffens under the power of kepweed.

Kira grimaces. She has what can help him, but she's already risked Nadia's life enough. If she gives Ruger the only antidote they have, she'll never be able to leave Nadia alone again. Glancing at her bathroom cupboard, she brings her eyes back to Ruger. Kira can't stand seeing someone inflicted with so much pain. She could just grab it, and end this. Closing her eyes, a tear rolls down her cheek. "God fix this. I can't give him the antidote, I just can't. Not him over Nadia."

The voice is low but unmistakable.

"Save him."

Goosebumps cover Kira's arms, while her chest floods with a warmth that can only come from the Holy Spirit. Her eyes open to see Ruger's body is still contracted in pain.

"Okay, God." Kira opens the bathroom cupboard, yanks out the antidote from where it was taped behind the pipe, and runs over to Ruger. She takes the cap off, and her heart drops. This antidote expired two months ago. Without debating if it'll work or not, she glances at the ceiling. "Please make this work," Kira prays before injecting it into his thigh.

He takes a deep breath, and his body contracts even tighter before his muscles relax. His eyes close, and if it weren't for his breathing, Kira would fear that the antidote killed him. "Ruger?"

His eyes open halfway. They're bloodshot, and only partly aware. "What did you inject me with?" He whispers before shivering.

"The antidote." She wraps his arm around her shoulder to help him on the couch and covers him with a blanket. "You're going to be okay now."

His hand grips her wrist, and while it doesn't hurt, his strength surprises her. "Why are you doing this for me?"

The worldly foolishness behind her actions causes Kira's eyes to tear. In all retrospect, what she is doing is murder for Nadia, and suicide for her. "Because I love God, enough to obey him, even when what he asks doesn't make sense."

Ruger let's go of her wrist. She can't tell if his eyes water because of the kepweed, or her words. "You will be rewarded."

"Yeah," Kira looks down and can't help her sarcasm. "Maybe in heaven?"

His chin tilts before a weak smile crosses his face.

It's so handsome, Kira can't help but to return it. "I'll get you some medicine."

She tosses the syringe in the fireplace, and digs some tree bark sealed in the last plastic bag inside of her cupboard. She smashes it with a wooden mortar and pestle, while the water boils over the fire. Kira carries it up to

Ruger and has to help him sit up to drink it.

Ruger takes a small sip and cringes. "What is this?"

"Willow bark tea. It's not the best tasting, but it should reduce your fever."

He can only take one more sip before collapsing in her arm. "I know..." He shivers. "Why God let this happen to me." He swallows and winces in pain before bringing his eyes to hers. "Last time I was shot, I barely noticed it." His eyes close for a moment, as though against his will. "I got cocky." He opens them. "God wants me to rely on him instead of my own..." His eyes close, but this time they stay shut, before he whispers, "Strength."

He is heavy in her arms, but Kira can't bear letting him go. Her heart is pulled for his condition, but more so for his humility. She's never heard a man talk like that before, let alone a soldier.

His breathing changes into the long, deep breaths of sleep. She gently lays his head on the pillow. While he sleeps, his face seems so innocent. Her cheeks flush.

Kira abruptly stands. That antidote was meant for her daughter. She has no business feeling this way. She shouldn't feel any peace at all. Guilt won't help her get through the day. What's done is done, now she has to get rid of her daughter's only weapon. She walks to Nadia's room, to find she's still asleep. Kira grabs the spray bottle and empties the kepweed infused water down her bathroom sink. The smell of kepweed is always rancid, making Kira's nose wrinkle. She can't chance anyone refilling it. Even rinsing it out could splatter the poison on her hands. Without the antidote, she'll have to toss the bottle down the waste hole, so no one can use it against them.

Setting the bottle on her counter, for now, Kira checks on Ruger to find his forehead is blazing hot. He doesn't seem to be in pain and isn't wheezing, showing some improvement. The antidote usually takes a few days to work. He'll either overcome this or die.

She can't handle thinking of what it would take to hide his body. That cold thought sends a boulder to her stomach. She feels connected to him, which is absurd. She should be calloused, but instead, her heart is warm. Shaking her head in frustration, Kira leaves Ruger to wake up Nadia.

"Good morning to you," Kira sings.

Nadia's eyes open and she sits up. "Is the stranger still here?"

"Yeah." Kira smiles to help calm Nadia's nerves. "His name is Ruger." She caresses Nadia's hair. "He seems to be a devout Christian."

"That's good."

"It's promising, but..." Kira tilts her head. "We still shouldn't trust him, just yet."

"Okay."

"Right now, he's sleeping and very weak. The kepweed took a toll on him. I had to give him the antidote. I'm sorry, but your spray bottle is too dangerous to keep without it."

Nadia gasps before hugging Kira tight. "You won't have to leave me anymore!"

It takes a moment for Kira to hug her back since Nadia's joy causes guilt to rip at her heart. She can't bring herself to tell her there's no other way they can get food. No. Kira hugs her back and allows Nadia the time to enjoy this happiness, no matter how temporary it might be.

\*\*\*

Nadia sits at the bottom step, smiling. She's been on cloud nine all morning.

Kira has to milk Feisty and gather the eggs. She looks back to make sure Nadia is out of sight from the yard, before stepping outside.

It's nerve-wracking to leave her daughter alone with a stranger in the house, but Ruger is still too sick to do anything, not that she believes he would. Kira's always had a soft spot in her heart for Zyandites, but she's not gullible enough to trust him just because of that.

She rushes through the mist. It's not as thick today, and some of the clouds break apart enough to see tiny patches of blue. Kira fumbles with the keys on her wrist, and smiles at the sound of Feisty's mooing. "Good morning," Kira greets, before milking her.

Basket in hand, Kira feeds the chickens, and gasps once she discovers their eggs. Instead of the usual two, there are three. "Thank you, God," Kira whispers. This additional provision couldn't have come at a better time. She figures it must be a reward for her obedience.

Kira locks both deadbolts on her shed door, before carrying the treasures into the house.

"Betsey laid an egg?" Nadia asks.

"Isn't that amazing?" Kira grins before getting a large, cast-iron pot ready. "I need you to boil some water."

"We only have one bucket left."

Kira bites her lip in frustration. She doesn't want to venture too far, and the stream is further away than the shed. "I know. I'll gather more water soon. First, I have to plant the vegetable seeds. There's some sunshine today, so there'll be lots of light for you to color at the table. I'll be on the other side of the window. Once I'm done planting, I'll make egg drop soup for dinner."

"Yummy." Nadia grins.

It takes her longer than planned, but finally, Kira plants the last seed. The soil is cold over her dry hands. Several tiny cuts on her hands stings when she brushes the dirt off. Looking up at the fading light beyond the patchy clouds, it's almost time for the patrol. Fear sinks into her stomach.

Kira steps inside their house. Nadia looks up from coloring at the dining room table and smiles at her. Kira hates having to make her daughter hide alone with a stranger, but if he's found, they'll die. "It's time."

Nadia closes her book and frowns. "Do I really have to hide with him?"

Fighting tears, Kira nods. "I'm sorry, but at least he's a Zyandite."

"You keep saying that, but why does it matter?"

"Cultures are defined by behavior, and Zyandite's culture is better than Auctairea's. That's not to say bad people don't exist there, but the likelihood of a Zyandite being bad is very low. They are taught that God holds us accountable for everything we do. They know he's always watching. Whereas Auctaireans, no longer believe God exists. To them, there is no accountability, which is very dangerous."

Nadia slouches before walking up to her hiding place.

Upstairs, Kira finds Ruger hasn't improved. She places a hand on his shoulder. Shivering in a fever dream, he doesn't respond. Running out of time, Kira grabs under his arms and drags him down the hall. Gritting her teeth, his body weight crushes her effort.

The mechanical voice of the drone sounds from the crossroad. Kira looks up at her covered window and gasps. "God, please, help me," she whispers, before struggling to drag Ruger across the carpet. Reaching the shadowed bathtub, Kira hears Nadia move out of the way. With one last pull, she gets Ruger in. Amazed the movement didn't wake him, Kira doesn't have time to catch her breath. She rushes through her house, opening every curtain.

She can hear the drone's presence approaching. With all but her bedroom windows exposed, Kira knows Nadia must be terrified. She stops outside the bathroom and whispers. "Nadia, if he does anything to you, scream. Just scream."

Nadia's voice is so soft, Kira barely hears her. "But they'll kill you."

"Maybe not. We'll say he forced us to take him in, or something."

"That would be a lie."

Kira cringes. "You're right. God never blesses a lie."

The drone is in her driveway.

She almost trips before reaching her bedroom windows. Flinging her curtains open, the sight of the Langton's house causes her to gasp. The front door rests on the ground, untouched by last night's fire. The first half of the house is nothing but charred wood, broken, and jagged. The interior of the home is exposed, revealing the staircase she's walked upon many times before. Like the rest of what's standing, it too is charred black. Kira feels a sob coming on, but can't cry, not now.

"Neighbors…"

Chills move down her spine. She can't stare at the damage for long. Straightening out her hair, she wipes her brow and walks downstairs.

The drone is at her kitchen window. Kira ignores it and casually walks over to her fireplace. There she stirs the soup, before slowly taking a bite.

"Watch out for your neighbors, by reporting violations now. An enemy to Auctairea is an enemy to us all. The war has reached Hanover…"

Kira's heart skips a beat at the change. She must hear the rest of the recording, but the drone is checking her upstairs windows. Slowly, she walks up the steps to listen.

"A Zyandite pilot crashed and is now on the run. Authorities are searching for him now. The reward for his capture is two hundred rations."

Kira stops. She has to grab the banister for balance, or else she'll fall.

Two hundred rations. Kira's first reaction is to lie. She can say she's being held hostage by the Zyandite. All she has to do is scream, and the drone will stop. Then she can report the pilot to it. Opening her mouth, her heart races and her voice readies to cry for help, until a sudden peace covers her. The warmth of God's Holy Spirit calms her heart.

The peace may calm her racing heart, but not her mind. Two hundred rations. Maybe that's why God sent this man here? She knows better. Ruger is a Christian. For that reason alone, she has to protect him. But for the first time in her life, Kira wants to ignore the peace of God…

# CHAPTER 7
## BUTTONS AND SCATTERED MEMORIES

"Neighbors…" The drone slowly flies away.

Biting her lip so hard, Kira can taste blood. She will not rely on the help of her state, God is too big to betray. Even so, a tear rolls down her cheek at the lost chance before her.

Once there is silence, Kira closes every window covering. "It's safe now."

Nadia rushes out to hug her. "He didn't wake up."

"Good." Now Kira dreads having to drag him back to her couch.

Kira manages to get him back into her room. Her shoulders hurt from the exertion, now that her adrenaline isn't kicked into gear.

With one last pull, Kira sets Ruger on top of the couch. Rolling her shoulders, she looks up to find Nadia hiding behind the door frame.

"Why is he so important?" She whispers.

"I don't know why there's such a huge reward for him." Kira wipes her brow, staring at Ruger, amazed he slept through all that.

"That's not what I meant." Nadia frowns. "Why is Ruger so important to God?"

Kira places her hands on her hips. "We're all important to God."

Nadia looks at Ruger, who sleeps as though nothing has happened. "Yeah, but why does God want you to save him?"

"I don't know." Kira brushes her hair out of her face. She's exhausted and so hungry she can hardly keep her knees from shaking. "Why don't we discuss this downstairs?"

Nadia's face brightens before she follows her mom down.

Kira serves two small bowls of egg-drop soup, and the last apple sliced on a plate. "I know this is hard for you." Kira says while watching Nadia eat from across the table. "It's hard for me too, but when God charges us to do something, we should obey."

Nadia chews and stares at her food. Her face scrunched in the deepness of thought. "So, God will bless us, right?"

Kira grimaces. "Not necessarily. If we only obey God because of a reward, then that's not really love. We should obey him, even if we don't benefit from our obedience. Who knows what plan God is weaving? The part we play by obeying him might really bless someone else. We could be the answer to their prayers. I know that eventually, in heaven, we'll get to see and feel the satisfaction of knowing we were a part of his masterpiece. This life doesn't last very long, but heaven is forever. We have to remember that, always."

Nadia wiggles in her seat. "I believe in heaven, mommy, but I would like God to bless us now."

Heart struck, Kira fights tears. "Me too, sweetheart, but we must have faith. God refines our souls the way we refine gold. Hardships are—"

"The fires that make us better." Nadia blushes for interrupting. "I know that, mommy, but you know what?" Nadia whispers and leans forward.

"What?" Kira follows suit and leans in close.

"Since God is so big, I've been asking him to save us from Auctairea. Do you think he may use Ruger to do that?"

Kira frowns. She doesn't want to mislead her daughter with false hope. "No, but keep praying. We should never put limitations on God."

Nadia smiles with a hope Kira won't allow herself to share.

The last light of day peers in above their curtains. "It's time to clean your room," Kira says, before wiping down the dishes.

Nadia runs upstairs, while Kira makes a small bowl of soup for Ruger. Crushing some willow bark with her mortar and pestle, she pours boiling water in a mug. Using a white serving plate to carry Ruger's dinner upstairs, when Kira first sees him, she fears he's dead. Hands shaking, she sets the tray on her dresser. Her heart thuds at the fear of having to hide his body. Carrying him across the hall was difficult enough. She can't imagine what it would be like to have to take him downstairs and across her property to the waste hole.

Leaning in closer, she can hear his breathing. She lets out a quiet sigh before feeling his brow. He's so hot, she pulls her hand away. After receiving the antidote, he shouldn't be in as bad of shape as this. Her hope that the antidote's expiration wouldn't matter begins to fade. "I brought you dinner." Kira whispers.

She's not surprised that he doesn't respond.

He hasn't had any fluids since this morning. With how much he's been sweating, Kira knows how dangerously close to dehydration he is. She kneels and spoons some willow bark tea on his lips.

He doesn't even move.

There's nothing more she can do, but give this to God. Placing her hand on his brow, Kira closes her eyes to pray. "Dear God, you've asked me to save this man. Help me to do that. Heal Ruger Anstone, in the name of Jesus, amen." With her hand still warm from his brow, Kira takes the mug of tea and sits on the couch beside him. Lifting Ruger up, she braces the back of his shoulders. "Please, drink." She carefully parts his lips with one hand, while holding the medicine with the other.

He grasps her hand with the mug, spilling some of the tea on his blanket. "I couldn't..." His breaths are jagged. "Save. Her."

"Shhh, drink."

His arm falls limp. He surrenders and takes a sip.

"More," Kira whispers.

Ruger manages to drink half of it, before his weight heavies on her lap. "She…" He shivers. "She's gone."

Kira knows he isn't coherent, but it's late, and she must tuck Nadia into bed. "I'm sorry," She whispers, before leaving him in his fever dreams, alone.

There's no longer light above Nadia's curtains, yet on her shadowed floor, a hundred circles varying in size and color greet Kira. Surprised to find Nadia's button family hasn't been put away, Kira places her hands on her hips. "You were supposed to clean this up while it was still daylight."

Nadia looks up from her play and gasps. "Sorry, mommy."

Kira frowns before setting the lantern on Nadia's dresser, while Nadia picks up her mess with her tiny hands. Kira resists the urge to help her. It would save time, but it wouldn't do Nadia's character any good. It's bad enough these are all she has to play with. Once Nadia was old enough to stop putting things in her mouth, Kira gave her all of the spare buttons from her clothes. She named each one as though they were her dolls. While Nadia carefully puts her buttons away, Kira examines the outfits that are hanging on the bar in her closet. Nadia only has six things to wear now, but once she outgrows those outfits, then what? Things were so much easier when Nadia was just a baby. Kira was able to carry her around everywhere, and she didn't require as much fabric for clothing. Since Kira never took up sewing, all she could do was stitch her own clothes into pieces small enough for Nadia. Having an extensive wardrobe helped, of course, but that's dwindling, and Nadia won't stop growing.

As Kira watches Nadia diligently put her buttons away, it's hard to believe she was once a tiny baby.

Nadia was seven pounds and six ounces when she was born. Kira will never forget that night…

George was visiting the tiny nation of Huqeletz, a GPU controlled country across the sea, for a diplomatic mission on behalf of Prime Minister Joplin. And Nadia decided to be born a week early.

It was in the middle of the night when the contractions became fifteen minutes apart. Kira had no other choice, but to call her friend Maggie Langton.

Maggie lived just across the street and showed up to Kira's door within minutes. Her blond hair was done up in a loose bun over her sun-kissed face and youthful blue eyes that were ready for action. Back then, vehicles were still legal for personal use, and Maggie owned a red truck.

Though Kira was in pain, the thirty-minute drive felt peaceful, until they reached Quandii's Center Hospital. There, peace became chaos.

After making it through the line of metal detectors, the waiting room was overflowing. Kira's contractions began to intensify, and there was nowhere to sit...

Maggie looks at the overwhelming sorrow and human neglect around them, before hugging Kira. "It's alright, you'll get through this."

A woman further in labor than Kira, stands against the wall across the room. Her dark hair is drenched in sweat, while her husband asks every nurse in passing, for help. Most roll their eyes, but every one of them walks away. Kira hasn't needed care since the government took over the hospitals and didn't realize it was *this* bad. "I don't think so," Kira whispers before another contraction makes her wince.

"Kira Westin?" A woman in yellow scrubs shouts over the crowd. Her red hair is cut short, over a face covered with sweat. Her blue eyes gush over Quandii's First Lady. She has to fight her way through the mass of patients, just to get to Kira.

"Please, help my wife!" An older man pleads, but she continues on towards Kira, without even looking at him. Ignoring him, the woman grins at Kira. "I'm Doctor Ryan, and you don't have to wait here. Come along this way."

A large crowd of desperate patients and their family members surround them, all begging Dr. Ryan to be seen.

Doctor Ryan whistles, and one of the two machines guarding the entrance to triage marches over to her, its mechanical feet scraping across the tile.

The yellow smile on the painted face was designed to make these machines look friendly, but is too jarring, and has had the opposite effect. The shape of the face is too narrow to be considered human. The animated smile below rows of rounded black cameras with red lights above them, make the machines appear sinister.

Immediately the crowd backs away in fear at the sight of it.

Now that a path is cleared for them, Doctor Ryan smiles at Kira before leading them through the double doors of triage.

"Oh, Kira Westin, please help me!" A young mother shouts, with her baby coughing in her arms.

"Out of the way." Doctor Ryan is not kind as she stares at the poor woman like she's less than human.

"But every store in Quandii is out of medicine. I just need something to break her fever." Tears roll down the woman's face.

"My contractions are still fifteen minutes apart, she can have my place." Kira offers.

"Thank you, Kira Westin, thank you!" The mother exclaims.

"Um, that's not necessary." Doctor Ryan fakes a smile. "We'll have that taken care of in a minute." She opens the doors to triage, but Kira doesn't move.

"She just needs medicine." Kira's eyes are insistent.

"Okay fine, get in here." Doctor Ryan allows the woman with a feverish child to run into triage first, before leading Kira and Maggie through the coveted doors. Everyone else in the waiting room watches with envy, but are too afraid to protest.

Now behind the line, the chaos isn't any better. All the hospital beds are filled. People are even lying on the floor.

"Get this baby a dose of acetaminophen for her fever, then get them out of here!" Doctor Ryan orders a frantic male nurse who fearfully obeys.

"Can't I have the whole bottle, in case her fever comes back? I'm willing to pay for it." The mother asks.

"You get what you get," Doctor Ryan says.

Kira stiffens, afraid this woman may be the one to deliver her baby. Another contraction takes over. "Oh, my gosh."

Doctor Ryan smiles. "Don't worry Miss Westin, you won't be receiving care here." She helps Kira to an elevator located on their left. "As soon as I saw your name come up in the queue, I called in our best OB. He'll be here in ten minutes."

Inside the elevator, the quiet reveals just how loud triage was. Four stories later, it's like they've entered into a different world.

The floor is clean, shiny even. A long counter with eight staff members awaits them. Rows of doors down the hall are opened to empty rooms, each with their own bed.

"This is where we treat our VIP's." Doctor Ryan whispers.

"I see," Kira says. She and Maggie exchange uncomfortable glances.

Dozens of people are on the ground downstairs, and these empty beds could help them. But they are not in the position to complain.

"Is that Governor Cantura's wife?" A nurse with blue hair asks. The hair dye washes out her complexion, and matching lipstick doesn't help. Behind her, a staff of nurses who could be treating patients downstairs sits around joking, waiting for someone like the Governor's wife to come in.

"Hello," Kira manages to say through another contraction.

"That baby's ready!" The nurse motions her hand towards an open room to the right. "I just love how you dress. It's so different and cute," she says. "I think it's so progressive how you kept your maiden name. Then again, Kira Cantura doesn't have the same ring to it, as Kira Westin." She laughs before showing Kira to her own room, where a large bed, a view of the city, and a private bathroom await her.

Kira can't help but feel guilty for this favoritism, when many are suffering just a few stories below her feet. Yet as the contractions increase, she has no choice but to accept this luxury.

Nadia was delivered by the best OB doctor in Auctairea and was the most beautiful sight Kira had ever seen.

While holding her most precious treasure, Kira hears a woman yelling down the hall.

A few moments later, a baby's screaming fills the air.

"Another delivery," Maggie grins.

"You share a birthday." Kira kisses Nadia's soft little forehead.

It's a wonderful moment, even with the mother yelling down the hall.

"Why won't it stop crying?" The brash woman demands.

"That's what babies do," A nurse replies. Kira can tell by her voice that it's the same one with blue hair and lips.

"Well, shut it up!"

Maggie gasps at the sound of a mother being so hateful towards her own child, while Kira protectively holds Nadia into her chest.

"I can't do that." The nurse says.

"Then, I change my mind here," The woman shouts before crying. "Now, I'm going to need six surgeries, just to get my body back."

Kira's eyes harden. The journalist in her wonders who this disgusting woman is before terror fills her heart.

"Is that your final choice?" The nurse asks.

"Yes! Get it out of here!" The woman screams in disgust.

Maggie holds her hand to her chest, before the baby's crying becomes louder. The nurse carrying the baby stops outside of Kira's open door and smiles. "Oh, look at your sleeping child Kira Westin. You lucked out and got a good one."

She closes the door, but Maggie stops it with her foot and follows the nurse down the hall. "My family breeds the finest racehorses in Auctairea. If that mother just refused her child, I will happily adopt it."

With the baby still screaming in her arms, the nurse turns, her face indifferent. "Our hospital appreciates the generosity of Auctairea's prosperous citizens, but once a mother deems her child unwanted, the tissue becomes property of the Government." The nurse forces a smile, but instead of it being kind, it's menacing. "And what the Government owns is non-negotiable."

Leaving Maggie speechless, the nurse carries that poor baby into another room, and a few seconds later, its cries stop.

Horrified, Maggie covers her mouth to hold in her scream. She notices the staff intensely watching her.

"Are you okay, horse breeder?" A male nurse asks. His disdain for the rural community is evident, while his hand hovers over the intercom.

If she causes a scene, he'll call in a machine to escort her out. Rendered powerless, Maggie says nothing, before running back into Kira's room.

"What happened?" Kira asks.

"They're actually doing it, they're killing babies. I didn't think the law would result in such evil." Maggie whispers. "What are we going to do? You know God's going to punish our land for this."

That moment, Kira decided to never let Nadia into the hands of anyone in Quandii. She made her vacation house, her permanent home. Rumors of torture and death in the Education Centers made that decision final, even when it became illegal. Looking back, Kira now has the wisdom to see that civil servants, who promote government control over the people's lives, only do so because they want the best for themselves. Nothing is too low for the likes of them to gain power and wealth, not even the murder of the innocent…

"How does my room look now, mommy?" Nadia asks, pulling Kira out of the memory. Her arm is held out to showcase the clean floor.

"It looks fantastic, you did a great job." Kira praises, before pulling the covers back to help Nadia get into bed.

"Do you really think Ruger will survive?"

Fear causes Kira's eyes to scan the room, as though a solution was in the walls. "That's in God's hands, but I hope he will." She picks up the doll she made out of an old pillow. Kira did her best to make it pretty. Looking at it now, she understands why Nadia prefers to play with the buttons. "Trust that God will cover us, no matter what happens."

# THE HUNTRESS

Nadia takes her doll and yawns.

Kira sings a song about Jesus, before tiptoeing out of the room.

Embarking on her nightly routine, Kira checks all the doors and windows, making sure they're locked before checking on Ruger. He's sweating, again. A sign the willow bark is doing its job. Kira reaches to check his temperature. He grabs her arm. The heat from his skin radiates onto hers. His grip is so firm it hurts, but it's his eyes that alarm her. They're practically on fire with incoherent rage…

# CHAPTER 8
## *THE GREAT CLEANSING*

The hold on her arm tightens. She wants to reach for the gun tucked in the back of her pants, but she's afraid to move.

Ruger's eyes are bloodshot, fierce, and full of destruction. Before he blinks, they soften and transform into remorse. His grip becomes a caress before he removes his hand from her skin and lets it drop at his side.

Yanking her hand back, Kira nurses her forearm. Heart thudding like a drum, she backs up, far enough to be out of his reach. She should've never brought a man into her home, let alone a trained killer. Fear distorts her breathing to where it hurts.

"I'm sorry, Miss Westin." Ruger winces in pain, before bracing himself on her couch to a stand. His leg is wobbly, and his face pale. His eyes are sincere enough, but she can't trust him. "For a moment, I thought I was in Kaddain. My mind is not where it should be." He frowns. "In Kaddain, they used their women to take advantage of our Zyandite honor and manipulate it against us. I thought you were one of them. Please, forgive me."

A lesson from fifth-grade replays in Kira's mind. It was so impactful that it gave her nightmares. The women of Kaddain are forced to fight with the men in battle. All of them are slaves, but the more barbaric they are, the more likely they'll move up into a better position. Attributes celebrated in other nations, like kindness, selflessness, and generosity, are seen as weaknesses in Kaddain, and even warrant death. The idea that any civilized human could survive fighting the Kaddains is unthinkable. She couldn't imagine being anywhere near one, but that doesn't matter. The pain throbbing in her arm proves that.

"I can't risk that happening again. I must go. Thank you for everything." Slowly, he limps towards the stairs.

If she lets Ruger go, she risks being caught for harboring him. Kira convinces herself that's better than having a threat inside of her home.

It takes far too long for him to make it to the first floor. Shaking, Kira listens for the backdoor to open.

It doesn't.

Silently begging God to protect her, Kira keeps his gun drawn, and sneaks downstairs. Wondering how she could be stupid enough to think all Zyandites are safe, it seems that her professor was right after all. Zyandites only see women as the weaker sex, and possessions to control. She should've never brought him into her home.

The moon's rising allows some light in above the curtains, but it's not enough to see if the lock is turned. Reaching the bottom step, Kira's mouth is suddenly covered, and the gun yanked from her hand in one move. She can feel Ruger's body heat radiating against her back while her heart races out of control. Now, she's under his grasp, and there's nothing Kira can do.

"Shhh," Ruger whispers above her ear.

God has never misled her before, but maybe he didn't lead her to save this man after all? Perhaps she's lost her mind? Regretting not reporting Ruger to the drone, Kira wonders how she could fight a Zyandite soldier and actually win.

A red beam shines through the edge of her back door.

Kira's eyes widen. She should have heard a machine.

The laser light is heat-seeking, and moves across the living room, then towards the kitchen. It's a struggle for him, but Ruger manages to move them into the half bathroom. Slowly, he uses his foot to close the door without making a sound. "I don't have the strength to fight them," he whispers. "My vision's blurred. I can't trust my aim."

Scraping sounds from the driveway.

Heart still racing, Kira tries to control her breathing.

"It's okay," he whispers, yet he won't let her go.

A thud against the house echoes before the scraping moves on. Each stroke of metal against the asphalt is troubling enough to rattle her brain. Once it's out of earshot, Ruger finally releases her.

Taking in a deep breath, Kira peers out the doorway. It doesn't look like her entryways have been breached. She walks towards the window on her backdoor. Heart pounding, she reaches to pull back the curtain to check on her livestock. A warm hand stops her.

"Don't risk it."

Knowing he's right, Kira takes a step back.

"I'll wait for an hour and leave. That way, if I'm caught, no one should be able to tell that I came from here," Ruger whispers.

Kira's stomach churns. "No." Even though he's a Zyandite, she'd rather fight a human than a machine. "You'll leave at dawn."

"You're sure?"

Scraping sounds from the street. "I'm sure."

"Alright." After a moment of awkward silence, Ruger limps upstairs.

Making sure to keep her distance, Kira follows him to the light of her room. She stops at the doorway, terrified of sleeping in the same room with him. He may seem exhausted, but that look in his eyes when she woke him, still frightens her. She won't go near him.

"I'll be down the hall. You're not invited."

"Of course not." Ruger frowns. "I'm so sorry. It goes against everything I am, to have scared you like that."

"Scare me?" Kira's lips snarl. "You grabbed my arm!"

"I didn't mean to hurt you." His eyes are believable enough. "I would rather die than harm someone as innocent, and charitable as you."

"You mean naïve and stupid..." Kira didn't mean to say that out loud and bites her lip.

"What I did wasn't your fault."

Kira only shakes her head, wishing she would've left him in the meadow.

Outside, a distant bark dismantles their conversation. It's a dog, not a wolf.

It's been months since she's heard a dog's bark. Most either ran off into the wild or were eaten. The barking intensifies.

"Is that normal?" Ruger whispers, before shivering. The kepweed has made him as useless to save the poor animal as she is.

Kira tries to remember which neighbor still had a dog, and the Callahan's come to mind. They used to breed Dobermans, but the frantic dog outside sounds too small to be a Doberman.

Barking turns into a horrific screech.

A mechanical thud, followed by scraping, replaces the screech. Feeling her palms sweat, Kira closes her eyes for a moment. She hates being unable to help the dog and whoever owns it. Nadia has always come first, and couldn't be left to fend for herself, not even when Maggie needed help. "No." Kira finally brings herself to whisper. "It's not normal."

Jagged scraping followed by a crash outside, jolts Kira's very soul.

"At least it's far away now," Ruger whispers.

"It's looking for you," Kira says more spitefully than she should.

After a long pause, Ruger exhales. "I'm sorry to burden you."

He's either sincere or manipulative. Kira's guessing the latter.

There's another thud, this one, even further away, proving the machines surround Hanover. Kira's heart pounds hard enough to rock her bones. Exhausted, she sits on the floor, leaning her back against the doorframe.

"That can't be comfortable. I promise I won't hurt you."

With his handgun giving her some security, Kira glares at him.

The silence is deafening before human cries fill the air.

Like the dog, these cries are cut short. Kira's breathing intensifies. She's helpless to save them, just as she was helpless that night…

"Why would Joplin kill his own people?" Ruger whispers, before another mechanical shrill taints the night.

Kira's stomach sinks. "Joplin believes that people are bad for the planet, therefore, disposable."

"That belief is ridiculous. God's will specifically states: Now be fruitful and multiply, and repopulate the earth." Ruger says.

She has read the scripture he quoted, Genesis 9:7. Kira frowns. "Here, the government is god."

Ruger shivers.

The scraping shuffles. It's further away, but it sounds as though the machine is running. Frightful for whoever is being chased, Kira bites her lip. "This is just like the Great Cleansing."

"The what?" Ruger asks.

Kira glares at him. "You're from a neighboring country, how could you not know?"

"Zyandite hasn't had a missionary in Auctairea for over a decade. It became too hostile, without a large enough harvest to justify the risk." Ruger crosses his arms. "We stopped trading with Auctairea, once they decided to export tissue from the innocent." He hisses those last words with disdain. "With communications cut, how could Zyandites know what Auctairea's internal affairs are?"

Kira now believes him. "I'd rather not speak of it…" Leaning her head against the doorframe, the words still flood out of her. "The Great Cleaning of religion. We had no idea it was coming. When the convoy came down my street, I would've called my neighbors, but our tablets had just been confiscated. First, Prime Minister Joplin deemed civilian air travel was too dangerous for the environment. Auctaireans outside of the country were stranded. About six months later, our cars were taken. He said that, too, was to protect the planet. Yet the parts were used to make these machines, creating more pollution in the process. The irony is, most Auctaireans cheered. They wanted to be protected from our militant neighbors."

Knowing that was in regards to Zyandite, Ruger raises a brow, but Kira's too lost in memory to notice.

"Taking away our communication was the final nail in liberty's coffin. As a reporter, to not have the ability to find out why military action was needed on my street, felt like torture. Back then, I didn't know what torture was." She momentarily points at the window. "The patrol stopped at the Langton's house. The sound. That sound was the same, just like what's out there right now. I watched a mechanical fist pound on the Langton's front door. Without my tablet, I couldn't call to warn them. Meanwhile, Auctairean soldiers laughed from the tank. They spectated like it was entertainment, instead of an attack on their own people."

Scraping echoes again. It's off so far in the distance, Kira's shoulders relax.

"After the machine kicked the door down, it only took a few seconds before the head of the Langton family was dragged out into the street. I wanted to run outside with my rifle to help them, but Nadia was too young and helpless to leave alone." Kira stops her voice from rising with her heartbeats. "I just stood there and watched, helpless to do anything. One of the soldiers asked if he would renounce the existence of God." Kira covers her mouth to not let her sobs release a sound. "'Never,'" she whispers through a cry. "All Tim said was, 'never.' The soldiers laughed and mocked him for believing in a Creator. Then…" Kira's body shakes, but she maintains a whisper. "They killed him. The machine smashed his head in the street. I saw it happen. I screamed, but they didn't hear me. Nadia woke up crying. I took her and hid in my closet. My friend, Maggie, kept yelling for me to run." The tears flood, and she can't stop them. "She was like a sister to me, and I didn't even try to save her."

"Don't torment yourself with false guilt. You made the right decision. If you had tried to save your friends, both you and your daughter would have been slaughtered." Ruger whispers.

"No. I was a coward then, and I'm a coward now." She stands and wipes away a tear. "But I know I can't fight them. I can't even fight you."

"I will regret hurting your arm for the rest of my life. Please understand that I didn't realize where I was. I thought I was in Kaddain, and..." He looks away. "I would have never done that to you in a sober mind." He slowly brings his eyes back to hers. "You could never deserve that."

Kira smirks. "I thought Zyandite men were punished by death for striking a woman."

Ruger frowns. "I didn't strike you."

She looks at her arm. There aren't any red spots from his grip earlier, but the invisible wound remains. "It still hurts."

"That's why I meant to leave." His eyes darken, though lost in memory. "This fever has brought memories into focus that I've tried hard to forget. Not one Zyandite soldier was disciplined for defending himself against the kind of women in Kaddain." His lips curl in disgust at the memory.

"You sound genuine enough, but I still can't believe you were in Kaddain." Kira crosses her arms, her eyes speculative.

Ruger looks at her in shock. "We took it."

Kira's heart stops. She's always been terrified of the Kaddains. To think of them under Zyandite rule, should give her relief, but she still doubts him. "You defeated Kaddain?"

"Yes. And we'll destroy these monsters too. You have my word."

She enjoys the fantasy, if only for a moment. "We'll see." She keeps her distance, but steps up to the dresser across from her couch and leans against it. "I've heard the stories of what kepweed does, so I'm willing to forgive you for frightening me, this time."

Ruger smiles. "Thank you for your understanding and grace, Miss Westin."

Kira scowls at him. "However, if you do anything like that again, I'll kill you."

That same spark of admiration from before he knew her name, returns to Ruger's eyes. "It won't happen again, I promise."

The sound of the machines gets closer, giving Kira the shivers. She blows out the lantern, in hopes they'll think she's sleeping.

"I don't think either of us is going to get any sleep tonight." Ruger whispers.

"No." Kira whispers, her stomach tied in knots. Even after how badly Ruger scared her, she finds herself thankful he's here. It's a surreal predicament to be in.

The sound of metal feet scraping on the road makes Kira's hair stand on end. "You know, after the Langton's were slaughtered…" Kira whispers to the dark more than to Ruger. "The next morning, I promised God that even if that same fate was given to me, I would never forsake Him. I would never renounce my belief in Him. No matter what happens tonight, I won't break that promise."

"That's beautiful."

Kira frowns. "Nothing's beautiful here."

"Your heart is."

Her shoulders stiffen. Kira doesn't like the way her heart fluttered at his words. She can't let her guard down. "Yeah, says the man who nearly pulled my arm out of socket."

Kira marches down the hall. Thankful, she can't see his face. Kira knows she may be overreacting, especially if what he said about Kaddain is true. Closing herself into Nadia's room, Kira leans against the door. The scraping outside intensifies and surrounds her house. It's too loud for her to take. Feisty moos, making Kira nearly jump. Her first reaction is to run out and save her, but that would be suicide. Grinding her teeth, Kira covers her ears.

# CHAPTER 9
## *STRANGERS*

Darkness surrounds her. The machines are getting close. The sound of their dragged steps makes their presence known. Kira is alone outside, unarmed, and vulnerable. The scraping closes in, making her fall to her knees. Suddenly, a beam of light flashes before someone grabs her by the hand. It's warm, reliable, safe. She looks up to see Ruger. He smiles. It's confident and handsome enough to make her weak in the knees.

"Don't worry, *I'm* here." His voice is like a melody.

The machines stop…

Waking up in the shape of a pretzel, every one of Kira's muscles hurt. The irony of dreaming of a man she fears causes her head to hurt. Sunlight peeks above Nadia's curtain. Thankful to see her daughter's still sleeping, Kira walks out of the room.

Even from this far down the hallway, she can hear Ruger's breathing. She finds him feverish and almost curses out loud. He should be better, not worse! If only the antidote wasn't expired. Crossing her arms, Kira can't justify her dream, or the warmth she feels budding in her chest at the sight of him. Looking at her forearm, there's no sign of bruising. He obviously didn't grab her arm as hard as she had thought. Perhaps she should forget it happened? Disappointed in herself for even considering such a thing, she abruptly turns away. Downstairs, she carefully checks to make sure her home is still secure.

All is calm and far too quiet.

Pulling back the curtain, the back of her property appears undisturbed. Maybe Feisty survived?

"Mommy?"

Kira nearly jumps out of her skin before turning around.

Nadia stands halfway down the stairway and rubs the sleep out of her eyes. "Is everything okay?"

Motioning for Nadia to come downstairs, Kira runs to the bottom step to see if Nadia woke him. Judging by his breathing, Ruger remains asleep.

"Yeah." Kira wraps her arms around Nadia, and can't bring herself to let go. She doesn't want to worry Nadia with the details of last night. "I love you so much."

"I love you, too." Nadia wraps her little arms around Kira's waist.

Silently thanking God for this moment, Kira breathes in deep. "Are you hungry?"

"No. I'm thirsty."

Kira doesn't need to check the buckets to know they're empty. "Alright, stay here." She slides a chair by the dining room table. Pulling out Ruger's handgun, she keeps the barrel pointed to the floor. "This is very similar to mommy's rifle. If anyone tries to hurt you, shoot, and don't stop shooting." Kira taps her chest to remind Nadia of the best target.

"Stance, breathing, and squeeze the trigger, don't pull it." Nadia recites before she sits down and takes it. Kira smiles at how well Nadia handles the gun and makes sure to keep it pointed at the floor.

"That's my girl." With a glance upstairs, Kira grabs the handles of all four buckets and rushes outside. Marching to the stream, its babbling song should bring Kira comfort. Instead, it drowns out all other noise, making her nervous.

The hair on the back of Kira's neck rises. She knows she's being watched. Looking up, the many shades of copper in her eyes are met with two blackbirds. Perched on the barren tree branch above, they stalk her, with eyes lusting to feed.

The memory of watching them eat human flesh makes Kira shiver. Dropping to her knees, she dunks the first bucket into the creek. She must hurry, and fills two more with shaking hands. After filling the last, a crunching sound causes the birds to fly away.

Nadia screams.

Kira's heart races. Terrified it's Ruger, she turns towards her house.

The ravishing eyes of a stranger greet her.

Gasping, Kira nearly falls into the creek.

His balding hair rests at his shoulders while his smile reveals missing teeth. He's not a member of the Commons. The fact he's wearing a jacket proves he's not a Vag either.

Another man runs up from the side of her house and tries to break in the backdoor.

Kira has to protect Nadia. He draws her knife and tries to slash at the man in front of her. He blocks her with his forearm. She kicks his knee.

He barely flinches, before taking a swing at her.

Kira dodges it and brings her knife towards his neck.

In one swoop, he grabs her wrist and twists it down. The pain causes Kira to bend, but she doesn't drop her knife. Gritting her teeth, she uses her free hand to strike him in the eye.

He screams but doesn't let go of her wrist. His pupils are too large to be sober, causing Kira's heart to sink.

The second man stops trying to break into her house, and rushes up towards her.

A mixture of relief and fear covers Kira, before she tries to break free from the grip of the first man. She twists her arm back, but his hold is like a vice. His accomplice tries to grab her other arm. Kira flings it back. He swings at her. She ducks but is unable to block him, and he hits the side of her face. The pain isn't felt, but her ears ring. Trying to strike back, Kira's feet are kicked out from under her, and she falls next to the creek. Landing on her back, the pain travels across her whole body.

Her first attacker tries to pry her fingers off of her knife, but no matter how badly her fingers hurt, she won't let it go.

The other man hoots in excitement at her fall.

"God, please save us," is all Kira can manage to pray. Body shaking, she tries to get up.

"Christian? Ha! Is God helping you now?" The bald man is about to kick her, but a blur yanks him back.

The cream of the sweater she gave Ruger stands out in the gray landscape, but he moves too fast for her to focus.

Kira does not waste time. The shock of Ruger's attack allows her the chance to kick at the other man's knees, making him fall down. She doesn't hesitate to slam her knee onto this man's chest and is about to stab him in the neck, but he blocks her.

"Crack!"

The snap draws both of their attention.

Kira and her attacker look up to see Ruger toss the lifeless body of the balding man aside.

"Allow me," Ruger says, before strutting towards them. He moves faster than the injury on his leg should allow.

Kira releases her dominant position over her attacker and stands.

The once fearless man now fumbles his words at the sight of Ruger. He slowly stands, holding his hands up. "P-please. L-l-let me go," he stutters.

Still suffering from a fever, Ruger hesitates. "Scram." He nods towards the woods.

The man smiles and backs up. "Thank you." He pretends to retreat for a moment, before charging towards Ruger.

Ruger straightens his posture. The man tries to hit him. Ruger blocks it gracefully, before grabbing his neck and breaking it in one smooth motion. The snap makes Kira cringe.

Bending over, Ruger gasps for breath. The kepweed is still trying to overtake him.

Kira's surprised to notice that his handgun tucked in his pants, and wonders why he didn't use it.

Ruger straightens his posture. "Where should I dispose of them?"

"Behind the—"

Kira is interrupted as Nadia comes running out. "Mommy!"

"Get back inside!" Kira screams.

Nadia looks around in terror, before running back into the house.

"She's just worried about you," Ruger whispers.

Kira's shoulders drop. "I know, but she can't be seen." Noticing how hard her hands are shaking, she folds them behind her back. "I'm not supposed to have her."

Ruger's eyes widen.

She ignores his surprise and focuses on the dead strangers. "We can hide them over here." Kira points to the left, where the waste hole is. Her steps crunch the dried pine needles underfoot.

Ruger has to be in pain but endures it well. He tosses the man in. The hole is so deep, it takes a few seconds before they hear the crash.

Kira lets out a sigh of relief. "I'll get the next one."

"No," Ruger says. Even with his limp, he races her.

Kira watches him get the bald man, and this one is easier to drag since he's thinner. Ruger straightens his posture after tossing him in. "Why were you out here?"

"I um…" Kira takes a deep breath to calm her racing heart. "I had to get water."

He notices the pails by the creek, and his eyes soften. "You're not even safe on your own property. That's terrible." Ruger is about to grab all four buckets.

"Here, I'll carry them." Kira reaches out.

He scowls at her before taking them all in his hands.

Kira rushes to open the backdoor for him.

He stops to frown at her notion, before stepping inside.

Nadia frantically hugs her. "I'm so glad Ruger is here!"

"Me too." Kira whispers.

Ruger gives her a doubtful look, before setting the buckets on the counter.

"I have some disinfectant for our hands." Kira gets out her last bottle of vinegar, opens a high cupboard, and reaches for a cup, but her fingers are too hurt to grip it all the way. She accidentally drops it on the tile. Kira doesn't have many cups left and finds herself crying. "Oh, no."

"Relax, Kira, it's just a cup." Ruger kneels to clean up the mess.

Nadia rushes over, but Ruger holds a hand up to stop her. "Careful sweetheart, you don't want to step on this, or you might cut your feet."

"Oh!" Nadia stays put and reaches for her mom

Kira hugs her, while Nadia watches Ruger clean up the mess as though seeing a man do such a mundane task was foreign. She looks up at her mom. "I'm glad you're okay."

"Thank you." Kira kisses the top of her head.

Ruger holds up the broken stoneware. "Where should I put this?"

"The waste bin." Kira lets go of Nadia to lead Ruger to the bucket in the far corner of her dining room.

"I'll take this outside." He dumps the entire bucket into the waste hole, before scanning her property for any potential threats.

Nadia and Kira watch him through the window. "What if someone sees him?" Nadia asks.

"Maybe they'll leave us alone?" Not wanting Nadia to worry, Kira forces a smile. "Everything's alright now. Why don't you go upstairs and play."

"Okay, mommy." Nadia walks upstairs, just as Ruger returns with an empty bucket.

Kira appreciates how attentive he is to lock the backdoor.

Ruger's brow glistens with sweat, and his limp intensifies. "Do you think they were alone?"

"They aren't local, so your guess is as good as mine." Kira's adrenaline is still racing, making her hands shake as she reaches for the vinegar. Ruger takes it and pours it in the cup. "If they were local, I'd be frightened of more coming for social justice." Kira whispers.

"Social justice?"

Kira shrugs. "Revenge cloaked as justice... It's just another sick, Auctairean trend."

Ruger puts the vinegar away and holds the cup over the sink. "Ladies first."

Kira steps over and holds her hands out for Ruger to pour half of it on her hands. The vinegar stings, but it still feels good to cleanse the filth of the wicked man off of her skin.

"The water bowl on the counter should be full." Kira nods towards it.

Ruger grabs it and rinses off her hands.

The pain from drying her hands causes her to wince.

After Ruger cleans his hands, his eyes focus on hers. "In Zyandite, it's mandatory for every soldier to be trained in combat medicine. I can tell you're hurt."

Shame causes Kira to look away. "I should've been able to fight them off." Her face quivers for a moment. "I shouldn't have let them get that close, but I didn't hear them until it was too late."

With the light from the window behind her, is not too dull to highlight the peridot and specs of emerald in his eyes, stirring the same warmth she felt earlier. Kira blames the dream.

"It's not your fault that they attacked you." He reaches his hand out to hers. "May I?"

She cautiously gives her throbbing hand to him. "Guess I'm in bad shape if someone else comes looking for a fight."

"Don't worry," he smiles. "*I'm* here." His eyes become serious before they focus on her injury. His hold on her hand is the same from her dream, warm, solid, safe.

The dream replays in her mind, and Kira can't ignore the butterflies in her stomach.

"If anything I do hurts, or just makes you uncomfortable, please let me know." Ruger whispers.

The heat from his skin proves he still has a fever, as he holds her wrist up with one hand while using the other to press down on specific points along her skin. He's so careful, Kira finds herself trusting him. The man she feared last night has become her hero today. That alone should be terrifying, but her heart is drawn to it, like an insect to a Venus flytrap. She knows it's dangerous, but can't turn back now. His fingertips press down on the left edge of her palm, just below her finger, causing her to gasp in pain.

"Sorry," Ruger whispers before moving his search to her finger, where he gently bends it back a few times. "I don't feel any broken bones." He checks her other fingers, and his touch is so tender, she forgets about the pain. "They're sprained, but should heal quickly." He continues to put pressure on her skin, slowly moving his touch up her wrist. "You just need to rest it." They both know that's impossible. "Does your shoulder hurt?" He lets go of her wrist, and disappointment fills her.

"No."

"This might bruise." He caresses her cheek, where she was hit. "What a terrible time this has been for you. First, what I did to you last night, and now, this."

"Don't compare yourself to them!" Embarrassed, Kira lowers her tone. "I would've died if you weren't here. Nadia would have watched it happen, and once they were done with me, who knows what they would have done to her." Kira nearly loses herself in the compassion she sees in his eyes. "So thank you, really, for saving us both."

"It was my honor."

She tries to smile. "Don't hate me for this, but I'm glad you crashed into our lives."

His brow furrows. "I could never hate you."

Backing into the counter, her hand hits it, and pain shoots up her arm, increasing the vulnerability Kira already feels. She has to look away to try and contain her heart, but still, it bursts. "I have to be so careful. If I make the slightest mistake, they'll come. There's always someone who wants theirs. I messed up today, and it would have cost me everything if it wasn't for you." She brings her eyes to his. It's awkward, but she can't contain herself and wraps her arms around him. The warmth of not just his skin, but the rhythm of his heart causes her to close her eyes.

Ruger slowly wraps his arms around her. "You're a strong woman."

"No, I'm barely surviving. If it wasn't for God, I'd be nothing."

"That's true for all of us."

She breathes him in at those words, and her guard dissolves. Lost in the trance of this security, Kira's words slip, "I've never felt this safe in a man's arms before."

Ruger's closes his eyes and holds her a little tighter.

Kira's heart is enraptured by too many emotions to ward off. Her lips slowly move towards his.

Immediately, Ruger lifts his chin away. Kira's lips caress his jawline, making her frown.

She can feel his heart racing through her skin. "Guard your heart above all else, for it determines the course of your life." He whispers, quoting, Proverbs 4:23.

Kira feels slighted and pulls out of his embrace. "What do you mean?"

Ruger rests his hands to his sides. "Zyandite has stringent laws on affection to protect us."

"I only wanted to kiss you." Kira scoffs, her heart offended that he would think so lowly of her.

"A kiss means much more to us than it does to Auctaireans." Ruger takes in a deep breath before looking around. "I should go. This situation is too dangerous for us both."

"No, don't leave!" Kira didn't mean to shout and takes a deep breath to calm herself down. "You're not healed yet. I promise I won't try to kiss you again. Just please, stay."

"God led me here for a reason, and now we both know why. But that's not why I'm in Auctairea."

His words bring the dark clouds of reality to their situation. Kira stares at the floor. Her heart is overwhelmed with longing for Ruger, in a world where they're supposed to be enemies.

"At least I got to save you." He lifts her chin with his fingertips. "I would've come down sooner, but I was dreaming of a battle, and screaming filled the dream. It was a bright light flashing in my dream that pulled me out of it. It was then that I realized the screaming was real." He partly grins, but his eyes remain stoic. "At least we're even now."

"A life for a life." Kira whispers. "Thank you, and again, I'm sorry. I know your king would probably reprimand you himself, just for hugging an Auctairean."

His eyes widen before he looks to the floor. "It's not because you're an Auctairean. But you're right. Since the king is responsible for carrying out most disciplinary actions, I must be extremely careful." His eyes return to her with the longing she feels. "I've been very good at guarding my affections until today." He blushes. "A kiss is never *just* a kiss. It's a display of affection meant only for those who are committed to each other."

"I understand." Kira's heart is strengthened. His rejection wasn't personal. Regardless, she must let go of her attraction to him. "I was weak, and I'm sorry."

"From what I've seen of you, you're never weak." Ruger is sincere enough, but Kira figures he is just trying to reject her kindly. "But, I have to go."

"When you're well?" Kira eyes him hopefully.

He looks at his leg. Pressing his lips together, he finally brings his eyes back to hers. "I appreciate your hospitality."

"So, you'll stay?"

Ruger hesitates. "I need to show you something…"

# CHAPTER 10
## *CULTURAL CONFLICT*

Kira follows Ruger upstairs. His limp is worse with each step he takes. The fight obviously took a toll on him. Getting out his Bible, he caresses his thumb across the top of the back cover. It chimes and a thin, black tablet slides out. "I've been trying to message my men."

Her knees buckle. She knew there was more to that Bible. Otherwise, it would be far too odd for him to fly with it. Slowly she leans against her dresser. "You've been messaging them this whole time?"

"Only when I'm conscious." He smirks, it's the same smile from her dream, making her cheeks burn. "So far, nothing's gotten through, but once I do get in touch with them," He looks up and scrunches his brows together. "Zyandite has an open-door policy for Christians. I'd like for you and Nadia to move there. I promise you'll be safe."

Fear of discrimination makes Kira grimace. "What would be expected of us?"

"To love God, and follow our laws. Nothing you couldn't handle." He types on the screen and frowns once a red dot flashes. "I just have to get a hold of them first. You said your tablet was taken, but you wouldn't happen to have anything I could try to find an open channel with? A radio, perhaps?"

"No. All electronics were taken. I don't even have my laptop."

Ruger frowns and puts his tablet away. "In Zyandite, you'll get a new tablet, and won't have to live in fear of anyone taking it from you."

"That sounds wonderful." Kira lacks hope that it really is, but anywhere would be better than here.

"It'll be wonderful." The exertion combined with the kepweed has him worn, but still, Ruger's eyes are keen. "Once I return to my post, I'll have an extraction team take you and Nadia to Zyandite."

"We'll see." Kira won't accept his offer as anything more than a fantasy and decides to change the subject. "Are you hungry?"

His smile fades. "I'm actually quite thirsty."

Kira cringes with guilt since she forgot the reason why she got water in the first place. "Nadia's thirsty too. I'll get her a drink and make you some tea."

He takes her hand. "You're hurt. I'll get our drinks."

Kira watches him limp downstairs, and can't deny her heart is stirred…

\*\*\*

Nadia hasn't wanted to leave Kira's side since breakfast.

Trying to rest her wrist, Kira's spent most of the day in her old study. She doesn't like this room, and the layer of dust that covers the bookshelves proves it.

A long, rosewood desk where her computer used to be, rests with a layer of dust under the window. The rest of the walls are lined with bookshelves, most of which are empty. Kira bartered most of her books years ago. The ones she's kept are the ones that wouldn't get her into trouble. All Christian books had to be destroyed before the drones began patrolling. The few she has left are educational, and have served Nadia well.

Their afternoon of studying is over. The drone is coming.

Kira's stomach sinks. Ruger already milked Feisty for her. Between that and the fight this morning, he's lost all color in his face. He's been asleep ever since. With her hand hurt, she doesn't have the strength to move him again. Afraid of what he'll do when she tries to wake him, she stands in the doorway and frowns. "Ruger?" She whispers, before stepping back.

He doesn't flinch.

"Ruger Anstone?"

He leaps onto his feet, his eyes dark, almost terrifying before they focus on her. His muscles relax, and his eyes soften. "Is everything okay?"

"The drone is coming, and I don't have the strength to move you." She glances at her hand.

His eyes widen. "Move me?"

"Yeah, down the hall." Kira points her thumb back. "The second bath is the only room without a window. If I don't open all my curtains, the drone will search the house."

Ruger limps towards her. "I'm sorry I've brought so much scrutiny on you."

Kira shakes her head. "This is our daily routine. Nadia's already hiding." She carefully places a hand on his. "Please, be kind to her."

"Of course."

Kira leads the way to the bathroom. "In here."

Ruger looks at the carpet before stepping into the darkness. "I can't believe you carried me all this way."

"Dragged." Kira corrects before pushing the door open. "Nadia, are you okay?"

"Yeah," Nadia answers from her place on the tub.

Keeping his distance, Ruger sits on the rim of the tub. "Can we have a light?"

"No. And you must be quiet. If the drone discovers you, we'll all die." Kira leaves the door cracked, before running to open the curtains. By the time the drone flies up to her driveway, she sits at the table, sipping on some water. The static recording is the same as yesterday's, but this time, the reward doesn't tempt her.

Biting her lip once the drone is done evaluating her home, Kira closes her curtains, slowly.

Nervous for how Nadia's holding up, Kira wipes the sweat off her brow. "It's gone."

Ruger steps out of the room, his eyes genuine enough. His leg is still weak, so he leans against the doorframe.

Nadia skips out and gives her mom a hug. "Ruger wanted to leave the room when the drone was too far to hear, but I told him not to go until you closed all of the curtains."

Kira hugs Nadia back. "Good job." She brings her eyes to Ruger. "Thank you."

He stares at the floor, deep in thought. "That drone comes by every day?"

Nadia turns to him. "Yeah. You did good staying quiet." She gives him a thumbs-up.

He smiles at her. "Thank you." He turns to Kira, and his smile fades. "How do you live like this?"

Kira hasn't allowed herself to feel the reality of their situation and only shrugs.

Nadia glances back and forth between them. "So be strong and courageous, all you who put your hope in the LORD! That's Psalm thirty-one, verse twenty-four. We live by it."

"That's one of my favorite verses." Ruger whispers.

She smiles.

Kira doesn't like the bond she sees growing between her daughter and someone who will eventually leave them. "Let me help you back to my room. It's dinner time."

"Yay dinner." Nadia performs a little happy dance.

Ruger watches Nadia admiringly, before sitting down on the burgundy sofa. "You gave up two hundred rations to obey God?"

A forceful breath escapes Kira's lungs. "Yeah."

"I've never witnessed a faith that strong."

"You're a Zyandite. Your people eat, drink, and sleep faith."

"We Zyandites profess to have faith over fear, all while living safely behind our strong walls. Here you are, living out that faith in the most dangerous place for it. I've never seen a character so true in my entire life." He smiles wearily.

Kira has never been one to fall for flattery. Even so, his words make their way past her defenses. She has to distract herself from it, or else her heart will fall deeper into this trap. She knows only pain will be her reward. "I'll bring up your dinner."

Serving everyone a scramble of venison and egg, Kira enjoys watching Nadia eat, before she checks on Ruger. She's surprised to find an empty plate on her dresser. "You must be feeling better."

Ruger shrugs. "You're sharing your food with me. I had better eat every bite."

Kira appreciates that, but won't let it show. "It's a miracle that you have an appetite. The antidote I gave you, expired months ago."

His eyes don't show surprise. Instead, Ruger smiles. "Praise God."

Leaning against the dresser, she wishes she could quell this budding attraction to him, but it only intensifies. "You know, I've been out of the loop for a while and…" She blushes. "You said Zyandite took Kaddain. What happened?"

"It took us two years to defeat them." Ruger's fever causes his body to shiver. He grits his teeth for a moment, revealing the kepweed still has a hold on him. "We just came home last month, when your dictator decided to attack our borders."

Seeing the symptoms take their toll on Ruger, softens her heart. Instinctively, Kira feels his forehead for a fever. He's hot, but not enough to be delusional.

Ruger smiles. "It's true. God gave us victory over Kaddain."

"I don't believe it." Now she understands why Ruger has so many freshly healed wounds. Kira doesn't want to imagine how brutal a fight that must've been.

Nadia bounces up the stairs, her heart overjoyed with a full stomach.

Kira turns to see the sunlight has faded to a light purple above her blinds. "Hey, clean your room. It's almost bedtime." Kira watches Nadia curtsy before walking into her room. Kira's eyes return to Ruger to find him smiling. She won't let his admiration for Nadia distract her. "What started the fight?"

"The Kaddains attacked our ranchers. They used guerilla tactics." His eyes become distant. "What they did to the innocent…" He looks up and presses his lips together. "We had no choice but to destroy them."

Kira shakes her head in disbelief. She's feared the Kaddains all of her life, to hear that nightmare is destroyed, is still hard to believe.

Ruger crosses his arms. "What do you know about my society?"

"Growing God's kingdom is essential as self-defense to you, right?"

"Missionary work is our highest priority." Ruger straightens his posture. "What else do you know?"

"I know that Sampson Tidal is your king."

"Sampson Tidal was our king." Ruger politely corrects.

Kira frowns. She's always admired King Tidal. He was known to seek peace over war. "What happened to him?"

"He died almost two years ago, in battle." Ruger's eyes harden. "The election to replace him took months."

"Election?" Kira asks. She was taught that Zyandite is not democratic, and the king is chosen by a horde of bloodthirsty generals.

"Yes, election." Ruger grins at her indifference. "We have a three-tiered electoral process, led by the Church, the Generals, and the People. In order for a general to be crowned king, he must excel above the top two contenders in the mock battles. Then, he must proceed to win the most votes. This last election, we almost lost the war with the Kaddains, due to Lineage issues." The disdain for the word Lineage hissed through his teeth.

Kira's brow rises. "What do you mean, lineage issues?"

"The refined bloodline of true courage and purity," Ruger recites with a tinge of mockery before changing his tone. "Most Zyandite generals are Lineage descendants, and they are reverential to their heritage. The more soldiers in their family tree that have fought for Zyandite, the more likely they are to be promoted. Having a king in your bloodline guarantees a soldier will at least make general." He frowns. "I fear that pride in their bloodlines has contaminated their hearts with idolatry. Then again, my father was a preacher, so perhaps, I can't relate."

"I always thought it was the strongest Zyandite soldier who was crowned king?"

"That's how it used to be. This last election was the most trying in Zyandite's history. It wasn't conducted because of a timely death or retirement. King Tidal took to battle with so much revenge that he forgot to carry sense with him. We lost an entire division and most of the Lineage."

"Your King went into battle?" Nadia asks from the hallway.

Kira jumps in surprise. "You shouldn't be eavesdropping."

Nadia's smile is too cute for Kira to be mad at for long. As though reading her mother's thoughts, Nadia tiptoes closer, and eventually hugs her waist. Kira rests her arm on Nadia, lovingly.

"Any leader that sees himself as more important than his people doesn't deserve the right to lead them, let alone send them into battle. A Zyandite king always attacks in front of his army." Ruger then looks from Nadia to Kira, because the notion is foreign to them. "A king, who expects his subjects to protect him, doesn't deserve the crown."

"Mommy said Prime Minister Joplin never goes anywhere without his security drones," Nadia whispers, obviously disappointed by her country's leader.

"He justifies it, just like most world leaders do." Kira lets out a sigh before noticing the light above her curtain rod has faded. "But, it's late." She looks at Nadia. "Is your room clean?"

Nadia grimaces before running across the hall.

"She's precious," Ruger whispers.

"She deserves a better life than this."

"Why must you hide her?"

Kira frowns. "Four years ago, the Education Centers became live-in facilities and mandatory for all minors. With Joplin's law against religion, I knew Nadia would be raised as an atheist. I couldn't allow that. Also," she keeps her voice low, so there's no chance Nadia will hear, "the rumors of what they do to kids…" She closes her eyes and shakes her head. "It's unspeakable." Glancing down the hall to make sure Nadia isn't coming, Kira leans forward to whisper. "It's been said that anytime a child gets out of line, they disappear." Straightening her stance, she shivers. "I couldn't risk Nadia being killed. The thought of her remains becoming a product," Kira whispers before wiping away a tear.

"I know what Auctairea's greatest export is," Ruger whispers through his teeth. "Nothing even remotely like that will ever happen in Zyandite." Ruger glances down the hall, where Nadia plays in her room instead of cleaning it. His eyes are fierce, protective even. "I promise I'll get you both out of here. In Zyandite, you'll be able to raise Nadia without fear."

Kira's heart skips a beat at the chance to be free. "Do you really think they'll accept us?"

He picks up his Bible from under the couch. "I told you, we have an open-door policy for Christians seeking asylum." He pulls out his tablet and types with Zyandish words characters she can't read. "Children are sacred in Zyandite. So is motherhood." He gives her a knowing look.

She can't deny that motherhood is despised in Auctairea. Kira briefly pulls her eyes away from the screen. "That was mine and George's biggest disagreement. He didn't want me to raise Nadia. No one did." She tightly presses her lips. She shouldn't be discussing this with him, not if she wants the warmth in her heart to cool. Kira refocuses on the screen. "I had to fight, just to be the mom God designed me to be."

Ruger's cheeks show color for the first time since this morning. "I wasn't exaggerating when I said you're the strongest woman I've met. In Zyandite, you'll fit right in."

Kira scowls. "I'm not that strong."

"You'd have to be strong to go against the grain of what society demands out of you," Ruger says.

Kira shakes her head. "They called me weak because, in my country, a woman could be and do anything she wants."

"Except to be a fulltime mom?" Ruger's sarcasm is not lost on her.

Her heart softens to Zyandite, before a history lesson dampers the charm. "Is it true that Zyandite women are forced to be confined in their homes?"

Ruger chuckles as though that is the most absurd thing he has ever heard. "No. As a matter of fact, the King's Surgeon is a woman."

"Really?"

"We train our women to fight and shoot just as well as any soldier, so if ever our homeland is attacked while we're deployed, they can defend Zyandite," Ruger says with a half-smile.

"Your women have military training, and you call me the strongest woman you've ever met?" Kira turns her chin to the side, her eyes doubtful.

"Absolutely. Training doesn't equal experience, Kira." Ruger eyes her cynically. "Tell me then, how have you survived all this time?"

"God's grace and reloading my ammo."

"Yes, and God's strength resting on you like a crown." His eyes smile, but Kira looks down.

She's never appreciated flattery, but his words managed to penetrate her heart.

Ruger focuses on the touchscreen, and his fingers type in a blur before he pushes send. A red circle with bold, white font fills the screen, causing him to frown.

"It's not connected?" Kira asks.

"It's connected, but it's always the same response. For some reason, my handle isn't registering on ZyanBell."

"ZyanBell?"

Ruger doesn't look up from typing. "It's how we communicate. I'm going to try something new." He opens up an older conversation in a different tab in an attempt to respond to a soldier directly. The same warning comes on screen. Anger fills his eyes. "It's like I don't exist." He looks up, but keeps whatever revelation he had, to himself.

"Your invitation was a nice thought, but it's obviously not meant to be." Kira watches Nadia sneak across the hall.

"I will take you to Zyandite, I promise."

"Zyandite?" Nadia asks.

Kira caresses her hair. "Yes, the land beneath, remember?"

Nadia looks up and nods.

"Is that what you call us?" Ruger winks to show he's not mad.

Her cheeks redden before Kira smiles. Ruger returns it, and for a moment, things feel lighthearted. In their situation, that feeling couldn't be more out of place.

Nadia's eyes sparkle as she points at Ruger's tablet. "What's that?"

Ruger holds it out for her to get a better look. "It's my tablet."

"You can look up anything you want with them." Kira whispers.

"You used to have one?" Nadia's mouth gapes wide open.

"Yeah, I did. Back when the light switches worked."

Nadia giggles.

Kira stares at the floor for a moment, missing all that's been lost. "Back then, I could look up anything I wanted to and learn all about it."

"Anything?" Nadia asks.

"Yes, anything. Knowledge was everywhere, and it was free."

"Wow, so like an elephant, you could read about them?" Nadia asks enthusiastically.

"Not just read about them, but see them on a little screen in your hand." Kira's smile is full of nostalgia.

"Whoa." Nadia grins while Ruger watches them, his green eyes solemn.

"Nadia, you've never seen an elephant before?" Ruger asks.

Nadia shakes her head shyly. "I can spell the word, but I don't know what they look like."

"Would you like to?"

Nadia looks at her mom, who gives permission by nodding her chin at Ruger.

After a few swipes of his fingers, he projects the image of an elephant on the wall.

Nadia gasps at the sight. "An elephant, wow!"

"Everyone in Zyandite has this ability," Ruger informs Kira more than her daughter.

"I want to go to Zyandite, mommy!" Nadia exclaims.

"Now, now, young lady, the only place you're going is to bed." Kira is resolved.

"Alright." Nadia mumbles. "Goodnight, Ruger, and thank you for showing me what an elephant looks like."

"Goodnight, Nadia." Ruger smiles, watching her walk down the hall with a sulk.

"She has never seen a picture of anything before tonight, let alone a projected image," Kira states coolly, causing Ruger's eyes to widen. "I keep all of my pictures hidden. I don't want to hurt her with what's been lost."

"She deserves to know."

"Nadia deserves much more than she's been given, but what she doesn't know won't hurt her, the way it hurts me." Kira's eyes harden with the reality of their situation, before walking down the hall.

Nadia jumps into bed. "Do you really think we'll go with Ruger to Zyandite? Because that would mean God answered my prayers!"

The excitement in Nadia's voice alarms Kira. She was afraid Nadia was getting attached to Ruger, now she knows it. If he lets them down, that might risk harming Nadia's faith in God. Kira can't have that. "I know God will cover us, no matter where we are."

Nadia yawns. "Well, I want to go to Zyandite."

"Right now, you need to go to sleep." Kira playfully pinches Nadia's nose. Closing Nadia's door softly, her face changes when she looks towards Ruger. She will not let him hurt Nadia with delusions.

Ruger sits on her velvet couch with his tablet in hand. "I think I've found a back way through." He greets without looking up. "It depends on if someone catches it. There's a different network, it's just for fun, but I may be able to get someone's attention through there."

Kira leans against the doorframe and crosses her arms. All friendliness towards him is gone. "If they see it, tell them to get you in the meadow at dawn."

Ruger adjusts in his seat and grimaces in pain. "I thought you wanted me to stay. What's changed your mind?"

"Look, I appreciate what you did for me earlier, but I can't risk hurting Nadia." Kira sits on the couch next to him. "She's already got her hopes up, so enough of this fantasy, please."

"It's not a fantasy. I can get you and Nadia, on a plane to Zyandite within hours." He holds up his tablet. "I just need to contact my men."

"Your men?" Kira stands. "You said you're the son of a preacher. If Zyandite loves its lineage so much, what authority could you possibly have?"

Ruger's cheeks flush before his lips press together.

Kira wishes she could trust him, but she knows that look. Years of reporting gave her a thorough education on body language. He's keeping something from her. "Last I heard, Zyandite pilots don't make it past lieutenant colonel, and you're far too young for that rank. Stop pretending you can fix our situation. That's in God's hands, not yours. And I will not allow you to lead my child along with your delusion. She's been through enough."

"You've been let down a lot. Haven't you?"

The last memory of George, his face snarling before he walked out, stabs Kira's spine with needles. She has to look away from him, just to keep her composure. "You ask too many questions." Kira decides his leg is the best distraction from the subject. "Let me see your wound."

Ruger glances at his leg. "It's looking much better."

"Don't let Zyandite modesty affect your health. Besides, I've already seen you in your underwear."

Ruger's entire face reddens.

Kira kneels to check under his pants. The bandages are orange, and beneath them, black veins move up his thigh. "The antidote should've made this better, not worse."

"It is better. The black lines were at my stomach this morning."

Kira briefly closes her eyes. "The kepweed almost reached your heart. If that had happened, you would've died." She forces a smile. "God saved you. Now, let me change your bandage."

"I can't take any more from you. Zyandite medics will handle the rest."

"Yeah, whenever that might be..."

Ruger's eyes flare with sarcasm. "Tomorrow morning."

Kira glares at him before stepping into the bathroom, where she digs out her medical supplies. Kneeling beside the couch, she pulls the old bandage off. Ruger grimaces in pain but holds it in and doesn't make a sound. The sight of his wound is five times worse than it was yesterday. The smell is most alarming. Kira fears his skin is rotting. A tingling sensation covers her head, and Kira can feel every inch of her scalp before the tingling moves to her stomach. She can't pass out, not now. Kira swallows the sensation down but can feel her color drain with it.

"That bad, huh?"

She can't look him in the eyes. The center of each wound is black, and the skin around is swollen and covered with black lines that expand out like spider webs. "I need some disinfectant." She rushes into the bathroom and grabs her last bottle of peroxide. There's not much left. She uses every drop, but it barely covers both holes.

Ruger begins sweating. Kira knows it's from the pain and wraps the clean bandage on quickly. "There." She smiles at him to find his eyes intently staring at her. They are not filled with lust like her old fans, or the men at the Commons, but something else... And it scares her even more. "Are you alright?"

"I'm amazed."

Confused, Kira tilts her chin.

"I'm amazed by you. Going through all of this, instead of turning me in for the reward."

Kira focuses on cleaning up the medical supplies. "It's the Christian thing to do. Besides, God is all I need." She puts everything away and looks at Ruger. Expecting the sparkle in his eyes to fade, it only gets stronger. He's getting attached, which is something she didn't expect.

"Where's Nadia's father?"

Such a blunt question makes Kira gasp. She hasn't wanted to revisit those memories and is caught off guard by them rushing to her mind now.

"I can't," she whispers. Her eyes lost in the pain of that night. "I won't talk about *him*."

# CHAPTER 11
## *SYMBOL OF COMMITMENT*

Kira couldn't say another word to Ruger and grabbed the bowl from his dinner as an excuse to leave the room. She cleans the bowl, and her anger numbing the pain in her hand. Putting it away, the bowl almost falls. Reminded of the cup earlier, Kira sets it on the shelf, wishing the gnawing on her heart would stop. After what George did, how could she allow her heart to be attracted to another man? Biting her lip, Kira can't believe she tried to kiss Ruger. How foolish could she be? Conducting her nightly routine in hopes to distract herself, Kira double-checks the locks and windows, before tending the fire. She can't stay downstairs forever and carries her lantern upstairs to face Ruger again. Entering her room, she finds Ruger is asleep. Her heart is warmed by the sight of him when she'd rather it be cold.

Relieved to not have to speak of George, she steps into the bathroom to change. Closing the door, the lantern's yellow light reflects off Ruger's handgun that's tucked into her pants. He said this weapon was from Tunaunda. Kira can't bring herself to believe that and sighs before changing into red pajamas.

Letting her ponytail down, the tightness releases her scalp. While brushing her hair, her eyes fall to the white light off her chest. It's the only thing that can make her smile after reliving such torment. The platinum cross reflects the lantern's glow, making the flicker of the flame much like yellow ripples of water...

Warm in a white pool, she was eight years old and stood knee-deep wearing all white, the color of purity. The Missionary who baptized her was a Zyandite. His hair was golden, and his eyes, as bright and pure as the water. Her mother stood with the Missionary's family, his four children, and his beautiful wife. Her mother's eyes matched her own, though Kira's hair was a few shades lighter. Everyone else, their names, their ages, she can't remember. But the water...

She could never forget that.

It was a covenant, a commitment of the highest regard. It was the truest symbol of her love for Christ. When she was dunked, everyone said that she smiled. It was the best moment of her childhood. Once her hair was dried, and her clothes changed, her mother knelt down and gave her this cross. "This was crafted out of Tunaundan platinum, so you'll never have to take it off." She fastened it around her neck. It was much longer on her back then. "Just like the stones from the river Jordan were symbols for the twelve tribes of Israel, to remember the miracle and love of our Lord. This necklace is a symbol for you to remember your covenant with Christ, and of how much he loves you." With a kiss on her head so warm, Kira could almost feel it now, her mother hugged her. Closing her eyes, Kira doesn't bother wiping away her tears. Holding her chin up, Kira admires the cross, the symbol of Christ's love and victory.

She will never take it off, so long as she lives. "He is risen." Kira whispers, before wiping away her tears.

Returning to her room, Kira finds Ruger is deep in sleep. After setting his gun on her nightstand, she digs out her Bible. Kira has to make sure she isn't so comfortable around Ruger, just because it was a Zyandite who baptized her. "Please, God, please speak to me. I need your assurance that I'm doing your will." She opens her Bible right to the very chapter her mother spoke of when she gave her the necklace.

So Joshua called together the twelve men he had chosen—one from each of the tribes of Israel. He told them, "Go into the middle of the Jordan, in front of the Ark of the LORD your God. Each of you must pick up one stone and carry it out on your shoulder—twelve stones in all, one for each of the twelve tribes of Israel. We will use these stones to build a memorial. In the future your children will ask you, 'What do these stones mean?' Then you can tell them, 'They remind us that the Jordan River stopped flowing when the Ark of the LORD's Covenant went across.' These stones will stand as a memorial among the people of Israel forever.

Joshua 4:4-7

God's care for her heart and the confirmation of his love overwhelms her. Tears pour down Kira's face. "Thank you, God."

Just like God comforted her after George left, Kira can feel His love engulfing her now.

She blows out the lantern and slides under the covers. Kira takes in a deep breath, assured that God is with her.

\*\*\*

The dirt feels moist under her knees, almost like a cold cushion. Kira's hands tend to her garden.

Through the fog, a straggly man marches towards her. It's the Principal of the Commons, who once harassed her, every single day. His long hair hangs in an unkempt mess over a bare chest and tattered jeans. His brown eyes nearly paralyze her. They are hungry for her pain.

Caught off guard, Kira reaches for her rifle, but it's not there. Panic seizes her to fall back. She turns away from the wild eyes.

Ruger steps out of the house, and rushes in-between them. He is entirely well and fierce. He only glances at the Principal, and it's enough to send him running.

Turning to Kira, Ruger winks.

She dusts the soil off her hands. Unafraid of who's watching them out in the open, Kira wraps her arms around his shoulders. "Thank you for staying."

"How could I ever leave you?"

He kisses her. His lips are warm against hers before the beauty of their kiss fades to nothing.

Kira awakes to only the darkness of her room. Heart racing, she fumbles to light her lantern.

Ruger stirs in his sleep from the couch.

# THE HUNTRESS

Covered in sweat, Kira sneaks into her bathroom. Cupping a handful of water from the bucket on the floor, she splashes her face and neck. It's not enough to cool the heat radiating from her skin. Surprised she could feel this way again, Kira blushes. Waiting for her heart rate to return to normal, she pats her skin dry and walks back into her room.

"Bad dream?" Ruger asks.

Kira stops before the couch to look at him. She would never tell him the details, but can't help that a part of her wishes the dream were real. She knows the desire is primal, but nevertheless, it is there, and she can't make it go away. "I wish it had been a bad dream."

Hoping he didn't catch her innuendo, Kira crawls into bed. She doesn't know if Ruger is feverish or not, but his lack of response is probably for the better.

It takes him so long to respond that his voice surprises her. "Whatever is bothering you, don't lose sleep over it. I may be injured, but I'm here. I'll do everything I can to protect you and Nadia."

Kira squeezes her eyes shut and holds in a gasp. His words only make the desire that caused her dream to only grow stronger. If this keeps up, his leaving will be devastating. Her heart begs to say things that would convince him to stay, but that wouldn't be right. No matter how beautiful the dream was, she has to separate herself from this desire. He has a duty to his country that she shouldn't break. Even so, his words help her fall into the deepest sleep she's had in years…

\*\*\*

Across town, Cheryl Fletcher is up. It's the middle of the night, and the Commons know she would usually be sleeping. From one of the many windows of their high-rise apartment, Meredith stares at the candlelit porch. She walks upstairs to the top floor to tell the Principal of the change in routine.

Reaching the only door in this hallway, she should knock, but this is an emergency, so she barges right in. His room is ten times the size of hers, but she's never noticed it before now. Frowning, she sees the Principal is in the middle of a pushup and is covered in sweat. Surprised, he leaps to a stand. "What's up, man?" His tone is casual.

"Military life died, didn't it, Prince?" She may have called him by his endearing nickname, but Meredith's lips snarled. Her eyes catch the layers of posters on his wall. They're old magazine clippings of Kira Westin. In each picture, her hair is done up, and burgundy paints her lips above modest clothing. Just the thought of wearing an evening gown hasn't crossed Meredith's mind before. She knows she could never be afforded such luxury, but Kira's had several.

"I like to sweat because it draws me closer to Mother Earth's tears." The Principal whispers, before opening the safe by his bed. There's an envelope with only a little bit of sacred herb left. It's not enough to control her mind. He frowns and tosses the envelope back.

"Look at all of those dresses," Meredith whispers. Standing before the wall, she crosses her arms. She hasn't been this sober since moving to the Commons. Meredith realizes that the pictures of Kira's late husband have all been covered with images of the Principal. They're old photographs, taken from back when he was in the military and clean-shaven. "What do you see in the capitalist witch?" She turns to glare at him.

He grimaces. He's not used to the subjects questioning him and could curse the Prime Minister for not sending a drop-off. "Kira Westin is my muse." He faces Meredith and smiles. "So, what brings you here, man?"

Meredith rolls her eyes. "The Mayor's up."

"At this hour? What's up with that, huh?" He struts to his window and pulls back the ratted black curtain. Only the Principal is allowed to cover his window, which tonight, he wishes he wouldn't have.

"Jeb thinks she's getting a drop-off."

"Is that so?" His tone was too harsh. He mends it by laughing. "That means there's got to be something for us."

Meredith slams her hands against her hips. "She'd better share."

"I'll go check it out." He leads her to the hallway and pulls a key from his jeans to lock his bedroom door.

Meredith glares at him, before walking downstairs. Before the Principal steps outside, he watches her whisper something to another female. They both watch him, suspiciously. Their conduct proves that he's losing control.

Without the herb, he knows he'll never gain it back.

Stepping outside, he finds at least a dozen Commons along the fence, staring at lights shining from the Mayor's house.

"What's all this?" He asks with the same, slow tone he addressed Meredith with.

Jeb turns. His blond hair and the whites of his eyes are all the Principal can see in the darkness. "If she gets a drop-off, we're going to catch it. No late-night shenanigans are going to get past us."

"Let me talk to her, see if maybe she's hurt or something." The Principal hears the low buzz and could curse at its timing, right before the drone flies overhead.

"Yeah, real hurt," Jeb's tone is not only suspicious but sober.

The Principal fakes a laugh. "It's time for some investigation. Stay here, man."

\*\*\*

Across the dirt road, Cheryl taps her foot impatiently. The supply drone has a scheduled drop-off, and it's late.

Her personal drone patrols her property in the same zig-zag pattern as always, directly over the gate. Her eyes sporadically check beyond it, to watch the Commons. Only a few windows have light, but she can feel they're watching, just as she hoped. Otherwise, she wouldn't have lit this many lanterns. The Principal will be notified, which is what she needs.

"Think it's passed the Commons, yet?" Gilligan asks.

Cheryl hardly looks back at him. "I hope so."

The familiar sound fills the air, making Cheryl smile.

Once it's close enough to be seen, this drone is five times the size of her patrol drone, with sensors that match Auctairea's flag, and a large crate hanging underneath.

"Oh, man, I'm so hungry," Gilligan whispers.

The drone flies over the gate. Their drop-off is in the safe zone now. Cheryl grins. "I take care of my boy."

Gilligan returns her smile before his eyes catch something behind her that makes him frown.

Approaching her gate is the silhouette of a man. With long hair bouncing, and a shirtless chest reflecting the little light they have, Cheryl knows who it is.

Boldly approaching the drone, the Principal sticks his chest out with pride. "This is Sergeant Billy Yarn, Principal of the Commons. I'm here to see the Mayor."

Cheryl glances at the control panel on her wrist. She couldn't deny him entry, even if she wanted to. The smile fades from her lips as she watches the Principal gain access to her property.

The gate shuts behind him, while Sergeant Yarn struts up to her porch. "I see you've been keeping secrets." His voice is normal. The slow, laid back tone he uses with the Commons is gone. His tone is clear and stern.

"Oh, Billy," She steps off the porch to greet him, her eyes pleading in the low light of the lanterns. "Why don't you give up on them, and just go. You could be reassigned to city. You'd never have to think of those fools again. After all, Quandii is where you belong."

"I'm not going anywhere without *her*."

Cheryl laughs. "Still chasing that golden ticket?" She shakes her head. "Kira won't ever leave Hanover, not willingly that is."

His face curves into a scowl. "Kira will. She'll leave with me. She just needs more time."

"Well," Cheryl looks down. "Prime Minister Joplin wants her to work for him again. He's just not sure if she's ready yet. Losing George hit her pretty hard."

"I'd be a better Governor than him."

Cheryl's eyes sparkle. She didn't realize Billy thought he'd gain *that* level of favor after winning Kira's heart. Now she knows this isn't just a mere attraction, making her promise to Joplin all the more likely to unfold. She's about to open her mouth to give away Kira's secret, but her voice stops in her throat. Thinking of when Gilligan was a child, her hands shake. She looks down, her heart discouraged from her original plan. Trying to hide her shaking hands, Cheryl looks at the stacks of cases piled on the crate in her yard. "Help me unpack." She walks towards her drop-off. Whiskey, she needs whiskey.

Gilligan stays close. His eyes watch Billy, suspiciously.

Trying to not be frantic, Cheryl digs to find the whiskey. Instead of sending two cases, Joplin sent four, and there are eight bottles in each. Cheryl yanks out the first bottle she can get her hands on and chugs it down. She's been out for two days, and the heat quenches her throat. Gasping for air, she offers a bottle to Billy.

His lips curl into a snarl. "I prefer to be sober."

"Sobriety makes life boring." She takes another drink.

"It makes everyone the fool, except me." He smirks. "Speaking of that, you got any herb?"

"Gilligan, see if the Prime Minister sent Billy any potion." She laughs, but her heart doesn't feel it. Watching her son obey, makes her guilt morph into shame. How could she turn Kira in for wanting to raise her own child? Forcing another gulp of whiskey down, she reminds herself that when she raised her son, it was legal to do so.

"Here." Gilligan pulls out a small box and hands it over to Billy.

He opens it and frowns. "That's it?" His eyes fall on all the whiskey, and his brown eyes burn with jealousy.

Cheryl doesn't need to turn her head to see what he's glaring at. "In Quandii, the Vags are never late delivering supplies."

"I don't do this crud!" He glares at her. "But I can't get half of them under control, with just this." He momentarily points at the Commons.

"I know, and I can help you, but you've got to promise that you won't share my little secret with anyone, not even Prime Minster Joplin."

His eyes turn to slits. "I never promise anything."

Cheryl holds her hands up, and the glass bottle reflects the flames. "Then I can't help you."

He frowns and watches Gilligan sort out some food into a small box. "I don't need that. I've got my own stash of rations. If they see me coming with that, they'll rip me apart." He lets his arms fall. "I've had to double the herb, just to get them inline. This lack of food has been making them act up, more than normal. They're even questioning me." He shoves his thumb into his chest. "So when am I going to get a drop-off?"

Cheryl takes a swig and pretends to ignore him.

"Well?"

She looks at Gilligan's nervous face and rolls her eyes playfully, to ease his worry. "Well," Cheryl takes another drink before looking at the Principal. "The lowlifes of the Commons aren't worth a drop-off."

He takes a few steps back, before remembering the Commons are watching his every move. He doesn't know if they can see him smile or not, but he forces one. "Really?"

Cheryl glances at the fence line. She knows the smile is for the dozens of eyes watching, and returns it, widely. "Yeah. So, if you're smart, you'll either report to the Outpost or leave for Quandii. If you pledge your stripes to fight Zyandite, I'm sure you'll be taken care of."

"What are you going to do?"

"Wait for them to starve off." Cheryl shrugs. "What else am I supposed to do? The Prime Minister wants me here."

Looking down at the pathetic amount of herb in his hands, Billy's eyes fill with rage. "I can't abandon my post, but I can't manage the Commons with just this."

"That's your problem."

Even Gilligan is surprised by her calloused tone.

"What if I keep your secret?"

This is the breaking point Cheryl was waiting for. "You know I've always liked Kira?"

Billy's right eye twitches. "What's this got to do with her?"

Cheryl glances at her drone, before whispering, "She's raising her kid."

Behind her, Gilligan gasps.

Registering that Cheryl hadn't shared this information with her own son, Billy glances at him, before glaring at her. "Why would she do a thing like that?"

"Mothers are strange creatures, Sergeant." Cheryl's brows dance playfully. "Why do you think I couldn't turn her in?"

It's evident by Billy's scowl that he can't comprehend such empathy.

She takes a drink, but it doesn't quench the guilt. She has to take one more. "I can't convince her to send the kid away to an Education Center, but maybe you can?"

"How?"

"Tell the Commons they'll get a drop-off tomorrow night. Say it's the biggest one ever. After that, let Kira how much you adore her. Then, tell her that the Commons are out of your control. Stress to her that this is her last chance before they go wild. To protect her kid, she'll have no choice but to take her to an Education Center. You and Kira can go to Quandii and live out the rest of your lives in luxury." Cheryl smiles. "For bringing Kira Westin back to him, I'll bet Prime Minister Joplin will be so grateful, he'll grant you a commission." Her eyes widen to play into his fantasy. "Or, he may even make you a politician?"

Billy's eyes lighten, while his lips turn into a roguish smile. "You're one brilliant woman, Mayor Fletcher."

The compliment pooled with her whiskey makes her laugh before movement catches her eye. Cheryl watches behind the Principal, while several figures walk up from the Commons. One of them runs up and tries to jump her gate.

The charcoal drone shoots several tiny spears from its belly, causing sparks to brighten the night.

"Get back!" The Principal yells.

The other figures disperse back to the Commons.

"I can't believe they tried that while I'm here."

"That's starvation combined with sobriety. I'm just glad he died outside of the gate, so Gilligan doesn't have to deal with the mess." She chugs more whiskey. "As you can see, I'll be fine. Give it two more weeks, and they'll end up killing each other."

"Then what are you going to do?"

"Wait for my invitation to Quandii." Cheryl grins. "Now go, give them the hope they need. After that, go make your greatest fantasy, a reality."

Billy snickers, but his eyes are locked on course.

\*\*\*

After watching the drone shoot down Marten, he ran back to his room. Now, Jeb stands in front of a window on the fourth floor. Behind him is a room the size of most closets, with only a mattress on the floor and mildew on the walls. He watches Cheryl and Gilligan gather their supplies, and his stomach complains. Jealousy causes him to scowl, while his starvation churns into hate.

The Principal walks up the stairs casually and even starts whistling a tune. His long hair wild and bouncing off his pale skin, while his brown eyes dance at the plan Cheryl made. "Relax, everyone, this is no time to be upset, man." His tone is slow and nonchalant again. "Our supplies are coming, don't you know?"

Jeb rushes into the hallway. "Really, Prince? Because man, I'm starving."

"Yeah, it's good. It's all good." Billy chuckles. "Prime Minister Joplin is so proud of us, our next drop-off will be doubled the last one we got."

"When?" Jeb asks.

Billy shrugs. "Tomorrow night, man." He slaps Jeb on the shoulder.

While hysterical laughter fills the Commons, Billy looks out the window at Cheryl's house and frowns. There's only so much time, a lie can give. Getting Kira onboard is the hard part...

***

# CHAPTER 12
## *MEMORY LANE*

"Hey, beautiful!"

Kira opens her eyes to yelling. Only darkness and silence greet her, making her think it was another dream, except this one, a nightmare.

"Oh, Modest Beauty!" A man sings from the street. "I'm here for you, beautiful, Modest Beauty of mine." His tune is terrible enough to make anyone cringe.

Kira tosses the covers off and leaps out of bed. She's surprised to find Ruger's already at her window. "Friend of yours?"

She shakes her head while peering through the curtain. Recognizing the Principal, Kira shudders. "I knew he was going to do this."

"So you do know him?" There's enough sarcasm in Ruger's tone to make her smile.

The Principal paces the street, wearing nothing but the same tattered jeans he wore the last time he was here. That was a year ago. "He's the Principal, sort like a warden of the Commons." Kira's lips pucker. "He's had a thing for me, from long before everything changed. Occasionally, he drops by to harass me."

"That scrawny puke is a warden?" Ruger asks. His face rolled in perplexity.

It's been a long time since Kira's laughed. She tries to hold it in, but it feels too good.

Ruger's lips curve into a smile. Even with his loss of color and unshaven face, Ruger's still the most handsome man she's ever seen. Chest warm, she has to look away.

"I said, beautiful! Come out of there. Come to Quandii with me. This may be your last chance!"

She lights the lantern because she wants to be seen. Even though it's unloaded, she picks up her rifle. "He's been trying to convince me to go to Quandii with him for years. He must really like me because he hasn't tattled on me yet." She grimaces. "In Auctairea, anarchy reigns, but if anyone were to hurt a Principal, it would be worse than killing the Mayor. Believe it or not, they're military, just in disguise." She grabs the curtain. "Don't let him see you."

Ruger steps aside.

Yanking the curtain back, she pulls the window open. Kira sets her scope right on him. "Hey, death wish!"

The Principal throws his hands up. "Come on, Kira, why you always got to be like that? You know I can save you. The Commons, they're getting angry. There's only so long I can keep them from taking what belongs to me."

"I'll never belong to you."

"Aren't you tired of being all alone every night?"

The thought of the orgies they're rumored to have makes her nauseous, but Kira doesn't loosen her hold. Keeping the barrel of her rifle on him, she only wishes she had ammo. "No."

He grits his teeth and flaps his arms down, much like a child having a tantrum. "I'm leaving! The Commons, they'll come here. If you don't come with me, right now, they'll kill you!"

Kira knows the consequence for a soldier abandoning his post and doesn't believe him. "You have five seconds to leave, or I'll shoot. And this time, I won't miss."

Ruger peeps out of the window through a crack between curtains. He's fidgety. Kira knows it's hard for him to just watch this exchange. She appreciates him all the more for going against what must be his first instinct.

The Principal violently points at her. "You're supposed to belong to me!"

Kira stands. "I belong to no man." Letting out a breath as though her rifle were loaded, she counts down. "Five... Four..."

He runs off.

Sighing, Kira holds up her rifle, watching him go until it's too dark to see him.

"Think the Commons will come tonight?" Ruger asks.

Closing her window, she nearly collapses. "I don't believe any of that. If he were to leave his post for good, the drones would know and the machines would execute him for disobeying an order." Sitting on the floor with her rifle pointed at the ceiling, Kira looks at up Ruger. "Sorry, I'm a little flustered. I hate being called Modest Beauty. It was a term some of my fans once used to describe me, and it still creeps me out. The fetish guys had for me was..." Unable to find a word to describe it, she shivers. "Alarming, but it boosted the network's ratings, so they encouraged it. Believe it or not, at the time, it worked great for me. While everyone else on air degraded themselves, I was able to dress with discretion. An entire page was set up, just for discussing..." Her lips curve in horror. "Me. It was run by a Sergeant in the People's Army of Auctairea. Part of the qualifications to become a principal is to earn your stripes in the military. Sometimes, I wonder if that Sergeant is him."

Ruger slowly sits a few feet away from her. "Your stalker has had some training?"

Kira frowns. "I can't think of that, or I'll be terrified." She takes a deep breath. "Training or not, if he gets any bolder, I'm going to have to kill him." Her threat was confident enough, but without ammo, how will she fight him? "I just don't know how." She whispers while the reality of her situation closes in, like a dense fog over her heart.

Ruger tilts his head, and his eyes widen. "What do you mean?"

"Last time I shot at him, I was careful to aim just close enough to scare him. I didn't sleep for a month afterward. I thought every noise was a convoy coming to arrest me, for the attempted murder of their precious principal."

"If he comes back, I'll handle him. That way, you'll be off the hook."

She can't laugh, though his humor is appreciated. Her mind is too fixated on how vulnerable she is without ammo. She knows that she shouldn't tell Ruger, but her heart trusts him enough to show the empty chamber of her rifle. "I'm afraid you'll have to."

Ruger stares at it, before bringing his eyes to hers. "You pulled off quite the bluff."

The way he looks at her causes the desire to kiss him to return. Kira must distract herself. She stands up and carefully sets her rifle next to her bed, and then reaches a hand out to help Ruger up. He takes it but barely pulls on her while rising to his feet. For a long moment, he doesn't let go of her hand. This should feel awkward, wrong even, but Kira couldn't feel more comfortable.

Ruger seems surprised to still be holding her hand. "Forgive me." He pulls it away and bashfully looks at the floor.

She watches him retake his seat on her velvet couch. "No need to apologize." Kira sits on the edge of her mattress and hugs her knees into her chest. "In fact, I should apologize to you."

His brow furrows.

Guilt almost makes her lose courage. "I've been reloading my ammo for years, but I ran out of solid casings. I used my last round on that deer. I found the brass, but it was cracked. I took the risk to approach you because I thought you were dead, and I was hoping to find a weapon. Just like a vulture." She looks away. "I'm no better than the Commons."

"Don't ever compare yourself to them. You're a survivor. In Zyandite, reloading ammo is an art." His smile fades into an expression she welcomes. It makes her feel like she's valuable to him. "But you're quite proficient, Miss Westin…"

She grimaces. "So formal."

"As I should be."

Kira's eyes fling back to his. "I don't want you to be. I want…" Embarrassed, she stops her confession by pressing her lips together.

His brow rises suspiciously, while his lips curve into a smile. "You promised."

"I promised I wouldn't try to kiss you again." Her cheeks flush. "Flirting is another story."

His lips are tight, but his smile broadens. For a moment, Kira's assured he feels something more for her. "We have to be very careful."

"I don't want to sin if that's what you're worried about." Kira tosses a pillow at him.

He catches it. "I would never accuse you of wanting to, but a sin like that can take down even the best character. Look around, we're in the best place for it to fester." He holds his hands out to showcase her bedroom before throwing the pillow back.

She understands his concern but doesn't see it that way. They're under the same roof together, without any human authority to keep them inline, so she should worry, but she knows she couldn't sin against God like that. "Zyandite standards really are amazing," Kira whispers, wishing it was like that everywhere.

"Accountability, character, my reputation, those aren't the only reasons I'm worried." His brow creases, and his slips are stern. "If only those things were at risk, I wouldn't be concerned."

A little frightened for what he means by that, Kira expects an insult and frowns. "What else is at risk?"

His lips press so tightly together, she's afraid he won't tell her. "My heart." He looks away. "All my life, I've been reserved. Zyandite traditions include many dances, but I've always preferred dancing with my sister, over other girls. They made me uncomfortable. I felt like they expected something out of me that wasn't there." His shoulders shrug. "God put it on my heart to be a career soldier, and it was easy to walk away from the only girl I had an interest in. In fact, I knew it was better that way. She married a man who only did mandatory service, and is there for her, every night. I chose this life, and I love what I do. To have another dragged down by the weight of my career, wouldn't be fair. I admire beauty at face value, without allowing that attraction to penetrate my heart." He brings his eyes to hers, and there is nothing bashful on his face, but rather, resolved. "But the moment I saw you, my heart was struck. You were like a character from the fairytales I read as a child, beautiful, mysterious, strong, almost mythological. I was enraptured and kept telling myself the whirlwind of emotions I felt were induced by the fever. Now the fever's gone, and those feelings have only grown." He looks down for a moment. "My surgeon is a woman. I've had female nurses sew up my wounds, but to have you see me," His cheeks turn red. "Was difficult. I've never had a woman reel my heart in the way you do. Now, I know my accusations and fears couldn't be more wrong. I shouldn't allow these feelings to blossom, but the more I get to know you, the more I admire you."

Trying to ignore that his words warm her heart, Kira gives him a doubtful look, all while trying to breathe normally.

"I mean it. To live in a place where it would be easier to give up your faith and to love God the way you do…" He lifts his chin, which causes the lantern's glow to reflect off the green in his eyes. "You're diligent, strong, compassionate… No matter how much I fight it, I only want to know more about you. Kira, I'm captivated by you." He looks away. "And it's incredibly distracting from what I came here to do."

"That's the fever talking." Kira walks over to check his temperature with her wrist. He's warmer than her, but not feverish.

Ruger takes her hand. Her automatic response should be to pull away, but like a fool, she's lured in. The warmth in his eyes enchants the fantasy growing inside her heart. It's a dangerous fantasy, one that she can't let go of.

Caressing the inside of her wrist, Ruger stares at her, not with longing, but adoration. "I told you, my fever is gone. I'm of sober mind and mean what I say. You captivate me."

"You do realize you're talking to an Auctairean?" Giving that reminder stings her heart. Kira looks away.

Ruger smiles before his eyes focus on her hand. Continuing to caress it, his eyes are deep, almost pained in thought. "If only things were different…"

"If only…" The weight of being alone again isn't all that falls on Kira's shoulders. The invisible grief of missing a man she's grown attached to makes her shoulders drop. There are so many threats, just for one night, she wants to feel safe. She lies down beside Ruger. "Don't worry. I won't try to force any of my Auctairean ways on you." She smiles at him. He doesn't return her smile but doesn't try to stop her either. Placing a hand on his chest, she can feel that his heart's pounding. "I just want to hear your heart beating, all night." Resting her head on his chest, Kira closes her eyes. "I'll leave the light on to make you more comfortable." He laughs, and it's whimsical, especially through his skin. There's sweetness in the smell of his sweat. When his arms enwrap her, Kira feels security she's never known. "Thank you," she whispers.

"For what?"

"Making me feel safe." She nuzzles her nose against his chin and closes her eyes. "So many nights, I've had to fight the advances from men like the principal and my own fears." Kira breathes in deep, soaking him in. "Even when I had plenty of ammo, I didn't feel secure. Not like I do right now, right here, in your arms."

His arms squeeze her in, a little tighter. "I won't let anyone hurt you, or Nadia."

"I know. You're a better man than I could ever imagine."

Ruger rests his chin on her head, his brow furrowed. "Kira, what happened to George?"

Kira's eyes fling open. "I don't want to talk about him." She should pull herself away, but she's too comforted by his embrace to let go.

"I'm sorry you've been so hurt."

She closes her eyes and doesn't hesitate to drink the moment in and allows it to carry her into sleep.

Ruger caresses her back. Once her breathing changes, he prays in Zyandish. *"The great I Am, please, direct my steps. Help me know what to do regarding Kira. I don't want to let her go. If this displeases you, break the bond off my heart. You put our lives together. If this bond is your desire, bless it. No matter what happens, please, keep her safe."* He kisses the top of her head and carefully gets up. Kira stirs but doesn't wake up. Ruger covers her with a blanket before sitting on the floor. His Zyandite convictions are too strong to be reckless with his heart. It's wrong to hold a woman who may be married. Besides that, his heart is lured in too close to hers as it is. Careful to not make a sound, Ruger pulls out his Bible. He opens is, and his eyes fall to Mark 10:9: let no one split apart what God has joined together.

This particular verse is used in every Zyandite wedding ceremony and jolts Ruger's heart with conviction. While George may not be around, that does not matter; he and Kira may still be married. Ruger closes his Bible and decides to pray in silence, this time, on his knees. With his hands folded together on top of Kira's bed, Ruger closes his eyes.

*"The great I Am, please forgive me for desiring a married woman."* Ruger's heart stirs, making him open his eyes. He feels as though he may be off and glances at Kira. Eyes closed in sleep, it stings him to see the bruise forming on her cheek. The protectiveness he feels for her goes beyond anything he's ever felt. Maybe he's misinterpreting what God is trying to say. Ruger closes his eyes again to pray. *"Help me to not feel the way I do for Kira unless this is your doing."* Just the thought of him marrying an Auctairean seems impossible. *"If she's widowed, and this is your will to join us together, then I ask that you reveal that to us. If that is your will, I'll obey. In the mighty name of Jesus Christ, I pray, amen."*

A flood of warm peace covers Ruger's heart. Surprised by the strength of God's presence regarding this matter, Ruger lies on the stiff floor and falls asleep.

*\*\*\**

Dawn breaks over Auctairea, transforming the dark fog into a lighter shade of gray. Sergeant Billy Yarn marches down a dirt road, with tears streaming down his face. He's not walking towards the Commons, but to Outpost Four.

The road curves, until a single-story, brick building comes into view.

A drone, much like Cheryl's, patrols the gateway of the fence.

The shadows of the pine trees become smaller, as the morning casts its light. He introduces himself to the drone and is granted access. Wiping his tears, Billy turns the knob of the steel door. It's locked. "Sergeant Lopez!" He says before pounding his fist on the metal.

A man opens the door and squints at the faded morning light. He's wearing Auctairea's enlisted uniform, a brown top, and loose, matching pants, with a white undershirt tucked in. The Auctairean flag rests proudly on the right side of his chest, while his name and rank are sewn on the left.

Sergeant Lopez recognizes his old roommate from Partisan Training. "What are you doing here?"

"I can't maintain control of the Commons." Billy follows Sergeant Lopez into the room. To the right is a tiny kitchenette, with shelves full of rations, before a small dining room table with four chairs. To the left are a latrine, a sink, a shower, and a closet full of uniforms and boots. Against the back wall are two sets of bunk beds. Billy frowns to find two mattresses are empty, while only Specialist Compton sleeps. Like all government buildings, this outpost has electricity, and a single lightbulb hangs over the table.

"Where's Private Beyer and Specialist Cage?" Billy asks.

"They're in Quandii, on a pass." Sergeant Lopez sits down at the table and stretches his arms up to the ceiling before rolling his shoulders. "You sure do know how to give a rude awakening. What did the Commons do now?" He grins wildly, before opening a can of carbonated orange juice and taking a swig.

Billy sits down across from his friend. "They're being starved out, on purpose. Mayor Fletcher said they're not worth supplying anymore. So I'm relieving myself of duty."

The smile fades from Sergeant Lopez's face. "You can't do that. Machines kill AWOL soldiers on sight." He leans forward. "And they're everywhere right now, looking for that Zyandite pilot. I'm not going to cover down for you. If you go AWOL, you're on your own."

Defeat crushes Billy's shoulders. "Maybe I can request a different assignment?"

Sergeant Lopez shrugs. "There you go, that's a better idea, but I doubt they'll approve it."

"Oh, they'll approve it." Billy gets up to get his own juice and a couple packs of rations. "Especially when I tell them what Kira Westin has done…"

"Kira?" Sergeant Lopez frowns. "What did she do?"

Billy sits down and unwraps the processed bar. "She's been harboring her kid." He takes a bite and chews.

Crossing his arms, Sergeant Lopez leans back into his metal chair. "Wow, are you sure? She only gets enough rations for one, and I watch her patrol footage. There's no sign of a kid."

Eyeing his friend's body language, Billy can see Sergeant Lopez hasn't lost his fascination with Kira Westin. "That's what Mayor Fletcher told me."

"We need to look into that before we act." Sergeant Lopez smiles. "You know, you're the only one who tried to make my little thread about her realty. How'd that pan out?"

Eyes hard, rejection spoils his appetite. Billy could spit the food out of his mouth, but swallows, hard. "She's tried to kill me, twice."

Sergeant Lopez laughs. "She's rejected me too, but I knew better than to push too hard. The Prime Minister would put a stake through anyone's head who dared to have their way with the Modest Beauty." He sets his forearms on the table. They may be thin, but unlike the men at the Commons, they have some muscle. "If the Mayor's accusation is true, then we have to arrest Kira. Who knows, maybe we'll get the go-ahead to administer a little social justice?" His thick eyebrows dance.

Billy chugs down all of the juice, before slamming the can on the table. "That's what I'm talking about."

Sergeant Lopez smirks. "Alright, here's the plan. Instead of getting yourself in trouble, you're going to go back to the Commons, until tonight's patrol. That's when you'll request to make a report, but have the drone follow you here. I don't want the machines to take this one. We'll make negotiations with Outpost One, and explains our frustrations…" He squeezes the aluminum can until it crushes. "Who knows, they may reward our effort? I could certainly use the fun."

Billy stares at the table, his eyes harden. "I hate her."

Sergeant Lopez laughs. "You don't hate her, you just hate that your fantasy's been stomped on. I told you, she'd never come around."

"You're wrong. I do hate Kira." Billy's eyes burn with rage. "I want to watch her die."

Sergeant Lopez grimaces. "I doubt Outpost One will authorize that. This is the Kira Westin we're talking about." He smiles, but Billy doesn't return it. "Look, we might be able to teach her a lesson. Maybe even live out everything we wrote about doing to her."

The rage in Billy's eyes is replaced with lust. "You're right."

"Did I just hear Kira Westin's up for grabs?" Specialist Compton gets up out of bed. The artificial lighting reflects off his round, pale face.

Sergeant Lopez eyes Billy with caution. "That's the rumor."

"Finally!" Specialist Compton exclaims, making his companions laugh.

***

# CHAPTER 13
## *WISDOM*

Kira's eyes open to the dawn.

She sits up to find Ruger isn't there. She's a light sleeper and can't believe he got up without waking her. Flinging the blanket off, she rushes to check on Nadia. She's sleeping soundly in her room. Kira peers down the stairs before she hears footsteps in her bathroom.

Ruger steps out of the doorway, clean and freshly changed in George's black, long sleeve shirt and dark jeans. The shirt is so tight, if he flexed, the fabric would most likely rip. The jeans are about five inches too short, which does not strike her with George's memory like the turtleneck did.

"I hope you don't mind that I took the liberty?" Ruger asks. "The bucket of water was already there. I figured it was the perfect time to bathe." He limps to the couch with a pair of socks and a few drops of water falling from his hair.

"I don't mind."

"Good. How's your hand feeling?"

"It's better." Noticing his bare feet, she frowns. "I have some shoes you can wear." She walks into her closet to dig them out.

"My boots will suffice," Ruger replies.

"Oh no, I couldn't chance those being seen. I buried them in the waste hole." Kira gives him George's dance shoes and a pair of black dress socks. "Here, try these. They haven't been worn in over five years."

Ruger takes the shiny black loafers and puts them on. They are obviously one size too small. "Mind if I rip them up a bit?"

"Of course not."

Ruger breaks the back threading and peels the heel back a bit, giving his feet a little more room. "Thank you."

"Sure." She blushes. "And um… I'm sorry about last night. I was weak."

Ruger smirks. "We both were. I shouldn't have shared my heart with you, the way I did."

Kira crosses her arms defensively. "Are you taking it back?"

He stares at the floor. "I wish I could." His eyes meet with hers, and they are filled with sorrow. "Perhaps, after we leave and this war is over, we can get to know each other under normal circumstances, so long as you don't mind?"

Kira stares at the floor. Just the idea of normal circumstances feels impossible to her. "I would love to leave," she whispers, "but Nadia's terrified of the woods. She screams. It'll attract everyone, including the machines." Kira lets out a sign to release the horror of the few times she's tried. If only she had to fortitude to leave Hanover while Nadia was still a baby. "That's why I never take her hunting with me. I can't control her once she elevates to that level of a tantrum. In a way, I'm trapped."

"Why is she scared of the woods?"

Kira glances down the hall. Nadia's bedroom door is shut, but still, Kira can't risk the reminder and whispers, "Because of what happened to her father."

Following her cue, Ruger leans forward. "What happened to him?"

She looks back, unable to let Nadia hear a word of her father. "He's gone, and that's all you need to know."

Ruger tilts his head to the side, while his eyes soften. "I'm not looking to satisfy a desire for gossip, Kira. Obviously, my heart is invested in you."

"That's crazy, we just met." Kira manages not to cringe since the words stung her heart to say. Crazy or not, she feels the same for him.

Ruger's mind isn't changed. He raises a brow and tilts his chin. "I don't care if it's crazy. I care about your heart."

Gathering the courage to ask him what she fears he'll refuse. "If you mean that, if you really care about me, then stay."

Ruger slowly shakes his head. "I can't stay."

Kira crosses her arms. "Then, I can't tell you about George."

He smirks, his eyes proving her stubbornness caught him off guard. "Alright, Kira, I'll leave after nightfall, so no one will see that I came from here." His eyes are no longer smiling. "I'll be back with a transport to get you and Nadia out of here. You have my word on that."

Zyandites aren't known to lie, yet she can't believe he could orchestrate a rescue mission like that, especially for mere Auctaireans. Her lips tremble in sorrow for this being their goodbye, no matter how much he says otherwise. "We'll see."

Ruger's eyes dance at her, the same way she's come to love. "I need to show you something." He turns his head to the side and points at his ear.

Kira leans over to see a sticker that's the same shade as his skin, and no bigger than a fingernail, placed behind his ear. She covers her mouth in shock because she should have expected Zyandites to have a tracking device on their soldiers.

"My men already know where I am."

"Then why haven't they come?"

Ruger glances at the window. "It must not be safe for them, yet." His green eyes are bright, healthy even. "Zyandite never leaves a man behind." He points at his tracker. "This records my vitals, so they know I'm alive."

"That's intrusive."

Ruger grins. "It's only for those in uniform."

Kira's doubtful. After everything she's seen, it's hard to grasp there's anywhere in the world that's free. "Why don't you stay here until they find you?"

He frowns. "If I were still feverish, I could, but my fever broke yesterday and hasn't come back. The black lines are gone. There's a part of me that wants to go against my oath, but God convicts me every time I flirt with the thought. Since my men haven't found me, according to Zyandite regulation, it's my job to find them. Not only are the coordinates to your house logged on my vitals history, but I've memorized them. It'll be easy for the transport to get here."

Her doubt twists into remorse. She should have never opened her heart to this man. "If you say so." She bites her lip, trying to believe him, but she just can't. Letting her arms fall to her sides, Kira focuses on whatever distraction she can muster up. "I need to milk Feisty and gather the eggs. You've got a long journey ahead. Why don't you lie down a bit?"

"I've rested enough. How about I milk Feisty, so you rest that hand?"

"My hand is feeling better, and I'd hate for her to kick you."

Ruger grimaces. "She tried to yesterday, twice, in fact."

She lets out of a laugh. "Of course she did. It took over a year for her to warm up to me." Kira bites her lip. "I have two potatoes that you can peel."

Ruger humbly bows his head at her. "Alright."

Kira leads the way. Ruger may be feeling better, but his leg still can't hold his weight. His hands brace the banister with white knuckles, proving that he's in no shape to go anywhere. Kira's mind begins to conjure up ways to make him stay with her. She doesn't want to force him to go against his oath, but watching how poorly he walks, scares her. "Are you really well enough to go gallivanting around, looking for wherever your men are hiding?"

Ruger catches the sarcasm and presses his lips together.

She shrugs before pulling a chair out. "Here." She sets up a bowl for the skins and a plate for the potatoes. "I feed the skins to my chickens." Kira sets the peeler next to the plate.

"I didn't know they could eat that."

"So long as they're not green." Kira checks the russets and frowns. They're both mostly green. Frowning, she hands them over and steps outside.

After the attack by the stream, her sense of urgency is stronger than usual. Kira rushes to milk Feisty and is disheartened to find only two eggs. "Really, Betsey?"

Betsey ruffles her feathers and won't acknowledge her.

Inside, Nadia creeps downstairs, rubbing her eyes. She gasps in surprise upon seeing Ruger at the table.

He smiles at her. "Good morning."

Nadia looks around. "Where's my mom?"

"Milking the cow."

She peers out the backdoor, before taking a seat next to Ruger. "Are you feeling better?"

"Yes, thanks for asking." Ruger finishes peeling the first potato, before moving on to the second.

Nadia watches him work. "Mommy says I shouldn't talk to strangers, but you're not a stranger anymore."

Ruger stops peeling for a moment to look at her. "You're exceptionally wise for your age, but I hope you wouldn't be as kind as you are to me, to anyone besides your mom."

"Oh, no. I hate most of the people here. The men, especially." Nadia looks down before whispering. "You should hear how they talk to mommy, it's like they want to hurt her."

"That's because they do." Ruger's eyes lock with hers intently, before he resumes peeling the potato.

Nadia's eyes widen. "You never talk to her like that, though. You're nice."

Ruger twists his face into a disapproving grimace. "Some of the worst people in the world hide behind kind faces and even kinder words. The Bible says: So be as shrewd as snakes and harmless as doves."

"What verse is that?"

"Matthew ten, sixteen," Ruger says before he finishes peeling the last potato. "Nadia, you must be careful to never let a snake deceive you."

Nadia smiles at him, and her brown eyes sparkle. "I will tell mommy to read that later. It's a good one."

Ruger smiles but doesn't look up from the potatoes.

Kira steps inside and gasps at the sight of Nadia sitting so close to him. She doesn't understand why she felt so afraid of Ruger. Perhaps it's just instinctual jitters from being alone for so long? Kira sets the milk and eggs on the counter, locks the door, and turns to look at her daughter.

Nadia stands. "I thought it was okay to talk to him."

Kira lets out a slow sigh. "You're okay, Nadia. Having a man in the house is just something we're not used to."

Nadia blushes. "Yeah, it is kind of weird."

Ruger and Kira exchange an uncomfortable glance. After double-checking the lock, Kira returns her gaze to Nadia. "Why don't you go upstairs and play, so Ruger and I can talk."

After a moment of hesitation, Nadia obeys.

"She's a sweet girl," Ruger says while using the peeler to chop the skins into small bits for her chickens. "Zyandite will be blessed to have her."

Kira frowns. "If you break your promise, you won't just be hurting me." She crosses her arms. "I want nothing more than to believe you, I really do. But Nadia likes you too much. I can't let you hurt her."

"I won't." He begins to arrange the plate and potatoes. "If you're worried we won't win this war, let me ease your mind." He sets up four potato peels on the table. "Let's say this is Quandii..." Ruger places several pieces of potato peels to represent the four main highways into the city. "North," he points to the setup, "south, east, and west. Here's where my men are attacking." He grins. "The machines are about to fall. Once that happens, Auctairea will fall."

Kira looks at the table and frowns. "You think that's the Hive?" She points to where his finger rests. "That's just an old radio station."

Ruger's expression doesn't change. He's resolute in this lie. "Our Satellite Charge Commander hacked into Auctairea's communications himself. This is the Hive."

Kira sits back, her mind troubled. Whoever this Charge Commander is was either given wrong information or lied. She won't say that to Ruger, he is obviously too trusting of his own. "Joplin wouldn't trust his army to be controlled by anyone else but his brother." She bites her lip. She's already committed treason, might as well go all the way. "He lives here." She taps the northeast tip of the invisible square.

"The Hive is in a house?"

"He runs the machines like a video game." Kira points to the west end of Quandii. "It's heavily guarded, but the signal connects here." She points further down on his makeshift map. "Above the old Quandii tower, is where the antenna is hidden. If you blast this, then this," She points back to where Hugh Joplin lives. "You'll take down the machines."

Ruger's eyes fill with disappointment, before he pulls out his tablet from his pocket, and begins typing. "I have to save these coordinates."

She glances over his shoulder, not that she can read Zyandish. Above the message board is a small font written out in what looks like bullets. "Chad?" Kira asks, surprised that she can read it.

"Chadder, actually. He was one of our best infantrymen. After sustaining an injury in Kaddain, he's too hurt to fight in this war and came up with this network, to provide a place for soldiers to talk about current events, anonymously. His first name is Chad, so instead of chatter…" He winks.

"That's clever, but I thought you said your account was on ZyanBell?"

"I can only access Chadder." Ruger frowns. "My account on ZyanBell has been wiped. It's like a digital death." His mouth smirks, but his eyes are stern. "I have Chad's password and logged on to his account, but even so, I can't reach anyone." He shrugs.

Kira doesn't want to hurt Ruger, but to her, the betrayal is evident. "If your accounts are down, maybe someone on the inside is working with the enemy?"

Ruger eyes her face, doubtfully. "Spoken like a true reporter."

A thought stabs her heart with fear, deep enough to make her gasp. "What if Zyandite's lost the war?"

Ruger smirks. "That would never happen." He puts his tablet back into his pocket. "If the information you gave me is still accurate, Zyandite will forever be in your debt."

The sparkle in his green eyes is one she could look at forever. Kira's heart flutters. She has to look away. "You know what bothered me last night?"

Ruger leans back into his chair. "Other than a serenading, long-haired fool?"

Kira laughs. "Yeah, well, no. I'm talking about before that." She wiggles in her seat, fumbling for bravery. "I dreamed that you stayed." She watches his smile fade and almost loses her nerve. "In my dream, you scared off that serenading, long-haired fool, and kissed me." She looks down. "It was so real, so intense, that when I woke up, I had to cool myself down. That's why I needed to splash water on my face." She places her hand on his shoulder. "That dream only affected me so deeply because it was a reflection of what I want. Ruger, I want you to stay." She looks at his leg, knowing it'll be the death of him to try to reach his men on foot. "Please, stay."

He carefully takes her hand. "I want something better than that. I want to take you to my home. In Zyandite, there's safety, sunshine, and lots of guns."

Kira chuckles at that.

"I'm serious. You can have all the ammo you want." Ruger's eyes become stern, and his mouth straightens. "Another thing, no one will serenade you, unless of course, you want them to."

Kira doesn't appreciate the joke, but once his smile breaks free, it takes her barriers down with it. She laughs with him, but in her heart, their little fantasy just met reality. The moment he steps out of her door is the moment a target will be strapped on his back. Ruger can't outrun the machines, and she knows they'll find him. It's evident to her that only God can change

Ruger's mind. "Why don't we pray about it?"

Ruger raises a brow before he closes his eyes and bows his head. "The great I Am, thank you for Kira and Nadia. Thank you for leading Kira to me, and for her obedience to you. Please, bless Kira for saving my life. Help this information she gave me to be fruitful, and give us victory in this war. I ask that you guide me back to my duty swiftly. Keep Kira and Nadia safe while I'm gone, and protect Zyandite soldiers. Give us victory in this fight, and Kira and Nadia safe passage to Zyandite. We ask for your best solutions in all of this. In the name of Jesus Christ, we pray, amen."

Kira opens her eyes to find herself crying. She's never heard a man pray like that—so much heart, so much faith—it takes a moment for Kira to pull away her hand from his. "Let's see what he says." She walks upstairs slowly, to make it easier for Ruger to follow.

She pulls out his Bible. Ruger takes it, closes his eyes, and allows the warmth of the Holy Spirit to lead him. Kira watches him open it, and his index finger rests on a page before his eyes reopen.

"Who can find a virtuous and capable wife? She is more precious than rubies." Ruger reads Proverbs 31:10 aloud, before bringing his eyes to hers. Peace still covers his heart, but he fears this could be a warning, if Kira is indeed, married.

"It's probably a reminder of your wife at home. I'm sure you've got one." She playfully wiggles her nose at him.

Ruger's eyes bulge. "I can't believe you'd accuse me of that." He shakes his head before closing his Bible. "It would take a woman with a heart refined like steel to endure being my wife."

Kira wants to believe he is everything she sees in him, but her heart is reluctant. "You expect me to believe that someone as handsome as you are isn't married?"

"You think I wouldn't tell you that?" Ruger's eyebrows rise. "It would go against my Zyandite honor."

The flutters return in Kira's stomach, as the fantasy digs deeper into her heart. Could happiness be hers? Could this incredible man who fell into her life, be her future? Doubt sinks her hopes. "It's hard to believe you when you want to leave me."

"I have to leave you. Not because I'm married, or because I'm leading you on. Kira, I'm not Auctairean."

She glares at him for that.

Ruger frowns. "My country needs me. So much is at stake. I have to go." He sits down on the edge of her bed. "Why don't we at least try to take Nadia into the woods?"

Kira cringes and shakes her head. "I told you, she'll get us all killed."

"Then, our only option is for me to come back to get you."

She glances at his leg. His injury won't allow him to get very far. "Let's see where God leads on this."

Ruger's eyes dance as he watches her dig out her Bible. Doing her best to ignore him, she opens it to Psalm 10:14-18:

"But you see the trouble and grief they cause. You take note of it and punish them. The helpless put their trust in you. You defend the orphans." Kira feels a lump in her throat for Nadia, before she continues reading. "Break the arms of these wicked, evil people! Go after them until every last one is destroyed. The LORD is king forever and ever! The godless nations will vanish from the land. Lord, you know the hopes of the helpless. Surely you hear their cries and comfort them. You will bring justice to the orphans and the oppressed, so mere people can no longer terrify them." Kira takes a deep breath and looks at Ruger.

"He's going to protect you and Nadia." Smiling, his fingertips caress her neck, sending warmth down her spine, before lifting up the chain that's tucked under her shirt. "Don't hide your faith, live it."

Heat rises to her cheeks, while a mixture of fear and joy blur together within her heart. She sets the Bible on her nightstand, right where she used to keep it before it was illegal to have. "Alright, but..." The heat on her face intensifies. Kira has never shied from asking tough questions, and won't stop now. "In Zyandite, what's to come of us?" She can feel herself blushing to such a degree that she has to look away from him.

Ruger turns her chin to face him. "That all depends on what God wants. I'd like to make to make you forget all about this wretched place."

"So, I'll see you again?" Kira can't help but ask.

"Yes."

Ruger's assuring enough. Kira should appreciate that, but disappointment tugs on her heart. "Good," she says, even though her heart isn't playing along. Once he leaves, he'll either be ordered somewhere that he'll never get back to her or die. "But I'd still rather you'd stay." She stands, the task of making breakfast for Nadia pulling on her mind.

Ruger says nothing, but she can see the longing in his eyes.

\*\*\*

Cheryl sits on her porch, sipping whiskey. Her new wool duster hangs it's green, yellow, and orange plaid all the way to her ankles, above her white turtleneck and tan pants. It's been a year since she's had anything new to wear, and she's enjoying every minute of it.

Gilligan steps out of the house with a roasted turkey leg in hand. He grins.

"They sent us the best this time." Cheryl smiles. "They'd better do that from now on."

He chuckles in-between chews.

The clouds can't conceal that daylight is fading, and even the Commons are quiet. It's a peaceful evening.

The sound of her drone flying back and forth over the gate is like white noise. Soothing, secure. Until it drops.

Charcoal sensors hit the ground and shatter like glass. The noise echoes throughout the countryside.

Cheryl and Gilligan frown. Their eyes fall on the Commons.

They saw...

# CHAPTER 14
## *EERIE SILENCE*

It's nearly dusk, time for the patrol.

Nadia slips into her faithful hiding place.

Ruger limps across the hall. Kira grabs his hand and steps on her tippy toes to reach his ear. "Not a word about our plans. Don't get her hopes up."

"You're used to being lied to, but that's not me. When I make a promise, I keep it." Ruger's eyes are firm.

Kira takes in a jagged breath. She wants to believe him more than anything, but Nadia's heart would be shattered if he can't deliver. "I understand that, but please, don't mention it to her."

His eyes soften before his chin tilts down once. "I'll still leave tonight if that's what's necessary, but may we at least discuss her going into the woods?"

Kira would rather not, but there's no time to argue. "Maybe during dinner?"

"Thank you."

While Kira feels better in leaving them alone today, the dread for this horrid routine drags down her heart. Noticing that she left her Bible on her nightstand, Kira gasps. She places her Bible in its hiding place, before tucking her cross necklace under her shirt. After opening every curtain, she's too emotionally drained to pretend everything's alright. The cloudy sky is still bright by comparison to her drapes, but not even the few rays of sunlight can cheer her heart. Not when the Langton's house lies in decay before her. She can't stand seeing it and lies on her bed facing in the opposite direction. There's no way she'll fall asleep here, but she can't fake being relaxed without lying down. Her heart is going to lose Ruger, one way or the other. He speaks of a new life in Zyandite, but a promise like that seems impossible for anyone to keep. Her heart has fallen for him, and eventually, that will bring nothing but disappointment and pain. She rests her head on her hands. Kira doesn't care if anyone watching thinks she's weak. Right now, she feels weak, too weak to pretend…

\*\*\*

Across Auctairea, nothing but an eerie silence fills the streets. The drones should be conducting their patrols, but are nowhere to be found. A few straggly civilians step out of an old farmhouse on the other side of the forest. The road that curves around their property should have been patrolled an hour ago. Instead of rejoicing, they back up into their house in fear.

Just a few miles away, screams of excitement fill the Commons…

\*\*\*

The Principal walks up the dirt road to the Commons. Staying under the tree line, his head is held low. This day has gone from bad to worse. Specialist Compton went to the Education Center to see how many rations they'd get for Kira's child, only to find out they haven't received a drop-off in weeks. After getting that news, Sergeant Lopez became doubtful their plan will even work. If it doesn't, Billy can't return to the Commons as their Principal, not after lying to them about the drop-off.

They'll kill him.

Cheryl's house comes into view. She and Gilligan are on the porch, but they don't notice him. Something dark and reflective catches Billy's attention. Focusing on the pile of broken glass on the ground, he stops once he realizes it is Cheryl's drone.

He doesn't hesitate to turn around and run back to the Outpost.

\*\*\*

An hour, maybe two, has passed by while Kira rests in silence.

The drapes of her bedroom windows are open, and the street is dark. The drone has never been later before…

She can't make Nadia and Ruger wait forever, and closes all the curtains in her house. Kira lights her lantern and carries it down the hallway. Whispering from the bathroom causes her to stop.

"You've never had cake?" Ruger whispers.

"I've had potato cakes."

"We'll have to remedy that. Pumpkin cream cake is my favorite, especially during Christmas time."

The memories of Christmas sting Kira's heart. She remembers the lights, shopping with her mom, the cheer, but most of all, the music. Tragically, Nadia's never experienced it. "I don't think the drone is coming."

Ruger limps into the hallway with a grin. "That's a good sign."

Kira's heart sinks. "No, it's not. Without order, the Commons will…" She doesn't want to scare Nadia and silences herself. "Never mind."

"Mommy," Nadia takes Kira's hand. "Ruger was telling me about all kinds of good food."

"Really?" Kira asks.

"We had to talk about something. Waiting for the drone took forever." Ruger gives a knowing look.

Kira looks around nervously, worried that the drone is just late. She knows Nadia's extra hungry, thanks to their conversation. Dinner can't be put off.

She fries the potatoes with her last onion and mixes in some jerky. After this, milk, eggs, and meat are all they'll have until her garden is replenished. Kira forces that worry out of her mind. She and Ruger carry plates for everyone to eat upstairs, just in case the drone comes, and they need to hide quickly.

Kira sits Indian style on the foot of the bed, with Nadia beside her. Two lanterns blanket the room with more light than they're used to. Kira can tell Nadia enjoys Ruger's company, far too much. Even while eating on the awkward spot of her couch, he displays refined manners.

"Nadia, what's your favorite kind of food?" He asks.

It doesn't take Nadia long to finish chewing to answer him. "Roasted chicken. Mommy only makes that if a hen stops producing eggs. When she uses rosemary, the meat tastes so good!"

"Betsey's on her way," Kira whispers, causing Nadia to giggle.

Ruger smirks at Kira before pointing his fork at Nadia. "Do you suppose if we imagine rosemary chicken hard enough, we'll taste it?"

Nadia closes her eyes to imagine it before taking a bite. "I do taste it!"

Ruger takes another bite. "Almost." He smiles. "Wait a minute... It works."

Even Kira can't help but giggle with her daughter.

A low sound dances outside of her window, making Kira turn sharply, her heart racing in fear that it's a drone, but it's only a breeze.

"Relax, Kira." Ruger whispers. "Who do you think took out the drones?"

Kira now understands why he's been so cheerful.

"Who?" Nadia asks.

She can't allow her daughter to believe Ruger's men are on their way to get them. What if Ruger's wrong? "We don't know anything for sure yet, but when we do, we'll tell you." Kira takes a bite and frowns. This food is far too gamy to resemble rosemary chicken.

"I hope it was my men." Ruger stares at Nadia intensely. "And I need to get to them very soon. But I don't want to leave you. Nadia, would you like to go with your mommy and me to find them?"

"Yes!"

He gives Kira a knowing look.

She rolls her eyes at him before focusing on Nadia. "Even if that means we have to walk through the woods?"

All color fades from Nadia's face. "No, not the woods…" She looks at Ruger and frowns. "The wolves live there," she whispers.

Regret for pushing the issue is plain to see on his face. "And if any of them come after us, I'll shoot them," Ruger whispers back, in a failed attempt to calm her fears.

Nadia shakes her head. "No. I can't go near them." Her tone elevates. "Not after what they did to my dad."

Seeing the trauma is rising in her, Kira gives Nadia a hug. "No one's going to make you go into the woods."

A few tears roll down Nadia's face before she buries it into her mom's shoulder. "I wish I were brave."

"You're the bravest little girl I've met," Ruger whispers, before looking at Kira apologetically. "I'll go find my men, and we'll come back with a transport. That way, you'll never have to step foot in those woods. Sound good?"

Nadia turns from her mom to look at him. "You're leaving us?"

Kira caresses Nadia's back to comfort her. "He has to. He took an oath to serve his country, and they need him."

"We need him too." Nadia runs down the hall to her room and slams the door.

Kira rushes after her. "Sweetheart, I didn't mean for this to happen." She opens the door to find Nadia sitting on her mattress with her arms crossed.

"Why does he have to go?"

"If I leave, I can get the transportation to take you and your mom to Zyandite," Ruger says from the hallway.

Kira looks back at him and frowns. "We've gotten way too attached." She returns her attention to Nadia. "But Ruger never meant to stay here. This isn't his home."

"Do you really mean it? You'll come back for us?" Nadia looks past Kira, at Ruger, who respectfully stays in the hallway.

"Yes."

Her lips quiver. "Okay. You can go then."

Heart stung, Kira wraps her arms around Nadia. "See, you are brave, very brave." Closing her eyes, she hates that her actions have hurt Nadia this way.

Glancing at Ruger, his eyes are so remorseful. Kira can't find it in her heart to resent him.

\*\*\*

# CHAPTER 15
## *TAKE HEART*

Adamant about helping Kira clear the plates, Ruger limps downstairs.

Still worried that the drone is just late and will inspect her house any moment, Kira decides to have Nadia sleep in regular clothes. It's so much easier to run in pants than her old pajama gowns, which are too big for Nadia as it is.

Nadia doesn't complain. She's still shaken about Ruger leaving. "You said you trust Ruger, do you really?"

Kira should say no, but can't lead Nadia on with something that may disappoint her. "I want to."

"Well, I trust him." Nadia turns over and squeezes her makeshift doll tight.

Heart shocked, Kira doesn't know what to say. She kisses Nadia goodnight and walks downstairs to help Ruger.

"I didn't mean to hurt her," he whispers.

"She was going to know you left anyway. At least now she has the hope that you're coming back."

"I definitely will."

Kira wants to believe that, but her mind screams otherwise. Searching for a distraction, Kira looks at her last scented candle flickers on the high counter of her kitchen, giving a warm glow with its two wicks. The smell of pumpkin and clove fills her nostrils, reminding her of why it was so easy to put this candle away. Even after a decent dinner, the aroma makes her stomach growl. Kira leans against her useless refrigerator, to watch Ruger use a wet towel to clean the plates, before drying them. His sleeves are rolled up, and the candlelight reveals the definition of his forearms. Kira blushes.

Looking at the floor, memories of George haunt her. He would've never been caught dead doing house chores. Allowing her eyes to take in the strong warrior, diligently completing commonplace housework makes her smile. "Thank you," she whispers, before reaching to help him put the dishes away.

"You need to rest that hand." He gently sets the plates in their cupboard. "See, all done." Ruger leans against the counter and folds his arms. The light from the fireplace highlights the peridot of his eyes.

Kira's so used to do everything on her own, she feels a little sluggish. "You didn't have to do that."

"It's no big deal. Considering I owe you my life. It's the least I can do."

"You're not obligated to me." Kira holds her hand up to remind him that they're even.

His lips curve into a thin smile. "There you go again, proving you're a ruby."

Kira blushes when she'd rather not.

"What happened to him?"

Her brow furrows.

"Nadia's dad..." Ruger raises an eyebrow. "Did wolves really kill him?"

"I'd rather not talk about it." Kira looks up at the short wall to the stairway to make sure Nadia isn't hiding there, eavesdropping.

"You possessed a Bible and a cross necklace before we met..." His finger lightly caresses her necklace, causing Kira to look down. "Both of which are punishable by death. Now you are helping me. Why are you so afraid of telling me about him?"

"I'm afraid of Nadia knowing the truth about her father." Kira looks back up at him. "It's bad enough that people made sure to come to talk to me about it, years after it happened. I didn't want Nadia to know, but she eavesdrops and has heard the details."

"So, what happened? Was he out hunting when the wolves got him?"

Just the idea of George hunting makes Kira smirk. "No. He would've never done anything like that." She looks at the door, the memories of that night replaying now. A new thought stops them. If she explains her situation, maybe he'll change his mind and stay? "Come on. I'll tell you what happened." She takes his hand and leads the way to her blue sofa.

Ruger carefully sits beside her.

Kira can't bring herself to look at him and stares at the beige carpet instead. "George wasn't a Christian, but I thought by marrying him, I would inspire him to follow Christ. It wasn't until after Joplin flipped on his policies that I realized George worshiped the government. When Joplin began taxing us for the very air we breathe, I knew in my core that it was too far. I watched the poor become poorer, while George and the other politicians like him got richer. There was no convincing George that his profits were wrong. I bought this house out in the country, to escape from the corruption. After Nadia was born, there was no way that I could live in Quandii anymore, not after seeing what it had become. George was too busy in the city he governed, to find much time to spend with us anyway. For over half a year, I was able to relish myself in motherhood. I was happy. I had the most beautiful child anyone could ever dream of." Kira smiles at the memory of Nadia's plump cheeks and toothless smile. "When George did visit, he didn't seem to love her. He looked at her like an annoyance." Her smile fades. "It was a surreal place to be, to love a man whose indifference toward our child disgusted me enough to resent him. It was as though I was torn in two pieces, one of hope for our love, and one of disdain for everything he'd become. I preferred it when George didn't come to visit. I had no idea what the future would bring." Kira's eyes become distant in memory. "Nadia was eight months old when personal automobiles were confiscated to make the machines."

"Prime Minister Joplin had to make robots to wage war because his men are too weak-hearted to fight."

"That may be, but an army that does not feel when it kills is easier to use on its own people."

Ruger sneers at that. "Did George ever come back?"

"Yes. He arrived by horse and buggy. An accomplishment of Prime Minister Joplin that took society back a thousand years. I was still naïve enough to be excited to see him. George was smiling, which was unusual. He explained the latest law from Joplin. He even brought me a script, finding it somewhere in his head that I would betray my God." Kira brings her eyes to Ruger. "I couldn't do that. Joplin thought that if my voice announced the law, people would renounce their faith, and he'd be spared the fight. I never thought I'd live in a country that would take away the very religious freedoms which make us human. It was by God's grace that Nadia was sleeping during this conversation because I collapsed. My heart just broke, and I fell on the floor." Kira turns as a tear falls now, to wipe it away before continuing. "I begged George to see what he was doing. To turn away from it, but he kicked me." She hugs her midsection now. "I couldn't breathe, I couldn't focus on my surroundings, all I could do was pray he didn't kill me in his rage. I was too scared to move. Finally, he stopped physically hurting me but said he'd fallen in love with his assistant. A young girl who knows nothing of the world, and swore to make certain I was executed for treason, so he could marry her." Kira's eyes harden. "Once he saw that his taxi had gone, George was unwilling to wait for Edgar to come back with the buggy. He stormed off on foot. I had no idea what was to become of my daughter once they killed me, but I was terrified that she would be forced into an Education Center. Back then, the Education Centers had just become popular across Auctairea, but they weren't mandatory yet. I knew they were secular. Who would teach Nadia about God? So I fell on my knees under that doorway. The trim was brown, that was before I painted it white. I thought the change would be enough to make me feel comfortable using that door again, but it didn't. It has remained locked ever since because I can't bring myself to stand there again. It's like it has been cursed."

Ruger's eyes trail off on the brightly painted white door, but only for a moment before refocusing on Kira's face.

"I came to grips with the fact that God is bigger than George, God is bigger than Prime Minister Joplin, or any man who's ever lived. So, I stood, not on my own strength, but on faith. I closed the door and went upstairs to get my Bible. I carried it to the rocker next to Nadia's crib. When I opened it, guess where my eyes fell?" Her shoulders rise, showing how much that memory strengthens her heart, even now.

"Psalm thirty-one verse twenty-four," Ruger whispers. It was not a question, but Kira still recites the verse.

So be strong and courageous, all you who put your hope in the LORD! Psalm 31:24

Ruger smiles, but it does not touch his eyes. "Then what happened?"

"I prayed, I prayed harder than ever before. I asked God to stop this injustice and protect Nadia and me." Kira's eyes tear up again, but this time she smiles. "The next morning, knocking at my door, woke me. I thought it was soldiers, coming to take me to my end. So, I caressed Nadia's face and prayed God's protection over her, no matter what happened to me. I walked downstairs, ready for my fate. When I answered it, my friend Maggie was the first person I saw, and she immediately hugged me." The real shock of that moment bewilders Kira's face even now. "Behind her was everyone, and I mean, everyone from town. They were all sad for me, and for Nadia." Kira looks at Ruger with her eyes widen. "George was found that morning, dead."

Ruger's cheeks flush. "God justified you, similar to how he justified Abigale."

"Yes." Kira's eyes widen in amazement. "I was led to read that passage shortly after it happened. And I cried. Her husband, like mine, was godless." Kira's face creases. "What happened to George was brutal. I was told it took them hours to find all of his remains. The wolves tore him to pieces. I should feel horrified, but instead, I felt vindicated." She wipes away a tear.

"He was going to have you executed and your child orphaned. He deserved it." He places a hand on hers. "It's incredible how God avenges those he loves," Ruger whispers. "Much like Psalm fifty-four, verse one."

"I don't know that one."

"Come with great power, O God, and rescue me! Defend me with your might." Ruger recites Psalm 54:1 naturally, and it's pleasing for Kira to hear such freedom in sharing God's word that she holds in a sob because she has had to hide her faith for far too long.

"That's exactly what God did for me. Even after I helped put into power a man who turned against Him, God never turned against me. I don't deserve such love."

"Just because Prime Minister Joplin turned against God, doesn't make it your fault," Ruger exclaims, obviously baffled by her guilt.

Kira shakes her head. "You may be right." She stares at the doorway, reliving the betrayal that stabbed her heart. If she hadn't campaigned for Joplin, none of it would have happened. The Langton's would still be alive. Every Christian in Auctairea would still be alive.

"Kira," Ruger gently turns her chin for her to face him. "Since God avenged and protected you in such a remarkable way, we can trust he'll take care of you and Nadia now." His eyes are resolved, like a battle in his heart was just won, and Kira is memorized by them. "Just wait and see. God isn't just going to avenge you like he did Abigale, he's going to bless you the way he blessed Abigale, too."

Kira smiles, but it doesn't reach her eyes. "We'll see…"

Ruger's eyes dance before he places his hand on her cheek. "Physical affection is significant in Zyandite, and we do not take it lightly." He then smiles, "Whereas to the rest of the world, a kiss is just a kiss, and there's no commitment to it."

Kira would love nothing more than to be committed to this man but is terrified of being vulnerable enough to be hurt again. She looks down.

Ruger carefully lifts her chin. "Auctaireans believe attraction is caused by pheromones, and that our hearts are merely ruled by chemistry." Ruger's voice is soft, but his words cut through her like a blade. "Nothing is beyond skin deep, yet Zyandites know better. For when two hearts come together, they are brought together by God."

Kira closes her eyes. "You're not making our goodbye any easier," she whispers, bringing herself to open her eyes to find Ruger studying her face.

"I'm not saying goodbye," Ruger says before he slides his hand from her cheek to her neck. His touch is so gentle, Kira leans into it. "Can't you see Kira, even in the darkness of oppression and war, God still showed His light by bringing us together? I didn't just crash here so you could save me, and I could save you." Ruger leans closer and gently kisses Kira's bruised cheek.

Kira closes her eyes, longing for him to kiss her lips.

Ruger gently rests his forehead against hers. "This was God's plan all along. He orchestrated our paths to cross, so our hearts would find each other." Ruger's eyes seem almost desperate, which is something she never thought this strong warrior was capable of. "I know it could be perceived as crazy for us to fall in love so quickly, but I don't live on the timeline of man. Everything I never thought I'd find in a woman, I've found in you. I've been fighting it, not just because of how soon my heart fell for yours, but because I thought you were married." He blushes. "As I told you before, I will say again, Kira, I am captivated by you."

All worldly sense has departed her. At this moment, Kira is so overwhelmed by the longing for him that she can hardly breathe.

"There's not a woman on earth even remotely like you, please, do not make me let you go." Ruger pleads. "I promise I will never let you or your daughter down. God willing, I will love and protect you both for the rest of my life and you," his lips curve into a smile, "will be my queen." Ruger's eyes flicker between relief and joy as his thumb caresses her lips tenderly, before pressing his own against them.

Kira breathes him in, as the passion of his kiss surprises her. She expected him to be more reserved, but he doesn't hold back. The dream she had of his kiss was nothing by comparison. Enraptured in this beautiful moment, their collided worlds and responsibilities fade into nothing but two souls drawn together by God.

Ruger's kiss is long and sweet before he pulls away.

It takes Kira a few minutes to catch her breath, as Ruger stares at her with adoration. There is nothing else, no threats, no duties, no pain, just their heartbeats, and the occasional crackling of the fire.

Ruger caresses the sides of her face. "My refined, beautiful huntress," Ruger almost kisses her again but stops himself. After closing his eyes for a moment, he glances at the stairs. "I will sleep downstairs tonight, and we'll leave in the morning." He stands and holds a hand out to her, the strictness of Zyandite standards plain to see in his eyes.

Kira's first reaction is happiness, even joy. Until reality sinks her heart like a boulder. "No." She closes her eyes. "Nadia…" Kira looks at Ruger, her eyes pleading for him to understand. "She won't cooperate. I'm sorry."

Ruger lets his hand rest to his side, and his smile surprises her. "It's alright. In fact, it's probably safer for you and Nadia this way." He presses his lips together, a new plan formulating in his mind. "Regardless of we get there, I'm excited for our future."

She doesn't want to hear about what may happen after he leaves. She wants him to stay. "You're still leaving?" Kira finds her lips desire to quiver, much like Nadia's did earlier. Embarrassed, she looks down. "After everything you just said…" She slowly brings her eyes to his. "You're still going to abandon me?"

Ruger kneels before her. "I'm not abandoning you. My goal is to come back for you. With all that God has done for you already, I'm assured you'll be okay while I'm gone."

Kira can't stop the tears that roll down her face. "I want to believe you. I really do."

"You don't have to right now." Ruger smiles. "I'll earn your trust."

Judging by his eyes, Kira knows there's no convincing him to stay. Defeated, she crosses her arms. "Be careful," she whispers.

"Keep everything locked. You'll know when it's me." He frowns. "I'd leave you my gun, but its fingerprint activated. Only a Tunaundan gunsmith can reset it. I'm sorry."

The irony is almost unbelievable. "No wonder you gave it to me so easily," Kira says. Bitterness creeps into her heart. She figures if he led her on about that, he probably lied to her about his feelings for her. How else could he go off and leave, if he really cared about her? Kira finds herself laughing, but it's not the kind that's pleasant. "You're totally okay with leaving me here, utterly defenseless."

"No." Ruger looks to the floor. "I've asked God for direction. I have to get to my men. I trust that He will protect you and Nadia. Otherwise, I could never leave you, armed or not."

"It's fine, just go. I've survived here for years before you came crashing into my life."

"I'm well aware of that." Ruger eyes her, before looking at the door. "But I don't intend to be gone for long."

Kira glares at him. She's too hurt to believe him.

His eyes soften. "When I flew in, I saw a military outpost about three miles away. If I can get a signal out through Auctairean airwaves, my men might hear it. Then I can coordinate for them to get me at the crash site. When they do, we'll come here."

"No." Kira's eyes harden. "If you do that, you'll invite every machine in Hanover to slaughter you." She reaches her hand to him. "I don't want to lose you, please, stay."

"There's nothing I want more than to be with you," Ruger whispers. "But I must defend my country. I've been gone too long as it is."

"You're injured. You shouldn't be going anywhere." Kira silently curses herself. Why did her heart have to fall for him? She knew he'd eventually have to go.

"When I was feverish, staying here was justified. If I could get a hold of my men, waiting for them here would also be justified. Now that I'm well, there is no justification to disregard my responsibilities to Zyandite. I took an oath, I must keep it. If my messages were getting through to my men, we could fly out. Then Nadia would only see the woods from the air. Our only choice is to flee on foot together, or for me to go and come back for you. I'm sorry, Kira. I'm so sorry."

No matter how sweet his words are, there's no doubt in her mind that once he leaves, he'll be out of her life forever. Looking up at him, her eyes almost lose the fight to her tears. "If you're going to leave, then go."

"Be ready, I'll see you soon." He walks over to the door and looks at her one more time. It's a look of longing, but more so, determination.

Kira knows there's no stopping him. Her heart is crushed, and her shoulders drop in defeat while she watches him walk out the door.

\*\*\*

# CHAPTER 16
## *DUTY STATION*

The cold causes Ruger's injured leg to stiffen. He pushes past the pain and walks through the darkness of Auctairea.

His eyes have adjusted to the darkness enough that he can decipher the ruins. So many concrete slabs and overgrown shrubs make it difficult for Ruger to pass. Eventually, he comes to the concrete road that leads to Outpost Four.

Lying low on the overgrown grass, Ruger sets his tablet to dark mode and uses his camera for night vision. The pieces of a broken drone reflect on the screen. He smiles and stands.

If his leg were healed, he'd run to the fence line. Ruger jumps over the gate, landing causes his leg to sting. Gritting his teeth, Ruger pulls out his sidearm. Using the pain, he kicks the door open.

Inside, the flickering of an artificial light above a pitiful dining room table, reveals a soldier, chained to a bunk bed. He's young, slightly bloodied, and unconscious.

There are four beds, making Ruger wonder where the other soldiers are.

Reaching out, his arm is three times the width of this young man's. Ruger notices some bruising on his forehead, before reading the name on his uniform.

"Sergeant Lopez?" Ruger inquires in Auctrah.

His brown eyes open. They squint, before widening in fear. "Zyandite!" Sergeant Lopez yells, before backing away. His shoulder hits the metal frame of the bunk, making him wince in pain.

"What happened to you?" Ruger asks.

"You…" Sergeant Lopez looks around suspiciously. "Speak Auctrah?"

"I lived here, once." Ruger stands. "You only have a few minutes to convince me to help you before I leave."

"Why would *you* help me?" Sergeant Lopez's entire face snarls.

"God's grace." Ruger walks over to the closet, where a radio sits on the top shelf. It's dusty. He sets it on the table and waves the particles before they can touch his face.

"You think that I believe in God?" He yells, lifting up his cuffed wrist the two inches he can, his face, strained in a snarl.

"No." Ruger scans the channels until he finds one that's clear.

"That's an open channel," Sergeant Lopez warns.

Ruger raises a brow. "Good." Lifting the square receiver near his chin, Ruger silently asks God for this message to be heard by his men. Pressing the button down, he speaks in Zyandish. *"Hear my voice. Those who know me, listen. The rain is on the sand."* He smiles at the perturbed expression Sergeant Lopez gives. *"I repeat, the rain is on the sand."* Looking at his tablet, Ruger is about to provide the coordinates for the crash site, but Sergeant Lopez's sobbing draws his attention.

"I don't want to die like this." He shakes his head. "No good deed goes unpunished."

Ruger slides the button up to stop recording. "What good deed did you commit?" He asks, with a hint of sarcasm.

"There's this girl. I've kind of had a thing for her, you know. Social Justice is one thing, but I don't want her to be killed."

"That's noble Auctairean, I'm impressed."

"She's way out of my league..." Sergeant Lopez looks up at Ruger, his eyes are bloodshot with tears. "My buddy was rejected by her. He wants blood. Specialist Compton agreed. I tried to stop them." He rattles the handcuff. "This is what I get for being what you call noble."

Discernment tugs on Ruger's heart, and he adjusts in his seat. The soldier said girl, not woman. It can't be Kira. Yet the pull on his heart screams it is.

"They even took the tank. Guess being a Principal for so long, finally made Sergeant Yarn go nuts."

Ruger closes his eyes for a moment. "They're after Kira?"

"How'd you know?"

A fire ignites in Ruger's eyes. He sends a transmission. *"If you know my voice, pay attention, the rain is on the sand. I repeat, the rain is on the sand."* The coordinates for Kira's house automatically flow from his lips in Zyandish.

Fear causes Sergeant Lopez to sweat. "What are you saying?"

Ruger drops the receiver and throws it against the wall, smashing it so no Auctairean can use it. Drawing his handgun, he marches over to Sergeant Lopez.

"No, no, no!" Sergeant Lopez grimaces, before looking away in fear.

Ruger flips a switch on his gun, and a thin tube slides out from the barrel. The blue flame is hot enough to melt steel and breaks the link of the handcuffs within seconds.

"Why?" Sergeant Lopez glances at the flame, before looking at Ruger in shock. "Why are you freeing me?"

Once the chain breaks completely, Ruger holsters his weapon and grabs Sergeant Lopez's uniform by the chest. Lifting him up, two feet from the ground, Ruger's eyes widen in anger. "I'm giving you one chance, just one, to be a man. You can take down the scum who did this to you and keep your life. Or you can stay enslaved." He lets go.

Sergeant Lopez falls to his feet. Slowly he straightens his posture. He's at least four inches shorter than Ruger and doesn't look up at him in fear, but reverence.

"Give me a reason to kill you, and I won't hesitate." Ruger eyes him, before turning his back on him and walking out the door.

Trying to run, his leg refuses to cooperate.

"Hey, Zyandite!"

He turns to see the young Sergeant holding up a set of keys.

"Want a ride?"

Ruger smiles.

Following the young man to the garage behind the Outpost, inside, there are four motorcycles, before a large, brown truck. Sergeant Lopez opens the door of the truck, while Ruger caresses the handle of one of the bikes…

"I really wish you wouldn't." His mother placed her hands on her hips, her blond hair, long, and shimmering in the bright Zyandite sun.

Ruger had just turned twenty and saved up his pay to buy himself a motorcycle. Living in the barracks didn't offer much space. Feeling the air and freedom of the open road, was his only real escape from duty.

Ruger grinned. "I knew you'd be upset, but I'm a pilot. I like fast."

She frowned and covered her mouth to hold in a sob.

"Mom…" His smile faded. "I'm going to die one day anyway. My fate is in his hands."

"Risking death for a righteous cause is admirable. Risking it for fun, puts our Lord to the test." She patted her heart and blinked away tears. "I expect better from you."

To honor his mother, he sold that motorcycle and hasn't ridden one since. Ruger looks at Sergeant Lopez, and the brown steel reflects the yellow glow of the single lightbulb overhead. "Key?"

Sergeant Lopez fumbles with the keys. Sliding one off the ring, he tosses it over.

Ruger catches it. Starting the engine, he straddles the seat and knocks the kickstand up. This is a righteous cause. Rolling the throttle, the sound echoes through the garage before Ruger rides out the door.

Even though the cold is worse at this speed, he enjoys it. The lone headlight guides him down the road.

A flicker of light in the side mirror catches Ruger's attention. He looks to see Sergeant Lopez riding a motorcycle behind him. Even the enemy follows him, making Ruger smile…

\*\*\*

# CHAPTER 17
## *THE COMMON RULE*

Night kisses the horizon. In the fading light, Cheryl watches every resident of the Commons walk past the thousand pieces of shattered glass that were once her drone. She should lock herself in the house, but they are carrying torches. Cheryl takes a long sip of whiskey. Trying to number the crowd, she loses count at forty-three. She glances up at the roof to see if the Principal is watching, but he's gone. There's no stopping them now, and it's all her fault. She shouldn't have encouraged the Principal to flee.

"They can't come here!" Gilligan runs out the door with his rifle in hand. His eyes bulge at the sight of the mob.

"Gilligan," she whispers, "take the back way out."

"No, Ma, I won't leave you."

Cheryl shoots him a glare. "You must leave now!"

Without a word, Gilligan backs away and runs towards the orchard.

Loosening her shoulders, Cheryl conjures up an escape plan. She must divert the leeches long enough to meet up with Gilligan. Their only chance is to escape to Quandii.

Meredith is the first to greet her. The purple paint smeared across her lips enhances the insanity in her eyes. "You're going to give me everything you have."

Cheryl hands Meredith her glass. Meredith chugs the whiskey down so fast, some of it drips out of the corners of her mouth.

"You can have it, all of it." Cheryl looks beyond her, scanning the crowd. If she wants Gilligan to live, she'll have to offer them something they hate even more than her. "Of course, my drop-off was nothing compared to what Kira Westin got…"

"Kira Westin?" Jeb asks. Some of the men hoot, making him smile.

"What'd she get?" Meredith sticks her face in Cheryl's.

Cheryl struggles to remain calm and only leans back a little. "She's working for him again," she lies. "As a thank you, Joplin sent her a personal drop-off. Kira didn't just get rations, she also got the finest imports from the GPU."

Meredith looks to the crowd. A bunch of thin, lustful faces grinds their teeth in anticipation. "The Modest Snob's next!" She yells.

"Okay, have fun. I was just leaving." Cheryl steps towards the edge of her patio.

A tall man grabs her arm. "Where are you going?"

"Yeah, can't have you warning Kira that we're free." Meredith snarls.

Cheryl's jaw drops. "I…" She looks to the road beyond the mob. "I just want to go to Quandii. I won't tell anyone about you. I swear."

The crowd laughs, and Cheryl frowns. Knowing there's no escape, she screams, "Run, Gilligan!"

Jeb knocks her out. Cheryl falls unconscious to the floor, and Meredith raises her arms in triumph.

Gilligan didn't take the backway out. Instead, he ran to the orchard and hid behind a tree.

Watching his mom knocked to the ground, Gilligan almost runs out of hiding. Fearfully, he cowers, and silently sobs, as a group of Commons surrounds her. In a blur, he does nothing while they kick and punch her so many times it's impossible to keep count. It's an enraged frenzy; they resemble ants on a corpse.

Meanwhile, the rest of the mob breaks into their house, stealing everything they can grab.

Knees shaking, Gilligan watches the crowd that was beating up his mom finally disperse. Her body is in a tangled mess on the porch, while the ones who attacked her, laugh. They actually laugh before looting her house.

Gilligan hides for an hour, quietly crying in the night until finally, there's nothing else to steal.

Hollering and laughing in almost a joyous percussion, the mob moves on.

They're proud, though never satisfied.

Moving on, this mob of fiends is ready for its next victim.

Gilligan's about to step out of his hiding place, until he watches a woman run back to his house, making him retreat. She's laughing in a wild, animal-like tone. There, she picks up a lantern from the porch and throws it into the living room window.

Several more of these animals see what she's doing, therefore, do.

His mother hasn't moved from that pitiful spot on the porch, even after the house engulfs in flames.

The small crowd of arsons bounces away together. High-fiving and laughing as they rejoin the large group down the road.

Now, with the Commons gone, Gilligan runs out of the shadows.

It's hard to see past the black smoke billowing out of the windows, but once Gilligan reaches his mom, he fears she's dead.

Grabbing the contorted mess that was once his Ma, he carries her out of the smoke.

Resting on a spot in the grass, while the orange glow of the fire reveals a face he can't recognize, Gilligan sobs aloud. "I'm sorry, Mama!"

Only one of Cheryl's eyes can open, but she can no longer see. "Gilli…" She whispers. "Don't…" Cheryl swallows, and it hurts enough to make her cringe. That alone sends pain across her face, like a thousand needles stabbing into her skin. "Let them hurt Kira's kid."

Gilligan looks up at the road that leads to Kira's house.

The torches the Commons carry are so far away, they look like fireflies in the night. "I can't beat them. I'll die too."

"No, cut through the forest." Cheryl's breaths become short. "Just warn them to run. Then, you go to Quandii, and never look back."

"No," Gilligan sniffles. "I'm carrying you to Quandii!" He stands to his feet, lifting her from the ground.

Less than a dozen steps later, before he can even pass the remains of their drone, Gilligan realizes that his mom is dead…

\*\*\*

Feeling like a brick was just slammed against her chest. Kira forces her weak knees to a stand and locks her backdoor. Rejection, fear, sadness, swirls inside of her, making it hard to breathe.

"God, why?" Kira shakes her head. "I believe in you, but I don't understand this." She presses her hand against her forehead. The thought of Ruger dying burns her more than the pain of him abandoning her. "Please, protect Ruger. Spare his life, please." Kira sobs. She should blow out her candle, but doesn't care if it's a waste of light. She stares at it and wants it to waste. The desire for destruction shouldn't fill her, but for tonight, she'll let it burn. Slowly, she walks up the stairs.

She checks on Nadia. Covers her tight and closes her bedroom door.

Walking over to her room, Kira sets the lantern on her dresser. Caressing the velvet of her sofa, it's empty, just like she feels.

Needing confirmation from God, she looks at the Bible on her nightstand. Kira's hands shake as she picks it up. "God lead me, the way you always do." She whispers. Peace covers her, almost enough to drown out her pain. Kira lets her Bible open. Her eyes fall on Mark 10:9 and widen. Voice shaking, she reads it, "let no one split apart what God has joined together."

Kira closes her Bible and hugs it against her chest. "You joined Ruger and me together. Please, let no man, not even Ruger, split us apart." Blowing out the lantern, she crawls into bed. Kira struggles to keep her cries silent, as torrents of emotion pour out. "Bring him back to me, please, bring him back."

\*\*\*

Several houses burn along the road from the Mayor's house, as the Commons wreak havoc across what's left of Hanover. There are just a few more houses left before they reach Kira's street...

\*\*\*

A low rumbling is felt beneath her body. Kira's eyes open. It's still dark, but her mind is groggy from sleep. Holding her breath, she strains to listen. The rumbling increases, and it's coming from her street. Only the glow from the candle downstairs fills her home with light. Wishing she had blown it out, Kira peers through the crack of her curtains.

Her chest rises with each breath, while her body desires to scream. Covering her mouth, Kira nearly panics at the sight.

The headlights reveal a tank as it rolls down her street before stopping at her driveway.

Kira's entire body trembles. "No, God, please, no."

Two men step out of the tank. The bright lights from the vehicle reveal that they are smiling. One of them is dressed like the Principal, with only a ratty pair of jeans, but his head is shaved. The other man dons the uniform of the People's Army of Auctairea.

Her knees buckle. "God, please, give me strength," Kira prays.

She has to hide Nadia in the attic. It's the only chance for her to survive. Reaching up for the chain, she pulls the wooden ladder down.

Kira can hear the doorknob downstairs wiggle and turn, but so far, the lock keeps them out.

Surprised to find Nadia's slept through the noise outside, it takes all of Kira's strength to lay her over her shoulder. Each step up to the attic is excruciating. Sweat covers Kira's skin, and her teeth chatter. Reaching the top, she lays Nadia down on the rug before her reloader. Covering her with her blanket, she backs away. "Nadia," Her tone is harsh enough that her daughter's eyes fling open. "Whatever you hear, don't make a sound. Don't leave the attic. Don't even move," Kira whispers, her face strained under fear.

Nadia's eyes begin to water. "Okay, mommy."

Pounding on the backdoor practically shakes the house, making Kira look back in surprise. She turns to Nadia, thankful to see she's staying still. "I love you," Kira whispers. Heart racing, she climbs down the wooden ladder. Pushing it up, she yanks the golden chain off the drywall. Without the chain hanging there, it's less obvious there's an attic. Shoving it in her pocket, she grabs Nadia's doll and clothes and hides them inside of a chest in her closet.

Relieved that Nadia is hidden, she lets out a sigh and heads down the stairs.

There's a pounding at the front door, which scares Kira so badly, she trips on the third step down, and lands on her thigh. She leans her back against the stair's low wall.

"Oh, Modest Beauty!" The Principal shouts through the door, before laughing.

She closes her eyes. This is worse than if it were just a random soldier. He's been rejected by her enough to be out for blood. Wishing she had ammo, Kira steadies her breathing. Rushing through her kitchen, she grabs as many glassware and knives that she can carry. Setting them along the front counter, sweat blurs her vision for a moment. Wiping her brow, a loud thud against her door makes her cringe. There's another, and another, each thud nearly stops her heart. She knows time is running out before they break-in and has to focus on getting her hands to stop shaking. Kira hears the door burst open, and ducks behind the counter.

"Hello?" A man whose voice she doesn't recognize asks, before snickering.

Squatting on the floor, Kira's fingers feel along the counter, and she grabs the first two objects she can reach.

Their footsteps are gaining.

Holding her breath, Kira readies her knees to jump.

The Principal holds his handgun out and is about to turn the corner when Kira kicks the gun out of his hands. He tries to hit her, but she shatters a measuring cup across his face.

"Hey!" Specialist Compton shouts, pointing his handgun at them, but he can't get a clear shot.

The Principal touches his face. Holding his hand out, he's surprised by his own blood.

Kira runs into the kitchen and throws several plates at them. He dodges most, but one smashes against his cheek, hard enough to break the skin. The Principal glares at her.

She grabs two knives, ready to strike.

Specialist Compton keeps his gun pointed at her. "Drop the knives, and we'll let you live."

Shaking, Kira looks at The Principal. His eyes are filled with rage. She knows she can't face him defenseless, but glancing at the gun, she knows her knife won't win this fight. She drops it and slowly holds her hands up.

"Whew!" Specialist Compton laughs before putting his gun away.

The Principal doesn't even look at his accomplice and lunges for Kira. The force of his chest against hers nearly knocks the wind out of her. Backing up to the counter before her sink, the edge of it digs into the small of her back. She tries to block his hand with her arm, but he knocks it away with his fist before grabbing her hair. Yanking her head back, he holds the tip of the knife under Kira's chin.

"We'd be in Quandii by now!" The Principal screams in her face. "Feasting with the Prime Minister, but you thought you were just too good for me."

Reaching behind, Kira's hand finds the faucet and pulls the hose from the socket. She uses it to hit him in the eye, hard enough that he lets her go.

Kira tries to hit the other soldier, but he grabs her fist and pulls her into him.

Specialist Compton digs his fingers into Kira's neck and yanks her back into his chest. Cursing at her through his teeth, a new sound silences him.

The Principal strains to listen. "What is that?"

Held too tightly to break free, Kira can hardly breathe under this pressure of the soldier's hold along her neck. Then, she hears it.

"Modest snob, modest snob, miss too good is going to cry. Modest snob, modest snob, tonight's the night you're going to die." The mob keeps repeating their jeer, over and over again. As their chant gets closer, shivers run up Kira's spine.

"The door!" The Principal runs over to try and put it back on the hinges.

Specialist Compton laughs. "They'll see the tank and run." His confidence loosens his hold on Kira, though only a little.

A full breath relieves her, before terror for Nadia stabs her heart. Kira never thought she'd pray for the Commons to break into her home, but silently, she begs God that he'll use them save her and Nadia from these soldiers.

The closer their chanting gets, the wilder it sounds.

A sudden pounding slams against the back door. "Kira?" Gilligan screams.

"That's the Mayor's son," The Principal whispers, his eyes wide.

"Don't let him in, Billy!" Specialist Compton squeezes his hold on Kira a little tighter.

Billy snarls at him. "We may need him." He opens the door.

Gilligan rushes inside, with his rifle in hand. He's sweating, and his eyes bulge when he sees the predicament Kira's in.

"Here to join the party?" Billy nods towards Kira and laughs.

"The Commons..." Gilligan's eyes tear up. "They killed Ma..." Gilligan watches Billy lock the door. "Where were *you?*"

"I relieved myself of duty." Billy looks at the front of the house, as the chanting outside gets louder.

"Soldiers are here!" A woman screams.

Instead of fear, there's laughter. A thud sounds against the front door, making Billy back up, his once confident eyes now frightened.

"You're nothing without your machines!" A man yells through the wood.

"The machines didn't fall with the drones, did they?" Specialist Compton whispers. His grip on Kira becomes more unstable.

Billy only shrugs.

Gilligan still won't take his eyes off of Billy. "You shouldn't have left."

Billy's upper lip snarls into a curve at Gilligan. "Don't blame me. It was your mother's idea to lie to them." He shrugs. "At least now's your chance for revenge."

Gilligan glares at the Principal and seems like he's about to cry, before his eyes harden. "I don't want vengeance. I just came here to save the kid." He looks at Kira. "Did you get her out in time?"

Surprised Gilligan cares. Kira wants to lie, so no one will know that Nadia is here. But God never blesses a lie. She looks down and doesn't say anything.

"Ma cared about her." Gilligan stares at the floor. "She cared about you, too." His eyes slowly rise to Kira's. They're no longer sad, but angry.

"I'm so sor—" Kira's words are cut short by pain, as the soldier yanks her back by her neck.

"Shut up!" Specialist Compton shouts.

"I'm going to go look for the kid." Gilligan stomps upstairs.

Horror fills Kira's heart. If she shows fear, the others will know she has something to hide. They'll look for Nadia, and she knows they'll find her. At least with it just being Gilligan searching, there's less of a chance her daughter will be found. Kira softens her shoulders and tries to appear bored.

The glass breaking causes the Principal to run over and start shooting.

Gilligan runs from the stairs and paints his rifle at the door, while Specialist Compton does nothing besides position Kira to be his shield.

After nine shots, the Commons are stopped, for now.

"Guess you're stuck fighting with us." Specialist Compton snarls at Gilligan.

"This is all your fault, Kira." Gilligan marches towards her in a huff. "If you'd only put that kid in an Education Center, none of this would've happened!" He yells.

Nadia's soul is more important than this mortal life. Kira will never regret protecting her daughter from being raised Godless. She glares at him.

"Shut up and get in position to fire on the Commons." Billy points at Kira's broken window.

Gilligan turns away from Kira to glare at the Principal. "Oh yeah, put me in the front, you coward!"

Kira watches the Principal's hand move towards his sidearm.

"Gilligan," she keeps her tone calm. "This is your chance to avenge your mom."

Much to her surprise, he nods. "You're right." Instead of pointing his rifle at the window, he points it at the Principal.

Billy charges and shoves the barrel of Gilligan's rifle up at the ceiling.

With Nadia in the attic overhead, Kira's eyes bulge as she silently begs God to not let the rifle discharge.

Gilligan is bigger than Billy, but training overcomes size. Billy never lets go of the rifle with his right hand and uses his left to hit Gilligan in the neck. Gilligan can't breathe for a moment, and fumbles back, giving Billy the chance to yank the rifle out of his hands. Pointing it at Gilligan, Billy shoots him with his own gun.

Gilligan grabs his chest. "It burns!" He screams before falling to the floor.

His body convulses into a seizure, while the kepweed goes straight into his heart. Within seconds, Gilligan's body stills, but his eyes remain open.

Kira knows he's dead and gasps.

Billy's nostrils flare. "Ewe, smell that?"

Specialist Compton shakes his head.

Billy holds up the rifle and grins. "Kepweed." He searches Gilligan's pockets and pulls out a box of ammo. Slamming it on the counter, he takes one of the dozen or so bullets and sniffs it. "Smell this." He waves the hollow point that's been stuffed with kepweed under Kira's nose.

The pungent stench makes her cringe.

"Suffering from this is the kind of death you deserve." He laughs. "That round is saved, for if you give me a hard time." He loads Gilligan's rifle as the chanting outside returns.

A soft glow shines in above each window, as the mob surrounds her house. Figuring they have torches of some kind, Kira fears that they may burn her house down.

Several objects are thrown through her windows, breaking them all at once.

Reaching for his gun, Specialist Compton loosens his grip enough for her to break free.

With the soldiers distracted by the Commons, Kira runs upstairs. Gunshots blare behind her causing her to cover her ears, but she doesn't look back.

Once on the second floor, Kira knows she has to figure out a barricade. Pushing her dresser across the carpet to block the stairs, Kira grits her teeth until she feels they may break. She has to turn the dresser horizontal to move it. Her arms and shoulders burn, she uses the pain and forces it in place at the top of her stairs. Barely hanging on the edge, Kira figures that if they try to move it, it'll fall down the stairs and crush them.

Relieved that Nadia's staying quiet, Kira rushes to get her trauma shears from the bathroom. Digging in her cabinet through the dark, she hears the

Commons yelling outside.

The gunfire stops.

Scissors in hand, Kira walks up to her window, she pulls back the curtain and nearly faints at the sight. The Commons are all on her lawn, running around with torches. They're in a frenzy, drunk on terror.

"The Prince is in there!" Meredith screams.

The crowd closes in.

Downstairs, several more shots are fired.

She leans against the wall and counts. After sixteen shouts are fired, the sound of glass breaking fills her ears, and what sounds like a pack of hyenas enters her home.

"Oh God, please don't abandon us." Kira holds her head down in prayer. The sound of fighting downstairs makes her cringe. "Protect us, please."

Several gunshots echo throughout her home. Kira's heart nearly stops. Could it be Ruger?

The Principal's laughter disproves her hope. "Tricked you!"

Screaming outside causes her to look at the window, from the sounds of things, the Commons are in retreat.

"It burns!" A man outside screams, making her realize they saved the kepweed laced bullets for last.

Hammering pounds the beams of her home, making Kira wonder if the soldiers are patching up where the Commons broke in?

Knees shaking, she rises to a stand. Checking out her window, she can see a few of the Commons are trying to figure out how to use the tank. There are at least three dozen of them left. A few stragglers run away down the pavement, but the rest of the crowd seems dedicated to destruction.

She backs away from the window. She doesn't stand a chance against a gun, but maybe she can figure out a way to take control of it?

The hammering downstairs stops, and a loud crash makes her jump. She turns to hear footsteps coming up the stairs.

Tiptoeing to the loft, she stands at the low wall, with the trauma shears ready.

Under the glow of candlelight, she watches her dresser move forward before it's yanked down the stairs.

The Principal laughs. It's crazier than normal.

Dismayed that her barricade didn't work, Kira slowly backs up.

He turns the corner of the low wall, before stepping up into the loft. Behind him, the other soldier follows suit. His eyes are just as insane as the Principal's. Whatever they're going to do to her, she can't let it happen this close to Nadia, or else she may come out of hiding. Without thinking of the risk, Kira runs to the ledge above her stairs and jumps over it.

The dresser breaks her fall, but landing on her side was far from graceful. Pain shoots up her leg to her back. Ignoring it, she braces her leg over the edge, and her feet reach the first floor.

She sees what the hammering was for. Pieces of her coffee table have been nailed over her windows and front door. The large cast iron pot once hanging in her fireplace lies dented on her living room floor.

"Get her!" The Principal screams.

The sound of wood breaking behind her causes her to run. She can't abandon Nadia by leaving the house. Kira fumbles to grab another weapon. Picking up the iron pot, all she has is this and her trauma sheers.

Both men shove her dresser into the kitchen, and the force is so hard, it breaks against the cupboards. Pieces of splintered wood and clothes explode from the crash. Kira can't focus on the destruction, and keeps her eyes on the soldiers. Like wild predators, they strut towards her. She flings the iron pot at Specialist Compton. His forearm blocks it, before yanking it out of her grip. He throws it into the living room and laughs. His pupils are larger than she remembers. Glancing at the Principal, his eyes are just as mad. Kira knows what drug they've done. She doesn't stand a chance.

A thud slams against her front door. "Your gun won't stand to the tank, Prince!" A man yells.

The Commons hoot and holler outside, making the intruders' exchange glances. They're not afraid, but rather excited.

Specialist Compton begins shooting out the window, to keep the Commons at bay.

Kira looks at the Principal, hoping he'll do the same. Instead of fighting the Commons, he runs towards her. Kira grits her teeth and shoves the trauma shears into his flesh, just below his collar bone.

He doesn't even flinch.

Watching the blood drip down, Kira's eyes widen in horror. He should've at least felt that. She's too shocked to move before Billy grips her arms. In a whirl, the room turns upside down, before her back is slammed against the dining room table.

Ringing fills her ears, before what sounds like the Commons screaming. For a moment, Kira thought she heard a motorcycle. How long has it been since she's heard one? Closing her eyes to the blur, a hand grabs her face.

"Don't you fall asleep on me," The Principal says with his nose against hers. "I've got plans for you, Modest Beauty." He sings, making his friend laugh.

The blur morphs into clarity. Kira can see his brown eyes darting back and forth. It's the darkest display of insanity she's seen. No matter what he does to her, she'll be quiet. She can't do anything to make Nadia come out of hiding. "Not like this, God, not like this," She lips without allowing her voice to escape.

"You'll see..." The Principal bears his fist into her midsection. The wind is knocked out of her, but she can't exhale too loud, or Nadia will hear. Something outside almost sounds like an explosion, but it could just be her mind breaking under the pain. "I always get what I want." The Principal's eyes are wild with rage. "You modest sn—"

Blood splatters, but all Kira hears is static, before the Principal's words are cut short. He falls on the floor. She turns to see the Auctairean soldier, pointing Gilligan's gun at Ruger. "No." She whispers.

Ruger shoots the soldier before he can pull the lever back. He rushes over to her and caresses her neck. "Are you hurt?" His voice is muffled. Her ears ring too loudly to hear him. His fingertips move down her neck and shoulders, then to her arms. He gently turns her on her side and runs his fingers down her spine. She smiles once she realizes he's checking her for injuries. "I'm so sorry I left you," Ruger whispers.

"No. I thank God…" She places a hand on the side of his face. "For you."

Her arm loses all strength, and her hand falls down to her side. The room becomes blurred before turning black.

\*\*\*

# CHAPTER 18
## *MISSION ESSENTIAL*

Rain falls in the night. It's torrent and bears down on Kira, more cumbersome than it should. She's trying to swim in a dark ocean. There's no chance for air, no chance for life. She begins to sink. Ruger pulls her out of the water, and she can breathe again.

Kira's eyes open to darkness. She sits up and heaves. Everything hurts. Waiting for her eyes to adjust, she recognizes Nadia's breathing. Reaching out along the familiar texture of her comforter, her hand finds Nadia's back.

Nadia squirms a little, but remains asleep.

The missing dresser causes the white wall in front of Kira to stand out. The rest of the room gives the security of normalcy, except, it feels colder than normal. Kira makes sure Nadia is extra covered up, before stepping out of bed. Kira feels like her entire body has been flattened under a steam roller. Wincing, she limps her way toward the stairs.

The glow of the fire flickers from downstairs. An occasional crackle pops before she hears Ruger's voice. Relieved, she momentarily closes her eyes before tiptoeing down.

The conversation is not one she expected, and she stops midway to listen.

"That's powerful," A strange man's voice whispers, "No wonder the government wants to destroy it."

"They can't," Ruger's tone is resolved. "Because of men like you, who help the gospel thrive and spread."

Eyes wide, Kira's excited Ruger found his men. She peers over the low wall and immediately frowns.

Every board that was hammered over her windows is broken, and her curtains are hanging down, eliminating her privacy. What really upsets Kira, is who's sitting on her couch. In his brown Auctairean uniform, there's Sergeant Lopez, listening to Ruger talk as though he's welcomed here.

Leaning back, Kira grips the banister. Her eyes turn into flames, burning at the memories of when he's harassed her at the drop-offs.

Ready to kick him out of her house, she grits her teeth and is about to stand.

"I heard my parents talk about it, but I never felt it myself. This warmth in my chest…" Sergeant Lopez sounds sincere, happy even. "It's so peaceful but still, strong."

"Now that you've accepted Jesus into your heart, that warmth will continue to guide you." Kira can hear the smile in Ruger's voice. "The more you listen to it, the stronger it gets. The more you ignore it, the more it fades."

"Man, I just can't believe God would receive me. When the machines came, I renounced him. I didn't do…" Sergeant Lopez sniffles. "What my brother did. What my parents did. They stood firm, but I betrayed God."

There's movement, making Kira strain to listen.

"Here, let me show you how much God loves you by reading Luke chapter seven, verse forty-seven," Ruger says.

"Wow, so that's the Bible that caught the bullet?"

Ruger chuckles. "Look at the pages."

"How amazing. I guess that's how God looks out for a righteous man."

"No one is righteous, but God. For all we know, my crashing here could've been for you. God loves you so much that He made certain you were found."

Kira covers her mouth with her hands and holds in a sob. While their countries are at war, Ruger is ministering to the enemy. All the while, she's harboring unforgiveness in her heart for this man, a man whom God's sought after to save. The conviction is overwhelming, but she knows how to make it right.

Downstairs, Sergeant Lopez sniffles, before Ruger reads the scripture.

"I tell you, her sins—and they are many—have been forgiven, so she has shown me much love. But a person who is forgiven little shows only a little love." Ruger reads Luke 7:47 and smiles. The soapstone cover of Ruger's Bible echoes when he closes it. "You've been forgiven a lot because God has a lot for you to do," Ruger's voice is resolute. "Whatever that is, requires for you to love, and love generously."

It's too much for her to stay still. She feels the urge to give something she never thought she could lose. Slipping back into her room, Kira digs out her Bible. Hugging it, her reluctance to give it away is replaced by peace.

"Mommy?" Nadia whispers.

"Hey, sweetheart, are you okay?" Kira slides into bed to hug her.

"I'm fine. Well, I'm a little sorry."

"Why?"

"I disobeyed you. I came out of hiding, but only because I knew Ruger was here. I saw him through the broken beam in the attic. He came here on a thin car that was really fast, and knocked it into the Commons before landing on his feet and fighting." Nadia pretends to do a left uppercut and a couple of right hooks. Her eyes widen as though remembering something. "Another man was with him. He got in the tank, and blasted the Commons away." She motions her hands apart like an explosion.

Kira realizes everything she thought she heard earlier was real. "That's amazing."

"Yeah, it was. I waited until Ruger called me to come down. He gave me a hug and asked me to watch over you while you sleep." She giggles. "Guess I fell asleep too."

"Oh, you brave girl." Kira embraces her. "I'm very proud of you."

Soaking in this moment, Kira silently thanks God for sparing them both, while enjoying the warmth of Nadia's embrace. "I have to go talk to Ruger, but I'll be right back up."

"Can I sleep in your bed all night?"

"Of course."

Nadia does a happy dance before snuggling under the covers.

Kira kisses her cheek and walks downstairs, where Ruger and Sergeant Lopez stand at the sight of her.

"How are you feeling?" Ruger asks.

"Alive." Looking around the room, she's surprised by how clean it is. The bodies of her enemies are nowhere to be found. Even the glass from her broken windows is picked up. Gilligan's rifle and a few rounds of ammo are on her counter, right next to her candle that's still burning. Glancing at Ruger, she smiles in appreciation, before walking up to Sergeant Lopez. "I hear you've made the most important decision of your life." She hands out her Bible to him. "I hope this helps you the way it's helped me."

"I don't deserve that." He shakes his head and even backs up a step. "Not after how I've treated you."

"You've more than redeemed yourself. Please, take it."

Sergeant Lopez does, and though he's quick to hide it, Kira sees his eyes tear up. "Thank you."

"Start with the gospels." Ruger turns the pages of her Bible to guide him. "Read Proverbs and Psalms, every day. Let God lead you through the rest."

"I will." Sergeant Lopez looks at the door and frowns. "You really think people will listen to me?" He brings his eyes back to Ruger.

"Yes, because God is in you. This is what he created you for. Your testimony proves that, and it is powerful." Ruger places a hand on Sergeant Lopez's shoulder. "May I pray over you?"

"Yes, please."

Ruger bows his head and closes his eyes. "The great I Am, thank you for the time you've given us. Thank you for Carl Lopez, and all the plans you have for him, not just in this life, but the next. I ask that you speak to him, guide him, and protect him. Show him those whom you are calling to you, and let him be the answer to their prayers. Thank you for creating Carl, and help him to know that your love doesn't die. Work through Carl, and bring forth your will on earth, as it is in heaven. In the name of Jesus Christ, we pray, amen."

Kira's amazed to see them hug before Carl walks to the door. He stops to wave goodbye, smiles, and lifts up his chin. Bible in hand, he walks away.

Ruger closes her broken door, the best he can.

"How did you convert him?" Kira gasps.

"I didn't. It was the will of the great I Am. My father always said that when God calls someone back to him, we're blessed to be the vessel the signal just happens to go through." Ruger's face beams. "Seeing that young man redeemed gives me hope for Auctairea."

Conviction gives her goosebumps. Kira crosses her arms to hug herself. "I never thought of that."

Ruger's brow rises.

"Saving them." Having a hard time getting the words out, she shrugs. "That they could be saved." She frowns. "This whole time, I thought I was such a good Christian, hiding my faith where it's illegal, when I should've shared it."

Ruger tends to the fire. "You have." He glances upstairs. "Motherhood is your greatest ministry." Placing the poker back on its hook, he gives her a sheepish smile. "I hope you don't mind, but I used your dresser for firewood."

Kira looks at the hearth. With her home exposed to the elements, the warmth feels good against her skin. The sight of what's burning causes her to gasp. It's not like she can go out and buy another dresser, it's gone for good. She shouldn't laugh, but it flows out of her, naturally. "Waste nothing," she says before her laughter boils into something more profound, moistening down to the root of her issue. She looks up at the ceiling, the corners, the walls, everything she thought she's kept intact all these years. "None of it matters," she whispers. "I thought I could maintain it until Nadia grew up, but I couldn't even save my furniture." She motions out to what's left of the dresser in her kitchen. "All my effort was in vain."

Ruger stands by the fire, watching her with his eyes flickering in grave concern.

"I mean it." She steps over to the backdoor and glances out the window. There are a few torches left by the Commons, which are still burning on the ground. As she suspected, Feisty and the chickens are gone. All that remains of her livestock is a broken shed and a few patches of feathers. No milk for Nadia. No protein. Gone. It's all gone. "I could put on a show to fool the drones every day for the rest of my life. I could hunt, I could reload my ammo. I've stayed strong during the coldest, loneliest nights of winter. I could cook and clean and educate my child. I could try to teach her of light, and grace, and beauty, in this dark, ugly, unforgiving place. I did it, but when it comes to saving any of it, that's out of my hands. I have no more control over that than you did in crashing here. Or Carl Lopez did in being found by you." She turns away from the pitiful sight of the feathers and looks at Ruger. "Only God is in control. My life, Nadia's life, your life, how long we have, how we die. How we live. That's up to him."

Ruger carefully steps up to her. "Considering everything that's happened to you, I think you're handling this very well."

Kira smirks at him. "I'm not having a breakdown. I've just finally, letting go." She looks at the table. All the memories of Nadia and her sharing meals there should bring her joy. But it's been tainted by one moment. "I thought I was going to die tonight." She brings her eyes back to Ruger. "I should've died tonight, but God didn't let me." She smiles. "He sent a vessel to save me, and now, I have no choice but to leave my greatest idol behind." Kira takes in a deep breath. "Relying on this structure, my home, has been my greatest sin. I'm finally free of it."

Ruger's brow lowers before he reaches a hand to her. "That's beautiful, Kira. I'm relieved that you're willing to go with me, but my leaving didn't have the outcome I had hoped for."

She takes his hand. "You didn't get through to your men?"

"I don't think so. If I had, then they would be here by now." He stares at her hand for a moment. Delicately caresses it, before lifting it to his lips. He closes his eyes and kisses her skin tenderly before letting her hand go. "Please forgive me, but when I found out what the soldiers had planned to do, I couldn't give the coordinates for where my jet crashed. Instead, I…" He looks down for a moment. Slowly he brings his eyes to hers. "I gave the coordinates for here. I wanted to make sure you were rescued, but my men should've come by now. I'm sorry."

Her heart should be crushed, but instead, it feels light. "All the drones must be down." Her brow scrunches. "The jets must be too, because," she shakes her head, "we'd already be dead."

Ruger slowly nods. "I know. Sergeant Lopez was very insightful on tracking a potential ambush. As it is, we've got about a half an hour before the machines get here."

The room spins. Kira's head should hit the tile, but Ruger catches her in time.

"I know this is the worst news you could receive." He gently carries her to the couch and sits down without letting her go. "It's the exact opposite of my intention for leaving, but nothing can change the outcome, or how much I regret it now."

"You were just going to let me sleep?" Kira asks.

"After everything you just went through, yes. For as long as possible." Ruger's eyes become distant. "I had hoped I was wrong about the message, and that my men would still show up." He looks at her and smiles. "I'm sorry I've let you down."

She's not mad at him. Part of her knows she should be, but she can't be. His intention was to save them. His action saved Carl. Trusting God to save them gives her peace. She leans her head under his chin and closes her eyes. "I forgive you," she whispers. "Without you, I'd be dead." Her eyes tear up. "Ruger, I love you."

Ruger pulls her close and kisses her lips.

Letting everything else fade, Kira enjoys the moment. The heat of their kiss intensifies. Out of all the loss and pain, at least they're together.

Off in the distance, the scraping of metal feet on pavement fills the night.

\*\*\*

Across Hanover, Sergeant Lopez rides his motorcycle down a curved road. Kira's Bible is tucked under his arm, and his eyes are full of hope.

A flicker of light catches his attention from a cornfield. He pulls up to the old farmhouse and walks up to the door.

A frightened elderly couple steps outside. "We mean the Prime Minister no harm." The man says, while the woman nearly falls to her knees.

Realizing it's his uniform that's scaring them, Sergeant Lopez shakes his head. "I'm not here to hurt you." He pulls out Kira's Bible. "I'm here to give you good news."

***

# CHAPTER 19
## *THE WINDOW*

Kira abruptly ends their kiss. A hot tear rolls down her cheek. "We're running out of time."

Ruger doesn't show fear and caresses the tear away. "No. They're still a good distance away." He frowns. "I've gone through our escape. We're both too injured to carry Nadia, and there's no way her little legs could make it that far, without the machines finding us." He leans his lips into hers. "I have to destroy them." He says between kisses.

Kira tightens her grip on his shoulders and pulls back to look him in the eyes. "How, with the tank?" Her eyes fall on how tightly he bolted her front door. She realizes this has been his plan since he returned.

Ruger smirks. "It's out of munitions."

"We can ride it." Kira's eyes widen. "If we hurry, we'll make it inside in time." She gets up and is about to wake Nadia, but his hold stops her.

"No. We'd run out of fuel before we could even make it past the woods." Ruger's eyes are bright, aware, and unwavering. "This is my battle to win." He walks over to the back door.

"You can't fight them. Our only chance is to flee." Kira tries to fight her tears, but it's useless.

He stops to look at her. "I'm trained and equipped to fight them." He draws his handgun and smiles. "Don't worry, as I told you before, this is an exceptional weapon." He winks and walks out the door.

How can he tell her not to worry? She's paralyzed by fear. The metal scraping outside only gets louder. She knows the machines are nearing her street. It's like the Great Cleansing all over again. "No…" Breaths jagged, she reaches for the deadbolt. This is Ruger's only way back inside. For Nadia's sake, she grits her teeth and turns it, locking him out. "I'm cursed," she whispers between heaves. So many people she's loved have been taken from her. Shaking, she swallows and almost chokes. The physical pain in her shoulders and neck, combined with the emotional turmoil in her heart, causes her entire body to tighten. She's so stiff, she can hardly move. Looking at Gilligan's rifle on the counter gives her enough strength to walk. She picks it up and flings it over her shoulder, before stuffing what little ammo there is in her pockets. Bracing herself on the banister, Kira makes her way upstairs.

The sound, that sound…

The scraping, the promise of death without remorse, digs its way closer and closer.

Legs shaking, her nails dig into the banister with each slow step up. Flashbacks from that night blur with her reality. Too scared to breathe normally, Kira reaches her bedroom. Ahead of her is the same window where she stood at to watch her friends get slaughtered.

She doesn't want to stand there now.

Violently wiping a lone tear away, she has to see Ruger. "God," she whispers in a heave, "let him survive." Hands shaking so badly, she can hardly move back her curtain. An orange glow radiates onto the street from various torches the Commons abandoned. Ruger holds out his handgun and points it towards the darkness. Beyond him, Kira looks at the Langton's house. Even though it's mostly destroyed by the fire, the memory of that night restores it, piece by piece in her mind's eye. The shadows of Tim Langton's end replay, just a few feet beyond where Ruger stands now.

Several red beams flicker from the darkness at the end of the street. At least twenty machines are scraping their metal feet along the pavement and now turn down her cul-de-sac. Marching in rows of fives, they advance in perfect formation.

# THE HUNTRESS

Ruger doesn't budge. His feet and arms are in a perfect isosceles stance, with nothing but a handgun, he aims it with a courage Kira wishes she possessed.

Suddenly, Maggie's screaming echoes in her head, making Kira tremble.

"Run, Kira! Run!"

Helpless, always helpless. Now Kira feels hopeless.

This is how it always ends, her watching, listening, with nothing but cowardice and shame. Except after tonight, there is no more hiding. The man she's fallen in love with will be slaughtered, then, they will come for her. She won't allow herself to think of what will happen to Nadia...

The machines make their way into the low light. Unlike the drones, their black encasement does not reflect their surroundings. The red lights blinking on each head, reveals the rows of cameras. Their feet scratch alone the road, just like the night of the Great Cleansing.

Cries of death and defeat continue to torment her mind. Tears roll down, distorting her vision, while nausea creeps into her core.

Gritting her teeth, Kira will not just stand here in this place and helplessly watch injustice again. She will fight, even if it costs her everything.

"Kira, run! Ru—" Maggie's last call makes Kira's lips tremble.

Wiping her tears away, this is not the time to beg God to let them survive. It's the time to have faith that God will give them victory.

"God, you are the maker of the cosmos. With your help, we will destroy our enemies." Kira prays, while courage builds within her. Remembering a Psalm, Kira begins to pray it. "Yes, they surrounded and attacked me, but I destroyed them all with the name of the LORD." Kira's voice cracks as she whispers Psalm 118:11 while looking at the mechanical demons that have haunted her nightmares for years. She kicks the window. The sole of her boot causes shards of glass to shatter out on the driveway. The low light of the moon and abandoned torches reflect off the shards like silver and gold confetti. She aims her rifle at the red light above one of the mechanical monsters. "God, I thank you ahead of time for your victory."

The lighting is poor, but the machines aren't trying to hide.

Ruger looks up at her, and nods once in solidarity, before refocusing on his aim. She doesn't know what he expects to accomplish with just a handgun but admires his fearlessness.

The machines are out of range for his handgun, but not for her rifle. She fires on them. Once, then twice, but the bullets bounce off.

"Stop wasting ammo."

She looks down to find Ruger smirking. Her heart quakes for this handsome man, whose bravery intertwines with folly. He doesn't stand a chance against these machines but is too valiant to know it.

The scraping intensifies, while the machines pick up their pace. The steel of their bladed arms reflects the flames of the torches while they sway towards Ruger.

He stands still, and unafraid.

"No God, not this man. No!" Kira prays before firing again. Each round is useless against the mechanical monsters. She tries a shot at the cameras and succeeds. Gritting her teeth, she keeps firing. Each machine has eight cameras above their face, and she intends to shoot them all. Her body aches, but the adrenaline rush helps her ignore her pain. Kira's ability to load the rifle and pull the bolt in haste becomes smooth until she runs out of ammo.

Digging into her pockets, there's not a single bullet left. Despair creeps in so thick, she can feel her muscles aching again. Fighting tears, she tosses the rifle on the floor. Chin held low, she turns away from the street. She doesn't want to look at Ruger. She doesn't want to watch him die.

A clicking sound echoes from the street, Kira turns towards it. The sight of Ruger's confidence isn't what makes her gasp, but his weapon...

Ruger's pistol builds on itself, piece by piece, transforming outward into a great hand cannon. The barrel spins and expands at the tip. The friction radiates into a blue glow, creating a halo of light around Ruger. His eyes are calm and focused on the machines. A blue flame bursts from his weapon like a flash, forcing Kira to cover her eyes. Static fills the air. It's almost hot enough to burn the hairs on her forearms.

Kira's hair stands on end before she squints open her eyes to see the blue wave igniting from his weapon hit the first row of machines. They disintegrate upon contact. Kira's jaw drops as they become nothing but glowing, blue ash.

Nadia rushes up behind her. "Mommy, what is that?"

"I don't know. Stay back," Kira whispers, holding a hand outward, to protect Nadia from the window.

The rest of the machines keep charging. Without sense or fear, they are only a game to their controller. As Ruger fires the next strange round from his gun, Kira does her best to keep her eyes open. Having to hold an arm up to block the intensity of the light, she's amazed to watch something beautiful, destroy so efficiently.

The bright glow is white at the center but is surrounded by blue flames that glitter in the night. It fires from his weapon like a shotgun shell, before expanding outward into a growing sphere. Once it hits the target, a dark blue flash fills the air with electricity. The moment the bright, shimmering blue light falls on the machines, it incinerates them. Kira gasps before Ruger fires another round, taking down the last of them.

"He let me hold that thing," she whispers to Nadia, who sits on the floor behind her.

Nadia giggles. "Ruger's a true warrior."

"He really is. Come look, the machines have fallen," Kira says while pointing out the window in complete and utter shock.

Nadia steps up to observe the piles of blue ash that shine with victory on the street.

Ruger holds up his weapon. "My Quhtarr. Specialized from Tunaunda, remember?" He activates a switch on the side, and it dismantles back into the size and shape of a typical pistol. He grins before holstering it. "So, are you ladies ready to take a stroll with me?"

Kira laughs. She laughs so hard, Nadia joins her. "What do you think?" She asks Nadia.

"Yeah, I'm ready."

She lifts Nadia up and walks downstairs.

Carrying Nadia out through the back, she looks at what's left of her shed, but the sight doesn't hurt the way she thought it would. Kira has accepted God's will, and that is for her to move on. She sets Nadia down, and they walk to the side of her house. There, Ruger is stepping up from the street to meet them.

Nadia runs over to him, "Ruger!"

Ruger happily picks her up and even gives Nadia a little spin, making her giggle.

Kira looks at her property. She should be terrified of leaving it, but oddly enough, she's at peace.

Slowly, she walks up to them and smiles. "So, are we going for a stroll, or what?"

Ruger smiles and bounces Nadia up a little higher. "It's going to be a dark walk, but the Outpost isn't far."

"I know where it is." Kira leans up to his free side, while Nadia keeps a firm grip on his left shoulder. It's like they're already a family.

Ruger leads the way up the street before a low buzzing fills the air.

Kira looks around. She may not be able to see it, but she knows that sound. How could she be stupid enough to believe they were safe?

"A drone…" Kira whispers.

# CHAPTER 20
## *A NEW DAWN*

"No." Ruger hands Nadia to Kira. "My men are here." He grins, before waving at the sky.

Looking up, Kira sees a shadow fly over her house. It slowly turns back in a circle, before hovering above their heads. Whoever is piloting this ship, must've noticed Ruger. The shadow drifts to the street. Kira follows Ruger to watch it land over the ash of the machines. Barely able to see its silhouette, she can tell it's an aerial carrier, large enough to hold a dozen people. A hatch opens at the side, and four soldiers run out. They are wearing armor over their uniforms, which make them intimidating enough for Kira to step back to the side of her house and hide.

"What's wrong?" Nadia whispers.

Kira hugs her tighter. "I don't know yet."

With layers of armor over his uniform and a dark green helmet to match, the first soldier approaches Ruger, and slams his right fist into his chest, in some form of salute.

*"You found me."* Ruger greets in Zyandish, before returning the salute.

The younger soldier grins and laughter chimes behind him. She can't understand a word they're saying, but at least Ruger's tone is friendly. Kira should be friendly, but her heart rattles within.

Kira's brow rises as she watches Ruger hold his arms out. Though on cue, two of the soldiers begin strapping armor and weapons on him. He glances back at her, his face stricter than she's seen. "Seems my message got through," Ruger says in Auctrah.

"Thank God." Kira musters the bravery to step out of hiding.

His face remains hard. "Yes, but the machines I took out were only the search party. Two hundred more are on their way." He motions towards the ship.

Kira stops and can't unbuckle her knees. She knows she needs to get Nadia onboard this strange aircraft, but she's terrified. She locks eyes with the first soldier to greet Ruger. He smiles. Kira doesn't try contemplating why, before forcing her legs to work.

"Are we really going to Zyandite?" Nadia asks.

"Yes. Don't be scared." Kira whispers more to herself than to her daughter. If she can't gain the bravery, she'll fake it. Slowly she approaches these men with her head held high.

"Whoa," Nadia whispers.

The sight of these soldiers helping Ruger into layers of armor causes her stomach to whirl. They look so dangerous. Mouth dry, everything in Kira screams for her to run off to somewhere better to hide. After a silent prayer, she forces her pace to be casual. The same way she would for the drone patrol, just to hide her fear.

Nadia bounces in her arms with nothing but trust displayed on her face.

Ruger and his men continuously speak their native tongue, and there's tension she can't understand. When Kira reaches him, all eyes soften at the sight of Nadia. Proving to her the rumors of children being sacred in Zyandite, are undoubtedly true.

Nadia waves.

Upon watching the soldiers return Nadia's wave, Kira's fear of them dwindles, though only a little.

Now that he is in armor, even Ruger looks intimidating. A lump forms in

Kira's throat.

Yet, Ruger's men don't look at her with eyes of accusation, but relief. It's almost as though they need him.

"Remember, these are the good guys," Ruger whispers in Auctrah.

Mustering up her courage, Kira forces a smile. "Okay."

His eyes soften for a moment before he addresses the soldiers. *"Let's go."* He says in Zyandish.

Kira adjusts carrying Nadia to the left before her eyes can focus on the aircraft. It's brightly lit. She counts only three soldiers inside, including the pilot. Once they see Ruger, each one smiles with relief.

Stepping on the ash, it still glows a dim blue. It's not hot, but she stops anyway. Beneath her feet is a victory that makes her heart leap with joy. "Thank you God," Kira can't help but whisper.

Ruger stops at the ramp, and motions for her to go first. Without hesitation, she carries Nadia right in and takes a seat. Ruger doesn't step inside until everyone is secure in their seats. He sits next to Kira and smiles.

As the aircraft lifts up, Nadia's eyes widen. "Wow!"

The soldiers laugh admiringly at her reaction.

"This is her first plane ride," Kira explains.

Ruger smiles and quickly translates. The soldiers look at Nadia as though she's precious.

Surprised by how quiet this carrier is, Kira looks out the window to see her house for the very last time. The remains of the Langton's home still hurts, but it doesn't have the power to weigh down her heart.

Seeing Feisty grazing in the field makes her smile. The meadow becomes smaller, and soon, she can't even see her property anymore. With open doors, much like a helicopter, the wind messes up her hair. She doesn't mind it. In fact, it feels good.

One of the soldiers hands Ruger a pair of boots.

Ruger doesn't bother hiding his gratitude before he takes off the small shoes she gave him. "Thank you for these, Kira, but may I?" He nods toward the opening.

Kira shrugs indifferently. She watches Ruger toss George's old shoes into the same forest his jet crashed in. Relieved to see them go, she smiles.

"Isn't this amazing, mommy?" Nadia asks.

"Yes, this is incredibly amazing." Their lives have completely changed. With as frightening as the unknown ahead of them might be, there is no going back now. Outside, the forest fades to rocks, before a cliff and the ocean. They're almost to Saffarion Airbase.

Nadia giggles. "Not just the plane, mommy. All of it. Be my rock of protection, that's what the Bible says, and guess what? God just was!"

"Psalm Thirty-one, verse two, what a brilliant girl you are to know that." Ruger praises before translating to his men what she said.

"Well, of course. Psalm thirty-one is mommy's favorite." Nadia says matter-of-factly.

Ruger translates, and even the hardened soldiers' smile at Nadia. Kira's heart quakes at how these seasoned warriors, are still warm-hearted enough to appreciate her daughter's knowledge of scripture. Kira notices that every soldier on this flight, besides Ruger, is wearing a wedding ring. She can't help but wonder if any of them are fathers themselves.

The warmth of safety loosens her back muscles. She hasn't felt this secure in years. Kira literally feels the weight of stress roll off her shoulders. "Psalm thirty-one," she whispers, suddenly fighting tears. These are not tears of sorrow, regret, or fear, but of relief and even joy. Inside, Kira's heart praises God for delivering her and her daughter from the evil that's haunted them for so long. "You have taught children and infants to tell of your strength," Kira quotes Psalm 8:2, making Nadia's smile widen.

Kira's heart rejoices over her daughter's wisdom for a moment before remembering the Psalm which was promised to her years ago.

So be strong and courageous, all you who put your hope in the LORD! Psalm 31:24

Kira begins to pray in silence, 'I have been strong and courageous, and you have been my hope. Thank you, God, for delivering my daughter and me. You are our strong rock and deliverer. Thank you for sending this man crashing into our lives. Thank you for your protection, in the name of Jesus, amen.'

Flying above the fog, Kira can see the sunrise. Cascading, fiery colors throughout the sky are so bright, they reflect off the ocean, before meeting back like two butterfly wings centered on the sun.

It's glorious, and in this moment, Kira feels glorious. It's been a long time since she's felt victory, so Kira smiles as she takes it all in, along with the view.

"I'm glad I was able to keep my promise," Ruger whispers in Auctrah, pulling Kira's attention from the sunrise.

"Sorry that I doubted you."

Ruger smiles, before looking at the second oldest man in the group, Lieutenant Coltner. *"I have been trying to get a hold of you since I crashed."*

Lieutenant Coltner responds in Zyandish. *"We lost your signal. If it wasn't for your message, we wouldn't have found you."* There's not much humor in his blue eyes that rest under a faded cut of blond hair.

Ruger frowns. *"I was hoping my digital death on ZyanBell, was merely a signal issue."*

Lieutenant Coltner's lips press tightly together.

Suspicions fog Ruger's mind. *"What all have I missed?"*

*"The lead we were given was a trap."* Lieutenant Coltner explains with eyes full of loss.

Ruger's muscles tighten. The information Kira gave him on who controls the Hive makes him lower his chin in anticipation of bad news. *"How many?"*

*"Seventy-nine,"* Lieutenant Coltner answers somberly.

*"Seventy-nine Zyandites, fallen."* Ruger looks down with regret.

Kira may not be able to understand their language, but the entire mood has changed. The aircraft is no longer a place for laughter. Kira's concerned but does not want to be rude. Gently, she places a hand on Ruger's shoulder. The soldiers glanced at each other in surprise at her invasion of Ruger's space. Kira immediately pulls her hand away.

Ruger's obviously not bothered by the soldiers' response to her affection. "Seventy-nine of my men have perished. I should have been with them," he whispers in Auctrah.

Kira shakes her head. "You didn't choose to be shot down."

Ruger's too lost in grief to absorb her words.

*"Sir,"* the first soldier who greeted Ruger says, with brown eyes full of concern. *"General Brice has to brief you. There have been other issues in your absence."*

Ruger looks up at Sergeant Groth, his eyes weighed down by suspicion.

*"There are many things you've missed,"* Lieutenant Coltner whispers. Kira figures he must be the head of this team, due to his age and demeanor. The intensity of how everyone stares at Ruger proves to her that he is their senior.

"What's going on?" Kira asks.

"They're briefing me," Ruger says in Auctrah.

Now it all makes sense to her. "Are you a general?" Kira asks. The saluting was one thing, but in watching them give Ruger his boots in the proper size, was her biggest clue.

"My name is Ruger Drew Anstone, King of Zyandite." Ruger's green eyes dance at her, showing he takes great pleasure in telling her his title.

"You're a king?" Nadia exclaims with her jaw dropped.

Ruger winks at her.

Kira's cheeks might as well be on fire. "I should have figured that out," she whispers.

"You guessed general, which is close enough. Considering that they think they're in charge, most of the time," Ruger says with a roll of his eyes.

"The King of Zyandite…" Kira can hardly believe it. "You're so young."

"The youngest ever crowned." Ruger's lips curve into a half-smile. "It's quite amazing how God used the crash and you, to save my life." His smile fades as his eyes gaze back to his men, who watch Kira and Nadia with curiosity. "The mission I came here for would have been suicide."

"The kepweed saved you." Kira beams. "Wow, praise God."

Ruger smiles at her before addressing his men in Zyandish. *"Be aware that the locals poison their bullets, with a man-made plant called kepweed."*

*"Is that what happened?"* Lieutenant Coltner asks. *"I've never seen anyone live through temperatures that high. Once your vitals dropped from radar, everyone assumed you were dead."*

Ruger's eyes fill with anticipation while he tilts his head. *"Am I still King?"*

Most of his men laugh, answering Ruger already.

Sergeant Groth remains deep in thought. *"That is what General Brice must brief you on, sir. If we had been one day later in finding you that title might not be where it belongs."*

*"I tried to message General Brice several times, but nothing went through."* Ruger lets out a sigh. The realization for what he thought was a digital death was meant to be a real one causes his muscles to tighten.

*"That can only mean one thing, sir, sabotage."* Sergeant Groth is resolved.

"A war within a war." Ruger stares off in anticipation of the battle within his own ranks. He knows the damage to morale from mere rumors can be devastating and decides to take these accusations with caution. *"I wasn't even gone a week."* His words spark much-needed laughter amongst his men. *"In the chaos of war, sometimes destructive ideas breed fear, even in the hearts of God's strongest warriors."*

Lieutenant Coltner leans forward. *"I don't mean to disrespect you, King Anstone, but sir, the complete loss of communication with you leads me to agree with Sergeant Groth. You must have been sabotaged from someone within our own ranks."*

*"No."* Ruger briefly shakes his head. *"Zyandite was sabotaged. Anyone who could orchestrate chaos and disorder in her ranks has selfish motives and the darkest of*

*intentions against our home. Whatever evil there may be, even amongst our own, we have to destroy it."*

All his men grunt once to show their agreement, causing Kira and Nadia some discomfort, since they can't understand a single word they say.

Lieutenant Coltner looks at Kira and smiles friendly enough before addressing his king. *"I believe that when God's hand is at work, even by delaying something, it is always for a reason."* He lifts his chin at her, approvingly.

Kira's mind is put at ease. She knows these men don't see her as the enemy.

*"That's right, Lieutenant."* Ruger smiles at Kira. *"Kira was once a reporter and knows the correct location of the Hive."* His eyes darken when they return to Lieutenant Coltner. *"We'll destroy Joplin's machines. In the meantime..."* He eyes each of his men, slowly. *"Trust that the truth will all be revealed in God's time. It's best to not draw our own conclusions while we wait. Conspiracies are the very poison that divides nations. I promise you, I will deal with any traitors to the full extent of Zyandite law."* Ruger's eyes are fierce, drawing respect from his men.

*"Perhaps the civilian knew who you were, and shot you with a laced bullet intentionally?"* A young private asks with brown eyes that are too stern to match his babyface.

*"These people are too primitive and unorganized to be able to pull off anything like that,"* Ruger says. *"They don't even have the internet."*

His men all look at each other, and Ruger can tell the conspiracy is still alive and well in their hearts.

*"This woman,"* Ruger points at Kira, who is nervous since she can't understand Zyandish, *"Wasn't even aware that Sampson Tidal is no longer our king."* He smiles at Kira graciously. *"Her name is Kira Westin, and she risked her life every day for her faith in our Lord."*

The soldiers' eyes show their approval.

*"She could have been killed just for having her Bible."* Ruger smiles at her admiringly.

Lieutenant Coltner looks at her with respect, but Kira only smiles uncomfortably.

*"She survived in this godless society, by reloading her ammo,"* Ruger adds.

His men grunt with respect since reloading ammo is considered an art in Zyandite. Not one of them would ever expect an Auctairean to be capable of mastering such skill.

Kira watches as the demeanor of Ruger's men changes towards her. She has never had such mighty warriors look at her with gratitude before. It feels undeserving, so she squeezes Nadia in tighter and looks at the floor. The uneven texture of gray and black metal doesn't help her process how drastically their lives just changed.

"Guess we'll never see Hanover again," Nadia whispers, peering out to watch the sunrise over the Atlantic.

"I don't think we'll ever see Auctairea again," Kira says.

"Your mother is right, that chapter of your life is closed. I think you're going to like Zyandite," Ruger says to assure Nadia.

"I think so too," Nadia whispers, filling Kira with pride at her daughter's bravery.

"I'm going to make certain of it." Ruger winks. He slowly reaches for the chain of Kira's necklace, which is only visible from the back of her collar. Kira doesn't flinch as Ruger's fingertips touching her skin before he lifts up the chain to reveal the platinum cross that was hidden under her collar. Ruger smiles as he watches the cross land boldly over her black shirt. "You'll never have to hide this again."

Glancing at her necklace, Kira is overwhelmed by the freedom to display her faith openly. It's been years since she's had that liberty. "Thank you," she whispers, doing her best not to cry.

Ruger doesn't say anything. His eyes prove he meant it when he said he was captivated by her.

Out of the corner of her eyes, Kira can tell there's an unspoken scuttle between his men. They are smiling, so she's not too concerned.

*"My King,"* Lieutenant Coltner breaks their moment. *"Since faith is illegal in Auctairea, do you suppose there are other Christians in hiding?"*

*"There will be, Lieutenant. An Auctairean soldier helped me. His willingness to come to God gives me hope for them. Regardless, Prime Minister Joplin must pay severely. Years ago, there was an event called the Great Cleansing. He murdered every Christian and potential threat to his reign that he knew of. He used the machines to do it, and from what Kira told me, it was brutal,"* Ruger explains in Zyandish.

Hissing and disgusted grunts fill the cab from Ruger's men.

Kira would be terrified that they meant their spite towards her if she had not understood Joplin's name between the words Ruger spoke under Zyandish tongue. Even so, her breaths become jagged.

"I just explained the Great Cleansing," Ruger tells her.

"Oh," Kira says, finding she can breathe normally again.

Ruger looks at each of the men in their eyes, one by one slowly, as he explains. *"Kira risked her life to save mine."*

Lieutenant Coltner looks at Kira with awe. *"Thank you, Kira."*

"He just thanked you for saving me," Ruger translates.

Kira shakes her head at Lieutenant Coltner. "I don't deserve thanks. God led me to do it." She smiles and watches as Lieutenant Coltner's eyes shine with a higher approval once Ruger translates.

*"As you can imagine, for rescuing me, Kira is now an enemy to her state. I must get her and her daughter, Nadia, to Zyandite, immediately. How soon can you get a flight ready?"* Ruger asks.

*"We have a few wounded soldiers who need to be evacuated. I already have a flight scheduled for this afternoon, but will change it."* Lieutenant Coltner then pulls out a tablet to begin typing the order.

*"How soon?"*

*"Right after we land."*

*"Thank you,"* Ruger says in Zyandish before turning to Kira and Nadia. "We're going to get you to Zyandite, very soon," He promises in Auctrah.

Kira smiles at him and caresses Nadia's hair. She can feel her daughter's breathing deepen, and looks to find her eyes heavy. It doesn't take long for Nadia to fall asleep. Relieved, Kira looks out the window. The sky is beautiful, but she can't focus on that now and instead prays in silence. She prays in praise for strength and protection, and she also prays for Ruger. As King, he has the power to destroy the evil that consumed her homeland. She asks God to help him to do it.

*"We're almost to the ground!"* The pilot announces from the cockpit.

"Brace yourself, we're about to land," Ruger informs Kira with excitement in his eyes she has not seen before.

# CHAPTER 21
## *FORMATION*

Looking out her window, Saffarion Air Base is larger than Kira remembered. The light of dawn accentuates the massive runway before rows and rows of Zyandite jets. Several hundred men are exercising in a nearby field, while thousands of soldiers march along another runway in the distance. Dozens of vehicles, armed with large guns and other weapons Kira doesn't recognize, drive in convoy towards the road beyond the fence line.

Flying closer to the open runway, the sight of at least two hundred soldiers standing in a formation makes Kira's eyes widen.

"They're here to pay respect to the crown. This formation is quite small. Probably all they could organize in such little time." Ruger shrugs with a playful smile.

The motion of their taxi comes to a stop. This is it. They may be on Auctairean soil, but it's evident that this portion of land belongs to Zyandite. Kira looks to Ruger and waits for direction. He stays seated while all of his men get off the aircraft. They are so considerate in passing, it surprises Kira.

Ruger places a hand on her shoulder. "I have to be the last one off the plane. It's tradition." He motions his hand towards the door.

Kira takes his cue and lifts Nadia up.

"Huh?" Nadia asks. Her eyes disorientated from sleep.

"We've landed," Kira whispers.

"Really?" Nadia perks up, but Kira carries her anyways. She's too uncomfortable to allow Nadia the chance to run off on her own.

Walking down the ramp, she sees the soldiers they flew in with all stand at attention on each side of the doorway before the massive formation of troops waits under the dawn's light.

Ruger steps out of the aircraft.

The sound of their salute is thunderous.

Nadia's jaw drops.

Kira feels a little frightened but does her best to hide it.

Ruger returns the salute. *"It is God's blessing on me to have returned to the presence of such righteous men. Thank you for advancing on the enemy, even in my absence. I will brief you all very soon."* He then motions for Lieutenant Coltner to lead the way. Behind them, the formation gracefully disperses.

Ruger's limp is still noticeable, though he manages to set a fast pace. Kira shifts her daughter's weight to her right, to keep up. Anytime a soldier recognizes Ruger in passing, their eyes fill with surprise. Each one holds a right fist to their heart in a salute. Kira can tell it's not just for his title, for their eyes contain sincere gratitude. It's apparent that they greatly admire him.

The closer they get to the main hanger, the more aircraft with the Zyandite flag painted on comes into view, and it baffles her. "I can't believe they got all of this here in just a few days," Kira whispers.

"We are very good at what we do," Ruger says. "As soon as you told me the drones had stopped, I knew my men had occupied this base. It took a little longer due to my absence, I'm sure." He leans down to whisper. "Regardless, they should have barged in to get me the very night I crashed."

That scenario plays out in her mind. Would Ruger's men have just killed her? Kira immediately thanks God it did not happen that way. "I'm glad they didn't."

"So am I."

He's sincere enough, but Kira finds that hard to believe.

They step into the shade of the navy blue hanger, where a white case on the wall catches Kira's attention. "Wait," she says to Ruger, who turns to watch her step over to the medical cabinet. With her free hand, she opens it and pulls out a syringe of the antidote for kepweed. "If you feel feverish again, take this." She hands it to Ruger, who smiles before placing it in his pocket.

"Aww, that's so sweet, mommy," Nadia says before resting her head on Kira's shoulder.

Ruger blushes before Lieutenant Coltner points towards the full opening ahead. *"We're almost there, my King."*

Ruger allows him to lead.

The rounded ceiling of this hanger is high enough to make it feel like a stadium, flooding Kira with memories of campaigning for Joplin. Guilt creeps into her core. She's let so many Christians down, she doesn't deserve to be here, much less honored by a king.

"Everything's okay, Kira, no one here will hurt you," Ruger whispers, obviously mistaking her guilt for fear.

Kira forces a smile. "I'm fine."

They follow Lieutenant Coltner down the hanger, where a large cargo plane is being loaded up with men on stretchers.

"This is your flight," Ruger says in Auctrah, before making his way up to shake the hands of every wounded soldier on the plane.

She may not be able to understand a word he says, but Kira can see he is sincere in his care for them. It's a love that's returned, and quite obviously so, by the way his men look at him. Ruger's age has no ill-effect on the respect he receives.

Carrying Nadia up the yellow ramp to the plane, the metal thuds under each one of Kira's steps. Once onboard, she counts nine injured. Only one man besides Ruger is on his feet. He is younger and wears the same uniform Ruger crashed in, with a large green backpack to match. His hair is blond, cut in typical military fashion, and his eyes are a sharp blue. Ruger's briefing him on something that makes him continuously nod.

"Kira, this is one of our medics, Private Hill," Ruger says. "He needs to check you and Nadia out. It's just a blood test, but it's mandatory before we can send you to Zyandite."

Kira catches her breath, "A blood test for what?"

"Everything."

"With one test?" Kira raises a brow.

"That's right." Ruger turns from her to motion for the medic to come near.

Kira worries for how Nadia will react. She hasn't seen a doctor since she was a baby. "Have you told him about your leg?"

Ruger grimaces. "I will."

Kira wishes she knew Zyandish. She would tell this medic herself. Watching the medic set down his aid bag, she expects him to pull out a syringe. She's surprised to see him pull a tablet out of his pack.

Ruger reads the Zyandish words to Kira. "Disinfectant Mode." He pushes the button for the medic. "Nothing could survive the temperature its compartment can reach." The tablet chimes. "Ready."

Kira sets Nadia to her feet, but she clings to her leg. This is Nadia's first time showing fear since Ruger's men found them. "Relax sweetheart, this is for our benefit too. They just need to prick us with a needle, very quickly, to make sure we're not sick."

"Will it hurt?" Nadia whispers.

"Only a little." Ruger gives her a knowing look. "But you're brave enough to handle it."

She smiles and releases her grip from her mom and steps forward. "Yes, I am."

"That's my girl," Kira says while caressing Nadia's hair.

Kira watches the medic step up to Nadia. His brow is raised, and his eyes silently ask for permission before sticking Nadia's arm.

Ruger holds his shoulder out to show her what to do.

Nadia follows suit.

The jab is quick. *"There."* Private Hill's shoulders drop in relief.

"I didn't even feel that." Nadia gives a thumbs-up.

"That's because you're tough," Ruger says with a wink, before smiling at Kira. "He's never worked on civilians before, let alone a child."

Relieved to know the apprehension she sensed wasn't discrimination, Kira lets out a deep breath. "Tell him he did a good job."

Ruger grins and translates.

Private Hill smiles. *"Mild vitamin deficiency, other than that, this child is healthy."*

*"Good,"* Ruger says in Zyandish, before translating for Kira.

"Thank you, God," Kira prays, before letting out a relieved sigh. "I've been so worried."

"God's been looking out for you both, in more ways than one," Ruger says before watching the medic reset his tablet, readying it for Kira.

She sets Nadia down and turns to hold her shoulder out. The prick is short, and she barely feels it.

Private Hill stares at the tablet. *"Like her child, she has a vitamin deficiency. She's also slightly anemic, but nothing contagious."*

Ruger's eyes close in relief for a moment, before translating the good news to Kira.

Before she can react, applause erupts from the soldiers onboard. Kira's heart flutters. She's surprised these Zyandite soldiers are happy for her eligibility to move to their homeland. It's so surreal, she has to clarify. "They're clapping for *me?*"

Ruger grins. "Of course they are. I explained the situation. Not only did you save me, but you're a Christian. I told you, Zyandite will welcome you with open arms."

She blushes and bows her head slightly to the smiling faces around her.

After giving each of the men a smile, the clapping stops, and Ruger looks at Nadia. "It's going to take a lot of bravery to move to a new country, but don't be frightened. God is with you, wherever you are."

Nadia frowns. "You're not going with us?"

"No sweetheart, but I will get you a pumpkin cream cake, as soon as I return."

Nadia sways back and forth with a bashful smile. "Good."

He winks before looking at Kira.

Kira's stomach sinks at the thought of leaving without him. The men around her are not only injured but kind. Yet, she is still nervous about being alone with them. "Here, I was selfish enough to hope you were going with us."

"I can't." Ruger's eyes are solemn before a new strength fills them. "My sister will greet you when you land. Her name is Rhonda, and she will be your translator until you learn Zyandish."

Not only the soldiers onboard the plane, but several more working in the hanger has eyes on them. Kira doesn't want to harm Ruger's reputation, but her heart must know. "When will I see you again?"

"When the war is won, I will find you and Kira..." Ruger's eyes are determined. "God willing, I will do everything I can to make you forget this terrible place."

He is so sincere that Kira's heart skips a beat. "Promise?"

"I promise," Ruger whispers.

Kira gently places her free hand on the side of his face. At this moment, her desire to kiss him overcomes everything else.

Ruger's eyes are filled with longing, but instead of kissing her, he turns away.

Kira knows she shouldn't expect affection from him in front of his soldiers, but the rejection still stabs at her heart. Fearing their love was only a fantasy, Kira knows she shouldn't expect anything else. If Ruger were a pilot, that would be one thing, but he is Zyandite's King. That changes everything.

Ruger looks back at Kira, and she sees nothing but love in his eyes, giving her hope that her fears may be in vain.

*"Take care of them,"* Ruger orders the soldiers behind Kira, who nod with vigor.

Kira watches Ruger walk away with Lieutenant Coltner. Her heart sinks as the hatch closes him out of her sight. Looking at the gray wall behind her, there aren't any seats, just loose, yellow belts hanging from the walls. She slowly sits down with her back against it. Nadia huddles next to her, but doesn't seem frightened.

Alone with strangers and a language barrier, there has never been a time when Kira should be more frightened. These soldiers may be wounded, but she knows they're all thoroughly trained on how to kill. On a flight to a foreign land she hasn't heard anything about for over five years, she shouldn't be comfortable at all. Yet, Kira knows God will protect both her and her daughter, the way He always has.

There is no turning back now. Instead of letting fear place its paralyzing pressure on her chest, Kira chooses faith.

\*\*\*

# CHAPTER 22
## *THE PROPHECY*

Age has been kind to a woman who sleeps with her long, strawberry blond hair framing her face like ocean waves. Her light skin is mapped by many lines, but still, a glow remains. The dream she is witnessing is torrent, and immediately her green eyes fling open.

"Brian." She whispers to her husband, who sleeps beside her.

Groggy eyed, Brian's alerted to his wife's plea. "What's the matter, Farrah?"

Farrah sits up, as the breeze from the open window of their modest bedroom, cools the sweat on her skin. "No matter what they tell you, King Anstone is alive."

"What did God show you?" Brian asks, his blue eyes sharpened with heightened alertness. His salt and pepper hair reflects the moonlight.

Farrah looks at his tablet that sits on the light oak nightstand.

Brian doesn't have time to follow her gaze before the call comes in. Answering it, Brian's heart drops once General Jordan Brice greets him with an anxious tone on the other end.

"We've lost contact with King Anstone. The generals demand that a new king be crowned immediately."

"Wait a minute." Brian tosses his covers and stands. "King Anstone's dead?"

Jordan's silence answers him.

If Farrah hadn't been given a dream, Brian would be in despair. "Do you have his body?"

"No," Jordan answers through the line.

Brian begins pacing. "Then, their demand goes against protocol. We can't begin a new election without proof of the King's death."

"I don't have a choice. King Anstone's fever was higher than most could survive when we lost his signal. Now the generals are enacting the Slayden Rule." General Brice says with the same shell shocked tone.

Brian's eyes widen. "They can't do that."

"Technically, they can since we don't have a stronghold on enemy lands. Brian…" General Brice's tone becomes soft, desperate even. "They're going to formally request the votes tomorrow evening."

Brian looks at Farrah, who stares at the blue covers of her bed, already knowing the news though she can't hear it.

"Who are the contenders?" Brian grimaces at the names given. "Alright, General Brice, I will be praying." He hangs up.

"Zyandite doesn't need a new king…" Farrah states before getting out of bed, and walking up to the window. The amber glow of artificial lights from the many high-rises of Zyandite's Capitol fills her heart with adoration. She knows God will protect her home. "We need a queen."

"God showed you this?" Brian asks in amazement.

Farrah turns to her husband, her eyes brightened with the fire only the Spirit of God can bestow. "Yes. She stood on our border with Auctairea, wearing a crown, with a sword in one hand, and a rifle in the other. Her dress was silver, the color of wisdom. Only her heart can save Zyandite. She's God's gift to us."

"Who is she?" Brian asks.

"I didn't recognize her," Farrah answers, her faith unwavering.

Brian's brow furrows. "Are you certain that she's Ruger's Queen?"

"Yes." Farrah is resolved. "The name Anstone was engraved across her crown."

Brian's never doubted his wife's dreams before, and steps into action. "Then, I will do everything I can to stop the generals' coup."

Farrah's chin humbly tilts, with absolute confidence in her God. "We must pray, not just for Zyandite, but for all of God's people. We're all at risk."

"God, save us," Brian whispers, before taking his wife's hands into his own. They bow their heads to pray.

"The great I Am," Brian begins in prayer. "Thank You for bestowing the gift of prophecy on my wife. Please open Zyandites ears to receive the message you have given Farrah, and grant us the wisdom on what to do. Please, the great and powerful I Am, protect Zyandite from all of our enemies. If Ruger's crash was the generals doing, please reveal that to our people, and to our King. Turn all injustice and wrongs into good. The great I Am, You know exactly where Ruger is. Save him with your might, and use even the most unexpected means to preserve his life. Save us God and direct our steps. To you be the glory, the majesty, and the praise, forever. In the name of Jesus Christ, we pray, amen."

"Amen." Farrah looks up at him with her eyes widen. "We have to alert the people. God does nothing without letting His prophets know first."

"I will use ZyanBell to read what God's putting on the hearts of Zyandites." Brian sets up his tablet on its stand on top of the shelf above his dresser. Through the digital communication of ZyanBell, he makes his projection to the people, live.

"Zyandites, I can't say good evening, for this message is not one of a good report. Brace yourselves, for I have just received word that King Anstone has crashed behind enemy lines in Auctairea, and all communications with him have been lost. He had a fever higher than anyone could survive without immediate medical intervention. The generals believe our King is dead, and are demanding a vote for his replacement, under the Slayden Rule. The contenders are General Baxton, and," Brian's face twitches. "General

Marshal. As the Lead Pastor of the Church of Zyandite, I can't go against my convictions from God. Otherwise, I would bear no right to lead you in any shape or form. Under the authority of my God-ordained title, no matter the choice Zyandite makes, I refuse to crown anyone king until I see proof of Ruger Anstone's death with my own eyes. This is my responsibility to our God, to you, and to King Anstone." Brian holds his head down in grief, only for a moment. "As you all know, God has bestowed the gift of prophecy on my wife. He has given her a clear and decisive dream. Before we reveal what God has told her, I ask that all prophets and prophetess of Zyandite, young and old, to reveal what God leads you to type on ZyanBell. We all know God does nothing without first telling His prophets. Once the keywords from all of you are collected, we will reveal Farrah's dream. Very soon, we'll know what God is telling us, all of us. As the Lead Pastor of the Church of Zyandite, I must inform you…" Brian clenches his fist against his chest. "I believe in my heart that our King is alive. I'm asking to delay the vote for a new king, just for a few days. Yet whatever the case, whatever happens, we must accept it is God's will. We must remain strong in Him and united. Pray for Zyandite, and pray for King Anstone. Under the authority of Jesus Christ, may God bless you all with His wisdom and comfort, amen."

Brian ends the message. Within moments, his tablet chimes. Zyandites received his message and are responding.

Farrah sits Indian style on their bed and watches as Brian projects the words from ZyanBell onto their wall. So far, two thousand messages have poured in. Most express prayers for their King and their country. Once the prophets begin to respond, the keywords are added up, and the top three are displayed:

Davidic.

Alive.

Queen.

Farrah covers her mouth and sobs in humility at God's love for her. "Who am I that he would grant such a powerful and intimate gift to me?" She wipes a tear as the confirmation from others who share that same gift pour in.

"You are his daughter." Brian smiles. "God wants to restore the Davidic line through King Anstone, and end the corruption of the self-seeking. Zyandite has been ruled by the three pillars of strength for centuries without any dishonesty, until now. We must trust that God will reveal all truth, in good time."

"Hereditary Monarchy will never be accepted unless God is behind it. Brian, I must admit, the idea scares even me," Farrah says.

"Trust God," Brian whispers. "King Anstone's crash and whatever has caused his fever, is a desperate attack on what God has planned, but have faith, God's will always prevails."

Farrah stands. "I'll get dressed, and share the dream God gave me with the people."

Wearing a teal sweater dress, she records the details of her dream for ZyanBell. Once the message is done, Farrah bows her head. Praying without ceasing is the only way she gains strength. The response pours in through ZyanBell. The people accept the prophecy and are even excited. "God is on the move," Farrah whispers.

\*\*\*

# CHAPTER 23
## *A GOLDEN GLOW*

There are no windows on the plane for Nadia to look out of, as they descend to a land they've never seen. Most of the soldiers have fallen asleep, but Kira's too uncomfortable to let her guard down.

Private Hill gives them a couple of protein bars and two water bottles.

Nadia has a hard time unwrapping the foil, but after Kira helps her, she takes a bite.

Her eyes widen. "Is this a pumpkin cream cake?" Nadia asks between chews.

"No, sweetheart." Kira doesn't want her eyes to water and holds in tears for all her daughter's missed out on.

"Well, it's the most delicious thing I've tasted!" Nadia says before devouring it.

From across the cargo hold, Private Hill watches them with compassion and gives Nadia two more bars.

"Thank you!" Nadia exclaims. This time, she unwraps them on her own.

Kira smiles at the young soldier. She's never liked being on the opposite side of charity.

Private Hill nods at Kira once, with eyes that genuinely seem to care, before retaking his seat.

Taking a bite of her own bar, Kira's ashamed that she used to think protein bars tasted like chalk. This one is strawberries and cream. It's one of the most delicious things she's ever tasted.

One of the soldiers taps the wall from his stretcher with his unfastened seat belt.

Understanding the prompt, Kira unbuckles herself and Nadia. She stands, and her legs are wobbly from sitting still for hours. Letting out a sigh, Kira readies her heart for whatever is on the other side of these walls.

There's a loud pulling sound, and the hatch to this aircraft begins to fold down. Sunlight peers through the opening at the top, and a golden glow increases in size as the hatch folds down.

The sunlight is as warm as it is blinding, and the air is thicker than Kira and Nadia are used to. But it smells sweet, with a watery freshness that must come from a nearby river.

Once the landscape comes into view, Kira soaks it in with a sense of comfort she shouldn't feel, but can't help. It's almost as though she was always meant to be here.

With only a few swirls of white clouds against the deep blue sky, sunshine reflects the layers of gold off of their matching brown hair, while a soft breeze welcomes them to this peaceful land.

A never-ending sky is kissed by high-rise buildings that stand proud, before low rolling hills. There are evergreens and yuccas on the hills. The smell from the breeze is fresh. There's a hint of algae from a river that runs through the middle of the city. Several objects fly above the city. At first, she thinks they're planes, but quickly realizes they are some type of car. Amazed by this advancement, Kira's mouth widens.

"Mommy, Ruger was right. Zyandite is pretty," Nadia whispers.

"It really is." Kira has never felt more at home in all her life. It must show because as a soldier limps up beside her on crutches, he points his finger at his home and gives her a thumbs-up.

Kira laughs. "Yes, it is beautiful."

Several soldiers from the ground help carry the wounded off the plane. Kira keeps Nadia out of their way. Private Hill walks down the ramp and smiles at them before following the wounded soldiers to an ambulance.

Beyond him, a lone woman in a green dress stands on the runway. She displays an excitement for their arrival that keeps her from standing still. Even from this distance, Kira can see she's smiling. Knowing that she must be Ruger's sister, Kira looks down at Nadia, who has not let go of her mother's waist since they landed. "Are you ready for this?"

Nadia only nods, her eyes full of the same admiration Kira feels for this place, even though she won't let her mom go.

"That's my brave girl," Kira praises, before walking down the ramp, caressing her daughter's hair as Nadia holds onto her.

Stepping out of the plane, Kira squints her eyes. The sun here is brighter than she's used to. The rays feel hot against her bare forearms. Kira looks down to see Nadia admiring the glow on her skin. A calm smile spreads across Nadia's lips, filling Kira's heart with joy. Before her feet can step off the metal and onto Zyandite soil, Kira stops.

"The air's a little bit thick here, though," Nadia says.

Kira can't help but giggle. "It is a little humid."

"I still like it."

"Me too."

Once she steps off this ramp, they will be out in the open, with nowhere left to hide. Kira touches the cross necklace on her shirt and feeling its exposure, makes her chin lift up. She'll never have to hide her faith again. This is not fake confidence, but assurance. Deep in her heart, Kira knows coming to this land was a gift from God. Looking around at the majesty of her surroundings, the fear Kira had turns into faith. Every day of her life, and Nadia's life, are in God's hands. Whatever happens next, will come to fruition because He has masterfully planned each step they take. Kira smiles because, for once, she isn't faking confidence. She doesn't need to. Shoulders loose,

Kira smiles at Nadia. "Alright, let's go."

She takes the first step onto this foreign soil, knowing it's exactly where God wants her to be. It's his gift for her and Nadia to call this beautiful place named Zyandite, home.

# EPILOGUE
## *A GENERAL WARNED*

After a torrential meeting with King Anstone, which undermined his Lineage, General Marshal storms down the hallway in a fury. His muscles are showcased under the dark green of his uniform. His black hair is cut in a high, military fade, over a pale face. Even with light skin, his blue eyes stand out before a straight nose and thin, mauve lips. His jawline is square, wide, and perfectly shaven. But the scowl on his face causes even his most attractive features to be repugnant.

A young Private catches up with him, his once pale face red from running. Red curls bounce at the top of his head, while his hazel eyes are stressed on a face that's covered with freckles. "General Marshal," he says, before stopping to catch his breath, "King Anstone is back."

"You're a bit late, Private Jensen." General Marshal rolls his eyes.

"I'm sorry General, but I had to wait for the runway to clear. The King had a group of wounded soldiers and a couple of civilians sent home." Private Jensen says through a jagged breath.

General Marshal was not interested in anything Private Jensen had to say until he heard civilians. "Were the civilians from our support team?"

"No. They were Auctairean."

"Two Auctaireans were sent to Zyandite?" General Marshal says. Scowl fading, he inquisitively lowers his chin. "Who?"

"Some lady and a little girl," Private Jensen leans forward and whispers, "You're never going to believe this sir, but I saw the woman touch King Anstone's face."

General Marshal straightens his shoulders with a newly gained confidence, while something dark and mischievous calculates in his eyes. "Is that so?"

To be continued…

# ABOUT THE AUTHOR

My name is Kimberly Humphreys, I am a Christian, tribal member of the Cherokee Nation, military spouse and I homeschool my three amazing kids. Writing is my passion, and while I enjoy writing fiction, it's amazing how God speaks through my blogs. You can follow me on Parler @KimberlyHumphreys. In my lifetime, I have learned that God can restore anything and anyone. I love my country and am thankful for my freedoms. In no time or place should words ever be silenced. I believe that socialism is evil, political correctness makes us weak, and dogs are awesome.

Made in the USA
Coppell, TX
14 December 2021